OTHER BOOKS BY KATE L. MARY

The Broken World Series:
Broken World
Shattered World
Mad World
Lost World
New World
Forgotten World
Silent World
Broken Stories

The Twisted Series:
Twisted World
Twisted Mind
Twisted Memories
Twisted Fate

The Blood Will Dry

Collision

When We Were Human

Alone: A Zombie Novel

The Moonchild Series:
Moonchild
Liberation

The College of Charleston Series:
The List
No Regrets
Moving On
Letting Go

Zombie Apocalypse Love Story Novellas:
More than Survival
Fighting to Forget
Playing the Odds
The Key to Survival

Anthologies:
Prep For Doom
Gone with the Dead

MAD WORLD

Book Three in the *Broken World* Series

KATE L. MARY

Twisted Press

Published by Twisted Press, LLC, an independently owned company.

Copyright © 2015 by Kate L. Mary
ISBN-13: 978-1502806857
ISBN-10: 1502806851
Edited by Emily Teng
Cover art by Jimmy Gibbs

To my husband, Jeremy, who has decided to let me love Daryl Dixon.
Thanks for being so understanding about my ridiculous crush on a fictional character.

CHAPTER ONE
VIVIAN

My heart beats against my ribs as Hadley and I run through the hospital parking lot toward the Nissan. I'm gasping and my legs tremble, but I force them to keep moving. Axl. I need to get to Axl. The van behind us is closer than the Nissan. Whoever it is, they're coming for us. Only, I don't have a clue why.

The Nissan is still at least fifty feet away when the van squeals to a stop at our backs. I hear the door slide open behind us, and my heart nearly explodes. The banging of the footsteps on the pavement matches the pounding in my chest, and I let out a scream of frustration. He's right behind me. So close I can hear every breath he takes.

I can't outrun him!

I grip my knife tighter as I spin around to face my attacker, swinging the blade through the air. He's a blur of black as he ducks and shoves me to the ground. My head snaps back. My body slams against the pavement. All the air rushes from my lungs, and my knife skids across the parking lot. Hadley screams. I can't figure out where she is, because I'm too busy gasping for air. The man in black grabs a handful of my hair and jerks me up. I scream as pain shoots across my scalp and down my neck. He hoists me up so my feet aren't touching the ground and takes off running. I kick and fight, but he just holds on tighter.

I can't get free.

My head bobs and the world around me blurs. I can barely make out the Nissan when it screeches to a stop.

It's so close.

The doors fly open. Axl and Angus start shooting, but the men in the van return fire. A window shatters right next to my head, and the man carrying me swears. He ducks, swears again, then tosses me inside the van. I land on the floor next to Hadley. Axl screams my name, but it's cut short when the door slams shut.

The van lurches forward, and my heart rips in two. I slam against Hadley. She's crying, and my own vision is blurred by tears. My hands shake so hard I poke myself in the eye when I try to wipe the tears away. More replace them, though. I clench my fists and dig my nails into my palms. Right into the little half-moons that haven't completely healed yet. I can't lose it. Not now. Now is the time to be strong.

Hadley grabs my arm and puts her face right up against mine. Her tears fall on my cheek. "Where are they taking us? What are they doing?" Her voice is so shaky the words come out distorted.

I wrap my arm around her and pull her against me. But I don't answer. There's really nothing I can say. There are only a few reasons men would abduct women, and none of them will make Hadley feel better right now.

The van bumps down the road, and we're tossed back and forth. The men move around in the front. Four of them. So far, though, they aren't paying attention to us. The broken window has their focus. They're busy covering it up with tape and what looks like a jacket. Yeah, that will keep the zombies out.

I can't get a good look at them. It's too dark in the back, and the sun shining through the front window makes it hard for me to see. The man who grabbed me has his back to me, but I know it's him. He's dressed completely in black. Like he's death, here to claim more victims. Maybe he is.

When they're done fooling with the window, the men finally turn their attention to us. The light in the back flicks on, and I squint, covering my eyes. It's a lot brighter than I would have thought.

"Holy shit!" someone yells. I open my eyes wider just as a guy crawls across the floor and grabs Hadley's chin, jerking her face toward his. It's the guy in black. "This is fucking Hadley Lucas!"

Everyone turns our way, and my body stiffens.

Shit. This isn't going to be good.

My eyes finally adjust, and I'm able to get a really good look at the guy in black, except now I wish I could go back to being ignorant. He's rough-looking. The kind of face you see in a mug shot or some reality crime show like *Cops* or *America's Most Wanted*. He looks to be in his mid-twenties and has dark, greasy hair that goes just past his jawline. His face is hard, and he has a scar going from the corner of his right eye all the way down to his chin. It jerks every time he talks, making him look lethal. Almost evil. There are two rings in his eyebrow and a few in each ear. He has a pierced tongue and more tattoos than I can count. They cover his arms like sleeves and creep out from the top of his shirt, curling around his neck like a serpent trying to choke him. The art consists mainly of demons and snakes and half-naked women.

You know, scary shit.

"No it ain't," another man with a twangy accent says. It reminds me of my years in Kentucky.

I tear my eyes away from Tat so I can check out the other guy. He's younger, probably only twenty. Overweight. His clothes are stained and made to fit a much smaller man. His filthy shirt stretches across his chest, emphasizing his man-boobs. A beer belly — or McDonald's belly is probably more accurate — sticks out from the bottom of his shirt. His face is round and sweaty and his hair is buzzed. He crawls across the van toward Hadley, probably hoping to get a closer look, and the stale smell of body odor follows him.

Something thumps against the outside of the van, and the driver swerves. Chubby grunts and topples over, right onto my leg. My kneecap turns under the weight of his huge ass, and I let out of yelp of pain. I shove him off me, but he doesn't even look my way. He's drooling over Hadley like she's the last cupcake on Earth.

"Damn! That is her," Chubby says.

"Anybody follow us?" New Guy asks the driver.

The driver shakes his head, and I catch a glimpse of him as he looks over his shoulder. Just like I thought, he's Hispanic. He's smaller than the other guys. Average-looking. Nobody I would've given a second look in the world that used to exist. None of these men look very scary—except Tat—but things are different now. Zombies aren't our only enemy anymore. We're living in a lawless country, and apparently someone has decided to start a new world where women are at the bottom of the pecking order. Again.

"That car at the hospital didn't come after us?" Tat asks.

My heart pounds, and I squeeze Hadley's hand tighter. Axl.

"The one guy shot at us for a while, but they never even tried to follow us." The driver glances back at Hadley and me. There's a wicked smile on his face I'd love to slap off. "Guess he was too much of a pussy to come after us."

Tears sting at the back of my eyes, and I have to look away. I can't imagine what Axl is going through right now. We were so close. If the van had shown up just a few seconds later, we would have made it. Hadley and I would be in the Nissan right now, on the way back to the shelter. Instead, Axl's left to wonder what happened to us and who took us and if he'll ever see us again. He has to be freaking out.

The van slows, and the driver looks over his shoulder again. "Get ready to make a run for it."

Hadley's eyes get even bigger. I didn't think it was possible. She doesn't look too hot at the moment, but Chubby can't stop drooling over her anyway. Her face is smeared with tears and snot and dirt, and her eyes are bright red from crying. But I can tell she's trying to put on a brave face. She's not going to take this lying down.

Neither am I.

The van screeches to a halt, and the driver and passenger climb back.

"Bobby and me will cover you guys," the driver says.

He slides the door open, and the bright Vegas sun shines in, blinding me. The air is sweltering and reeks of death. The moaning is so loud I know we're on the Strip without even having to look. It's the only place that could be this overrun.

I have my hand over my eyes to block out the sun, so I'm taken completely off guard when someone grabs me and jerks me out of the van. He tosses me over his shoulder and takes off running. His bony shoulder digs into my stomach with each step he takes. Between that, the stench of death, and the ball of dread in my gut, the urge to hurl is so strong I have a tough time swallowing it down.

But no way in hell am I going to just lay still and let this asshole carry me away. I squirm against his arm, ignoring the intense way his shoulder twists against my belly. At the same time, I kick my legs, trying to loosen his grasp on my thighs.

His arm tightens around me. "Stop fighting." I recognize the voice. It's New Guy. "There are zombies everywhere."

I can't see her, but I know Hadley's somewhere in front me. Probably over Tat's shoulder. No way could Chubby carry her, he'd be out of breath in seconds. She's screaming and fighting to get free. Her voice sounds panicked, and it makes my already pounding heart beat faster. All I can think about is the gleam in Chubby's eyes when he got a glimpse of Hadley.

No. We can't let these assholes get any further. We have to get away. Now.

I wiggle harder against New Guy's grasp and kick my legs like a swimmer trying to outswim a shark. Somehow my foot makes contact with New Guy's crotch. He grunts, and his hands are suddenly no longer holding me. He leans forward, probably to grab his damaged goods, and I can feel myself falling. The ground lurches up to greet me, and I instinctively put my hands out, bracing myself for the impact of the hard cement.

I land hard on my right side. Pain shoots up my arm, but I ignore it and roll onto my back so I can get a good look at my surroundings. The Monte Carlo looms in front of me, bringing to mind what my mom, Darla, said about seeing movement outside the casino. Tat is almost at the front door. He has Hadley slung over his shoulder and she's still kicking and screaming her head off. There's some kind of barrier set up they have to run through before they can actually get into the casino, though. Armed men stand behind it, and as I watch, they open a gate so Tat can pass through.

Hadley is out of sight within seconds. Shit.

The man I kicked in the groin is doubled over in pain only two feet away from me. The driver and Chubby head toward us with a group of zombies not too far behind. The two men are out of breath and covered in sweat. Chubby is having a hard time keeping up.

He acts like he's about to suffocate. Probably hasn't exerted himself this much his entire life.

I tear my eyes away from the men and look around, desperate to get away. But there's nowhere to go. I try to get to my feet, but New Guy grabs my ankle to stop me from moving. His face is twisted in agony, and his fingers dig into my skin.

"I have to get you inside," he says, grimacing.

"You can't handle carrying a chick in?" the driver says when he reaches us. He shakes his head at New Guy.

The driver reaches down to grab me, but New Guy suddenly finds his strength and pushes the driver aside. "I got her." He grunts when he lifts me up, then slings me over his shoulder again.

He takes off toward the hotel, but this time I don't fight. There's no point. Three men against just me are impossible odds. Plus, there's no way I could leave Hadley. I'd never be able to live with myself.

When we make it inside, I'm tossed onto a couch next to Hadley. New Guy glares at me and grimaces again. He grabs his crotch and bends over, and I'm torn between the desire to smile at his discomfort and the desire to burst into tears at the situation.

I inhale slowly, trying to calm my breathing and quiet my pounding heart. Then it hits me. The air doesn't stink and I'm not sweating anymore. The air conditioner is on. Electricity.

The hotel lobby is brightly lit, and there's even music playing from the speakers overhead. The place is clean and clear of bodies, and the people walking by—only men—aren't filthy. Even the four men who brought us here. They're sweating from the heat, but now that I get a closer look at them, they aren't dirty. Chubby's clothes are stained and gross, but they don't look like someone who's been fighting off the living dead. Which tells me he's just a slob. A slob who's been holed up in a hotel.

The driver glares at New Guy and shakes his head again, then jerks his thumb toward Hadley and me. "Watch them."

Hadley grabs my hand, and I squeeze it. We watch as the Hispanic man walks toward the front desk like he's checking into a room. He stops and talks to a man. A man dressed in a suit, which seems crazy and out-of-place, considering what's outside this hotel. Suit man is short, stocky, and balding, but he stands tall when he talks. Like he has a lot of power and he knows it. The driver points toward Hadley and me, and Suit Man grins like he was just told he won the lottery. My stomach turns inside out.

I have a very bad feeling about what comes next.

Men come out of the woodwork to gawk at us. Like we're freaks in a sideshow. Hadley scoots closer and squeezes my hand so tight my knuckles crunch together. I can't really focus on the pain, though. I'm too busy checking everything out. There are so many men here. I scan the room, counting. Ten. Fifteen. More than twenty. Where did they all come from?

A group of men stands in a cluster on the other side of the room, staring at the wall. I lean forward to get a better view, and when I catch sight of what they're looking at, I inhale sharply and grab Hadley's leg with my free hand. There are dozens of pictures of naked women lined up on the wall. Not pages taken from a magazine. Actual pictures. And they're divided into three numbered categories. I guess that explains the crazy code the men were using in the van.

Hadley's body trembles next to mine. She must see it too. She squeezes my hand again, and I scoot closer. We have to find a way out of here.

It isn't going to be easy, though. Not with the armed men at the doors. Plus, I really doubt we're going to be free to roam the hotel. New Guy, Tat, and Chubby haven't walked away or taken their eyes off us for even a second. They stand right in front of Hadley and me like guards, glaring down at us.

"What's going to happen?" Hadley whispers.

I swallow and work on controlling my voice. "Try to stay calm." The words shake.

She turns her green eyes toward me, and her lips tremble. She didn't miss the fact that I didn't answer her question, but I have no intention to. Thinking about what these men have planned for us is only going to make us panic, and right now we need to stay calm. Focused. Strong.

The driver heads back, followed by three other men. Suit Man and two big guys with broad shoulders. They look like they should be playing professional football or something. They stop in front of Hadley and me. Suit Man looks us over, nodding in approval. He obviously has some position of authority.

"Nice work." He steps forward and grabs me by the arm, then jerks me to my feet. "Hadley Lucas will be a three for sure. Looks like this one will be, too. We'll have to check them over, but this is definitely worth a two. I'll get you guys a receipt."

"Ain't it worth a three?" Chubby whines. "She's a movie star! We brought 'er in, we should get a go at 'er."

Suit Man's fingers dig into my arm, and his eyes narrow on Chubby. "It took four of you almost the entire day to bring in two women. You're lucky it's a two. If you have complaints about your compensation, you can take it up with the boss. I have to warn you though, he isn't the understanding kind."

Chubby clamps his mouth shut and stares down at his feet. He looks like a giant kid with his hands shoved in his pockets, kicking at an imaginary ball on the floor. It makes me sick to my stomach.

Suit Man nods, and the corners of his mouth turn up, making him look sinister. He jerks my arm roughly and shoves me toward the linebackers. "Take them upstairs to be processed," he says as he turns away. "I'll be up after I get their receipts."

Linebacker One takes over where Suit Man left off. He grabs my arm and pulls me forward. Hadley squeaks behind me as she's yanked off the couch by the other linebacker. They drag us toward the elevator, and men leer at us every step of the way. Fear twists inside me, but I focus on controlling my breathing. On staying calm.

The elevator door shuts, and Hadley sniffs. "Why are we here?"

The linebackers don't respond. They won't even look at us.

CHAPTER TWO
AXL

Somebody's yellin' and it rings in my ears, only it takes me a few seconds to realize it's me. It's hard to hear anythin' over the sound of gunfire as I run after the van, pullin' the trigger over and over again. My chest is tight, and my body's so tense it feels like I'm gonna explode. But I can't do nothin' but pull the damn trigger and charge after that fuckin' van.

"Axl!"

Angus's voice finally reaches me, and I lower my gun. I'm pantin', and I can't catch my breath. The van is outta sight, anyways. There's nothin' left to shoot at but the dead.

"Get in the car!"

I try to swallow the lump in my throat. It don't work. Feels like it's gonna choke me. I can't get any words outta my mouth, so I just nod as I run back to the car. Angus climbs in the driver's seat, so I go to the other side. The bags of medical supplies Vivian and Hadley was carryin' are on my seat, and I gotta throw them in the back. At least Angus remembered to grab 'em. It wasn't exactly on my list of priorities.

"Hang on," Angus growls as he hits the gas pedal.

He steers the car through the parkin' lot and 'round the crowd of zombies while I stare out the front window and try to find the van in the distance. It's long gone and I know it. I wasted time shootin' after them. I shoulda gotten in the car right away. Shoulda drove off and run that bastard off the road. Then I'd have Vivian with me right now, and them bastards would be dead. I know, because I'd shoot every last one of 'em. And like it.

But I didn't, and now she's gone.

My stomach hardens, and I stare straight ahead. "You see where they went?"

We're flyin' down the street, and Angus is swervin' like crazy. "We'll find 'em."

I grip the dashboard, cursin' myself for my own stupidity. Why the hell didn't I get in the damn car right away? We coulda followed 'em.

"Dammit!" I scream, bangin' my fist against the window.

Pain pulses through my palm to my wrist and up my arm. Somehow it goes straight to my heart. I clench my fist and press it to my chest, tryin' to hold it all together. This is exactly why I didn't want Vivian to come to Vegas. Why I wanted her to stay in the shelter where she was safe.

We don't catch up to 'em, and Angus eventually slows the car. I can't even argue with him to keep goin'. I don't know where she is any more than he does.

"What now?" I ask through clenched teeth.

I can't think. At least not 'bout where to go or what to do. My throat feels close to closin' and there ain't a clear thought in my head.

Angus grunts and pulls over. The dead start poundin' on the side of the car, and the sound vibrates through my body 'til I think I'm gonna explode. I wish they'd stop so I could think. Could come up with a plan and figure out what I had to do to find Vivian. But right now all I can do is picture the panicked look on her face as she ran toward us.

"I know you ain't gonna like it," Angus says, "but I think we gotta head back to the shelter."

I clench my fists. He's right. I don't like it. Don't mean I think he's wrong, though. "We can't just leave 'em."

I wanna say *her*, but that'd be a dick thing to say. 'Course, if I was bein' honest, I'd admit I didn't give a flyin' fuck 'bout Hadley. Not as long as I got Vivian back.

I can't say that, though. Not even to Angus.

"We got no idea where they took them girls and we got no backup." He puts the car in gear like it's already decided. "I say we head on back and get a group together. Then we can make a real go of it."

Angus don't look at me, and I know he's not sayin' what he really thinks. That they're gone for good and we're shit outta luck. It's a good thing he don't say it. If he did, I'd probably beat the shit outta him.

I swallow and nod, but I can't for the life of me get any words outta my mouth. Especially when he starts drivin'. My eyes sting, and I know any minute I'm gonna be cryin'. I ain't cried since our mom died, and the last thing I wanna do is cry in front of Angus. I don't ever like lookin' weak, but in front of my brother, it's about the worst thing I could do.

Angus drives, runnin' over the zombies that're too stupid to get outta the way. Their bodies crunch under the tires and for some insane reason, it makes the pain inside me less intense. If we can take care of the damn walkin' dead, we should be able to handle a few men. Right?

I don't say one word the whole drive to the shelter. It's nearly five by the time it comes into view, and the sun is gettin' pretty low. That damn rock in my stomach gets even bigger. We ain't gonna be able to go back out tonight. I understand how Angus felt now, that day Winston and Trey showed up at the shelter without Vivian an' me.

We'd gone on what shoulda been a routine supply run, but the Strip was swarmin' with the dead. The other car had kids in it, and sacrificin' myself was all I could think to do. My life ain't worth more than theirs, that's for sure. My only real regret was that Vivian was there, too. I hated puttin' her in that position. But we made it. Got out of a sticky situation thanks to Winston and some fast thinkin' on his part. After that, Vivian an' me spent the night on the roof of the Paris hotel. Angus came for us the next day. I knew he would. I could always depend on my brother, and there wasn't a doubt in my mind he'd find us. Zombies or not, Angus would be there. 'Course, when we got back to the shelter we found out what a prick he'd been to everybody else. Gave Winston a black eye, even.

I'm plenty pissed 'bout Vivian bein' gone, but I ain't gonna scream an' throw punches like Angus did. Bein' reasonable is the only way we're gonna get them back.

Angus pulls up in front of the gate and I hop out, shootin' two bastards in the head before I even step away from the car. They go down, and it feels good. Watchin' 'em fall. More of the dead head my way, but they're a good distance off. I unlock the fence while I wait for them to get closer. Angus drives through, but I don't follow. I tuck my gun into the waistband of my pants and pull out my knife. It's the huntin' knife Angus gave me for my fifteenth birthday. I'm pretty sure he swiped it from the place he was workin' at, but I didn't give a shit. Still don't.

The zombies sway toward me. They remind me of the guys I used to hang out with after a night of drinkin', the way they're staggerin' all over the place. I clench my jaw tight an' step forward to meet 'em, jabbin' the blade into the first one's skull. It slices right through the bone, squishin' into the bastard's brains. A few squirts of black gunk sprays out and lands on my arm when he falls to the ground. I jerk my knife out and wipe the shit off my arm, then stab the second zombie right through his eye. The bastard goes down, and I wipe my blade clean on his uniform while I look 'round for more.

The air's ripe with the stink of rot. The bodies are pilin' up outside the fence, and the voice of reason in my brain tells me it's something we gotta take care of. But right now all I can focus on is the rage buildin' inside. How it's threatenin' to crush me.

"Axl, you dumbass!" Angus yells from inside the fence. "Get your ass over here!"

I ignore my brother and pull my gun back out, firin' off two quick shots. The bullets hit the two closest zombies, and I watch in satisfaction as their heads explode. Brain and black shit and bone rain down on the sand. More of the undead head my way.

Angus keeps yellin', and another voice joins him. I jerk 'round, lookin' toward the fence so's I can see who it is. Winston. He must've seen us on them monitors. That rational part of me says to go inside and talk it out. Somebody'll have a plan. They gotta.

I ignore it.

A zombie moans, and I turn to face it. He's a big bastard. An' ugly. He ain't wearin' a uniform, so I got no idea where he came

14

from, but I don't give a shit. I put my gun away and pull out my knife. Two steps and I'm in front of him. One swipe and my knife is in his skull. The blade rips across his face and he falls down, but that ain't enough. He's still movin'. Twitchin' on the ground like he's havin' a seizure. My blood boils, and the muscles in my hands jerk. I can't focus on nothin' else. I bring the blade down, stabbin' him through the eye before pullin' it out and doin' it all over again. Over an' over I stab the asshole 'til there's nothin' left of his face but a black, messy pool of bone and rottin' flesh. I'm only a little aware of the screams comin' outta my mouth.

"Axl!"

Winston pulls me away from the body and back toward the fence. I'm shakin', and I can't focus on nothin' he's sayin'. He leads me through the fence, then shoves me down the stairs. Into the shelter. I'm still holdin' the damn knife. My fingers ache, I'm grippin' it so tight.

"Pull yourself together!" Winston yells.

We're outside the control room, and there's a group of people there, starin' at me like I've lost my mind. Maybe I have. Every muscle in my body is stiff, and I'm shakin'. Drops of sweat drip down my face and into my eyes, but I don't wipe 'em away. It stings. Just like the tears tryin' to get out.

No one talks, and my breathin' slowly goes back to normal. My heart's still poundin', though. Only they can't see that. Winston's face is tense. He scratches at his beard. He ain't lookin' at me, and I got a feelin' it's 'cause he don't want me to see the pity in his eyes.

"Now tell us what happened."

Angus clears his throat an' looks at me. That rock in my stomach gets heavier, and I curl my hand into a fist. I wanna punch him. The prick don't even look like he cares.

"Lost the doc at the hospital. He was a suicidal bastard. Threw himself into a horde and went down with a damn smile on his face. Helped the rest of us get away, though." Angus puckers his lips like he does when he's thinkin'. I hate it when he does that. Moron looks like he just sucked on a lemon. "Axl an' me got split up from the girls when we was tryin' to get out. They took off one way an' we had to go 'nother. We got to the car first and circled 'round the parkin' lot, lookin' for 'em. Finally found 'em just as a van drove up. Two guys jumped outta the back and snatched 'em."

"They just grabbed them and drove away?" Trey narrows his

eyes an' shakes his head like none of it makes sense. Which it don't. He gives me a look that's full of sympathy, but not pity. Trey's a good guy. Never thought I'd say it 'bout no black guy, but he's alright.

"You follow them?" Nathan asks.

My insides twist, and that rage starts to creep back up on me. I haven't forgotten how that prick made Vivian strip at Sam's Club when we first met him. Doubt I ever will. He said he did it to make sure she wasn't bit, but something 'bout it never sat right with me. I ain't blind, and I know he ain't neither. Vivian's got a body, and it's hard for me to believe he didn't just want a good look.

I tear my eyes away from that asshole. "We lost 'em." It's all I can manage to get out.

I'm so mad I start shakin'. Mad at myself for lettin' 'em get away. Mad at Angus for bein' an ass. Mad at Nathan for what he did to Vivian. Mad at God for puttin' us in this fuckin' situation to start with.

Winston shakes his head and scratches his chin again. He's starin' at the floor, thinkin'. It helps ease some of the heaviness in my gut. If there's a way to find her, he'll come up with it. I know he will. If I was thinkin' clear, I might have an idea or two. But I ain't. Winston an' me, we think alike. Something that took me by surprise. Didn't think I could have so much respect for a middle-aged black guy, that's for sure. Sure as hell never thought I'd compare myself to one. Angus would shit a brick if he knew what I thought of Winston. Not that I'm gonna tell him.

When Winston looks up, he don't look happy. His shoulders slump, and he won't look me in the eye. He don't have a clue neither. "Is it even possible to find them? Vegas is huge. They could have taken them anywhere."

My gut tightens even more, and I let out a noise I ain't never made before. It sounds like an animal tryin' to rip its way outta my body. Feels that way, too. I turn 'round and punch the wall behind me as hard as I can before slumpin' to the floor. And that's it. After that, I can't move.

People 'round me talk, but I don't listen. My hand throbs. I look down. My knuckles are covered in blood. I probably broke something when I punched the wall.

I get to my feet and stagger toward the stairs.

Angus comes after me. "Where you goin'? Don't get all crazy, you hear me? We'll find them girls. We just gotta think this thing through."

I wanna hit him, but my hand hurts like hell and that will only make things worse.

"Fuck off, Angus," I mumble. "It ain't like you liked her anyways."

Angus grunts, but he don't argue.

"I gotta take a shower." I walk off, and he don't follow.

I go to Vivian an' Hadley's apartment. I'm pretty sure Darla—that bitch who abandoned Vivian—moved into mine an' Angus's. I don't wanna see her. I'm sure she'll have some fake sympathetic bullshit to say to me, and the way I'm feelin' right now, I'm likely to punch her in the face. I ain't never hit a woman, and I ain't 'bout to start now.

Even if she probably does deserve it.

I'm hopin' the shower will clear my mind. Help me think of a plan. But when I'm washed off an' wearin' clean clothes—thanks to Vivian, who did my laundry before we left—I ain't any closer to a solution. I'm willin' to drive to Vegas myself if I gotta, but I don't got a clue where to start lookin' even if I do.

I grab some food and focus on everythin' I can remember while I eat. The van was white. The men that jumped out. One was a fat bastard that looked like he was 'bout to have a heart attack from runnin', and the other was covered in tattoos. Another guy with dark hair fired at us from the passenger seat. He was a shitty shot, didn't even come close to hittin' us. I never saw the driver.

The harder I think 'bout Vegas and the hospital and that damn van, the more I feel like I'm missin' something. Something that should be obvious.

I grab a bag of chips and try to pull it open, but pain shoots through my knuckles. The bag falls from my hand and spills all over the floor, and I bite down on my lip. My hand is broke. Dammit.

"Shit," I mutter.

I gotta find the doc and get this thing looked at. Usually I wouldn't rush off to the doctor—Angus woulda called me a pussy—but I can't afford to let it go now. Not with Vivian out there. She needs me.

Gotta go back to the common area. I'm pretty sure the doc was outside the control room when Winston dragged me down, but I couldn't say for sure. There was a lot of people there, and I wasn't exactly in my right mind. Not that I am now.

I head out, and just like I thought, the doc is there, along with most everybody else. I catch his eye when I walk in and jerk my head to the side, motionin' for him to come over. I don't wanna listen to them talk 'bout Vivian and Hadley gettin' taken, and I don't wanna see their pity. Not right now when my chest hurts like this. Not when I'm likely to explode again. I gotta get my shit together. This ain't me. This is Angus.

Joshua jogs over. He's a tall, thin guy. The type of kid I woulda picked on in school. Probably sucked at sports and studied all the time. Truth is, I was jealous of guys like that. They was goin' places I couldn't even dream 'bout. Who cares if I was good at football? The only thing it did for me was get me laid in high school. While that was great at the time, it didn't make my life no better once I graduated.

"What's up?" the doc asks.

"Think I broke my hand."

I hold it out for him to look at. He takes it and feels 'round, and I gotta bite down on my lip and resist the urge to cuss at him. It hurts like hell.

"We better get you an X-ray." His eyebrows pull together in a straight line and it kinda makes him look alien. He's funny lookin' on top of being so skinny. But I like him. Wasn't sure 'bout him at first, but he grows on you. "It's a good thing you were able to get all those medical supplies—" He stops talkin' and frowns. "I'm sorry."

I pull my hand outta his and head to the stairs. "Ain't your fault."

I NEVER HAD AN X-RAY BEFORE. A ZOMBIE APOCALYPSE brings all kinds of new experiences. Like being to Vegas for the first time or killin' a man. Or fallin' in love, only to have your heart ripped out. Things just keep gettin' better an' better.

"It's broken." Joshua points at the X-ray on the screen like I know what the hell he's pointin' at. "The fifth metacarpal bone here."

"So I gotta get a damn cast? Just great." That's gonna make it tough for me to head out on my own to find Vivian. I ain't exactly sure how I'm gonna shoot with a cast on my hand.

Joshua shakes his head. "It never occurred to me to ask you guys to get the stuff to make a cast. There are some hand braces around here though, and that's better than nothing."

"Great." At least a brace I can take off if I gotta. My hand hurts like hell, but if I gotta use it to shoot, I can work through the pain.

The doc goes to the other side of the room and roots 'round in a cabinet.

It's gettin' late. I gotta get some sleep so I can leave early in the mornin' and head back to Vegas. Sleep ain't an easy thing, though. Not since I was a kid. Vivian noticed, but I never told her why. Not really sure why I didn't. She wanted to know. Asked me a few times. That's something new. Nobody ever really wanted to know me or what I was thinkin' before. She did, though. And a part of me wanted to tell her 'cause I love her. But lovin' her hurts, too. More than my damn hand, that's for sure.

Thinkin' 'bout Vivian makes the rock in my stomach get bigger. I clench my jaw an' fight against the pain. It ain't gonna do nobody no good to let it out. Not me and not Vivian.

And Hadley! Shit. I keep forgettin' 'bout Hadley.

"We're not going to leave her, you know." The doc is suddenly back in front of me. "You don't have to go alone. I know that's what you're thinking."

He's holdin' a brace in his hand, and I let him put it on. I hafta swallow the giant lump in my throat before I can talk. "We gotta find her."

"We will."

CHAPTER THREE
VIVIAN

Hadley and I ride the elevator in silence. Linebacker One doesn't loosen his grip on my arm for even a second. Like he's afraid I'm going to escape. But there's nowhere to run. Even if we weren't in an elevator, the hotel is crawling with men.

Hadley's still shaky, but that doesn't stop her from giving Linebacker Two a dirty look. He doesn't even blink.

The elevator comes to a stop on one of the top floors. When the door slides open, Linebacker One's fingers dig into my arm so hard I yelp. His grip only gets tighter as he drags me down the hall. Luckily, we don't have far to go. We stop just a few doors down with Linebacker Two and Hadley right behind us. When Linebacker One knocks, the sound echoes through the empty hall.

And makes me want to hurl.

A gray-haired man who's probably in his sixties answers the door. He's wearing a brown tracksuit and a couple gold chains. His dark eyes sweep over me before moving to Hadley. He doesn't react. Not a smile or a nod. Nothing to indicate what he's thinking. He pulls the door open further and motions for us to enter.

Oh, shit. This isn't good.

Linebacker One drags me to the middle of the room before finally letting me go. I rub my sore forearm as the second linebacker shoves Hadley my way. She bumps into me, nearly knocking me over, but I catch myself just as the gray-haired man steps forward.

His face is tanned and deeply lined, and his eyes are perfectly expressionless. "Why don't you ladies go ahead and get cleaned up?"

He jerks his head toward the back of the hotel, and I look over my shoulder. The bathroom door is open and the light is on. There are towels on the sink. For us? He has to be crazy.

"Are you fucking serious?" I spit out.

He nods, but I still can't get a good read on him. Talk about a poker face.

I shake my head and take a step back. "No."

His hand shoots forward so fast I don't have a chance to react. He wraps his fingers around my neck, and he pulls me forward until my face is only inches from his. "You and your little friend are going to go into that bathroom and take a shower. When you are done, you're going to come back out here. Understand?"

Hadley starts to sob, and the man's fingers tighten on my throat. My lungs burn and my eyes sting. I claw at his hand, but he doesn't ease up. I can't get any air!

Panicked, I nod, and he finally lets me go. I stumble back, gasping for air, and Hadley catches me. She's sobbing, but I can't look at her. My throat feels like it's on fire, and my lungs are raw. I rub my neck while the gray-haired man holds my gaze. His eyes aren't expressionless anymore. They are as black and evil as the pits of hell.

He sniffs and calmly lowers himself into a chair. "Glad we understand each other."

I grab Hadley's hand and pull her toward the bathroom. My heart pounds harder than the bass drum at a rock concert. I'm pretty sure if I don't get away from those menacing brown eyes, I'm going to lose it.

"What are we going to do?" Hadley asks the second I shut the bathroom door. Her face is red and streaked with tears, and her clothes are filthy. No wonder he wants us to shower.

The pictures of naked women in the lobby flash through my mind. I swallow and pull my shirt over my head. "Shower."

She blinks, and her bottom lip quivers.

"That's all we can do right now. I don't know exactly what's going on, but right now our best option is to cooperate. We'll figure a way out, or Axl will find us..." I try to swallow again, but it doesn't work. A ball the size of Mount Everest is lodged in my throat. How the hell did it fit in there?

"So we shower," she says slowly.

"Yes." My voice is barely a whisper.

WHEN I'M DONE, I WRAP A FLUFFY TOWEL AROUND MY body and go back to the hotel room. I don't wait for Hadley. I want a few minutes by myself with these men. She keeps crying, and it's making it impossible for me to think. To get a good read on the situation. There has to be a way out of this.

The linebackers and the man with gray hair are still here, but Suit Man is here now, too. He frowns when I walk out. "You can drop the towel."

When I don't move, he takes two quick steps toward me and jerks it away from my body. My hand lashes out on its own and makes contact with his face. A bright red streak cuts across his cheek, and his jaw tightens. He walks toward me. I hold my breath and brace myself. He's going to hit me. I know it. There's no way in hell he's going to let this go.

He clenches his fist, but he doesn't hit me. He does take another step toward me, leaving less than six inches of space between us. "Watch yourself." The words hiss through his clenched teeth. "You are very lucky I've been instructed not to damage the merchandise. Otherwise, you'd be on your ass right now." He moves even closer until there's only an inch of fresh air separating us. His breath smells like stale coffee. "But I *can* make your life a living hell."

"Too late," I spit at him. Probably a stupid move, but I was never one to keep my mouth shut.

He snorts and steps back a little. "You have no idea."

My throat tightens. He's right. I don't have a clue what's going on here or what Hadley and I are in for. I should take my own advice and cooperate.

"Let's get this over with," Suit Man says, no longer looking at me.

23

The gray-haired man steps toward me. His eyes flick to my arms, crossed over my chest. He grabs my wrist and jerks my arms free. "Arms down." Then he circles me. Slowly. Like he's inspecting cattle at an auction. "Nice," he says from behind me. My eyes sting, and I squeeze them shut, fighting to maintain control. It doesn't work. The tears won't go away.

"Stand still."

He's in front of me again. I open my eyes just as the gray-haired man snaps a picture. He steps back and takes another, and I fight the urge to run. My feet twitch, and every nerve in my body screams at me to make a break for it. I clench my fists when he walks behind me, snapping another picture.

"Got it."

I try to swallow again, but the lump is even bigger now. Pretty soon I'm going to suffocate. I can't wait.

The bathroom door opens and Hadley walks out. She's wrapped in a towel, and her hair is dripping wet. She's shaking, and her eyes stretch to the size of golf balls when she sees me standing in the middle of room naked.

The gray-haired man tosses me a red T-shirt and a pair of skimpy underwear. "Get dressed."

He crosses the room to Hadley, and I turn away. I can't watch.

The shirt is huge. It would probably be big on one of the linebackers. When I pull it over my head, it almost reaches my knees. My hands shake as I pull the underwear on. I flinch when Suit Man starts talking.

"Hadley Lucas," he says. "She's got a skinny ass, but men will be crawling all over each other to get at her."

Hadley whimpers, and even though I don't want to, I turn to face her. The gray-haired man is circling her just like he did with me.

"They're both threes. Those boys did a good job." Suit Man grins. "Don't tell them I said so."

The gray-haired man laughs, then snaps a picture. He goes behind Hadley and takes another. When he's done, he tosses her a shirt that, like mine, is huge. She isn't crying anymore, but she's still shaking. Then again, so am I.

"I'm done with them," Suit Man says, not even looking at the linebackers.

Suit Man flips through the pictures on the camera with an evil little smile on his lips. More than anything, I want to grab it out of his hand and smash it on the floor. If I had a knife right now, I'd happily cut off his balls and shove them down his throat.

The linebackers don't have to be told twice. Once again, they grip our arms and drag us down the hall. Back into the elevator. They still haven't said a single word to us. Maybe they aren't human. They could be cyborgs. It's possible. A few weeks ago, I would have laughed my ass off at the suggestion that zombies existed, but now it's just a part of everyday life. Cyborgs could be real too for all I know. Along with vampires and fairies, maybe even werewolves.

My mind is wandering—off the edge of a cliff, if I'm lucky—but when the elevator door slides open, it snaps me back to reality. The hall reeks of death, and the air is thick and stale even under the stench. Hadley gags, and I cover my nose while Linebacker One jerks me forward. I stumble out of the elevator, trying hard not to breathe out of my nose.

We're in a short hallway with only a handful doors. I see the source of the stench at the end of the hall. Three zombies chained to the wall, blocking the door that leads to the stairwell. They moan and thrash as the men drag Hadley and me toward them, frantically pulling against their chains as they try to get free. My heart pounds and my feet stop moving. I struggle against the tight grip on my arm, trying to get away from the zombies just dying to rip me apart. But the linebacker grips me tighter, digging his fingers roughly into my skin as he jerks me forward.

The linebacker holding Hadley stops in front of a door. The zombies moan, and I jerk back while Linebacker One pulls me forward. Linebacker Two slides a keycard into the lock. A zombie screams, and Hadley whimpers. The light on the lock changes from red to green. Linebacker Two opens the door and shoves Hadley inside, and I'm pushed in right behind her.

I stumble forward and spin around. "What the hell?" I say just as the door slams in my face.

"What's going on?" Hadley says as I turn around to survey our surroundings.

We're in a suite. A huge suite. The kind that was probably reserved for celebrities and high-rollers. But it isn't luxurious anymore. The air is stuffy and the scent of decay has seeped its way in from the hall, filling the room with the pungent odor. The place hasn't been cleaned since probably before this whole mess started, and the room is crowded with women. Close to a dozen are gathered in the living room, and more come out of the bedrooms as Hadley and I walk forward. Blankets and pillows lay all over the floor like little makeshift beds. The women range from age fifteen to fifty, and they're every shape, size, and color imaginable. None of them look particularly well. Physically or mentally.

They all stare at us, but no one says a word. A woman in her late thirties stands in front of me, and our eyes meet. She's average-looking and slightly overweight, with greasy, chin-length brown hair. She's dressed like Hadley and me: T-shirt that's way too big and nothing else. She has dark circles under eyes, and there are bruises on her forearms exactly where mine will be after a few more walks with the linebackers.

"What's happening?" I ask.

She bites her bottom lip. Her eyes go over me, then move to Hadley. They widen. She recognizes Hadley, it's obvious. The woman takes a small step back, like she's afraid to be associated with a former celebrity or something, then glances around the room. Most of the other women don't even look our way.

The brunette shakes her head and stares at the carpet. "Do you really have to ask?" she finally says. "Use your imagination and you'll be able to figure out why you're here."

"But none of this makes sense!" Hadley says. "The men who grabbed us were talking in some kind of code. Twos and threes, and a bunch of other stuff that sounded like total nonsense. We just want to know what we're dealing with." Her voice shakes, but at least she isn't crying anymore.

The brunette frowns, but she doesn't look up. "You'll figure it out, just like the rest of us did."

She walks away, heading into another part of the suite that isn't visible from here. The few women who did look up when we first came in seem to have lost interest. They stare at the walls, the floor, their hands. The room is unnaturally silent.

"What do we do?" Hadley whispers.

I shake my head and slump back against the wall, trying to keep the terror threatening to rip me apart tucked away. "Axl will find us." It comes out flat, and Hadley flinches.

She swallows. "Until then?"

I bite down on my bottom lip. Hard. "Try and stay safe."

HADLEY AND I HUDDLE TOGETHER IN A CORNER OF THE room as night closes in. These women barely speak, and the silence is killing me. We've only been here for about three hours, but it already feels like days. My stomach growls, and in the absence of conversation, all I can do is think. Think about Emily, about Axl. About what lies ahead. My insides are one giant knot, twisting tighter and tighter as time passes.

We have one pillow and one blanket between the two of us. There aren't enough to go around, and we had to fight for these. The same goes for the food. Shortly after we got here, a few men came in and dumped a box of prepackaged snacks on the floor. The type of stuff you find in a vending machine, which is probably where they got it. The women scrambled for the food, and by the time Hadley and I figured out what was going on, all we could get was a package of brown sugar Pop-Tarts.

It's not even seven o'clock, but Hadley has already dozed off. Her head rests on my shoulder, and she's breathing heavily, blowing my hair into my face every time she exhales. It tickles my nose, but I can't make myself move to stop it. My insides are numb.

Most of the other women are still awake, but I have a hard time looking at them. The blank expressions in their eyes makes my stomach ache. They all act like they're waiting for something horrible to happen. Maybe they are.

There's a girl curled up under a blanket not too far from me. She has dark hair, and even though I can't see much of her face, I can tell she's young. Maybe seventeen. Her face is covered in bruises, and her eye is so black it's swollen shut. I heard someone call her Megan, but she hasn't spoken at all. Imagining what happened to her makes the Pop-Tart I ate threaten to come back up. I swallow and force it to stay down. I can't afford to lose what little food I get.

Hadley jerks awake when the door bursts open. The women around us shrink down like if they get close enough to the ground the men coming into the room won't be able to see them. It doesn't work, of course. The linebackers walk through the room, grabbing women and shoving them toward the door. This is the terrible thing all these women were waiting for. This is where Hadley and I find out what's going on. Now I'm not sure I want to know.

27

Hadley clenches my leg, and I freeze in place, holding my breath. She sucks in a deep breath. I guess she is, too.

The same linebacker who dragged me into the suite a few hours ago stops in front of us. He looks right at me. "You've been requested."

His voice is higher than I expected, and for one crazy second I think of Mike Tyson. When he grabs my arm, something between a giggle and a sob pops out of my mouth. Hadley's cries echo in my ears as the linebacker drags me toward the door, but I don't fight him. There doesn't seem to be much point.

He pulls me into the stinking hallway, then releases my arm and shoves me forward. I'm so panicked that I'm gasping for breath, and when I inhale the stench of death, my stomach lurches. The Pop-Tart jumps to my throat, and I have to swallow it back down for the second time. Other women are herded toward the elevator in front of me. I count six in all. Their sobbing mixes with the zombies' moans. My head pounds.

The other linebacker stands next to the elevator, holding the door open. He shoves the women inside, and when it's my turn, I almost fall. I bump into a black woman in her thirties, but she doesn't even look at me. Both linebackers step in and the door slides shut. The elevator lurches, then moves down, and my body shakes.

No one talks, but there's plenty of crying. My own eyes are amazingly dry.

We stop after two floors. Linebacker Two grabs a couple women and pulls them from the elevator while Linebacker One holds the door open. When the first man comes back—alone—we continue down. My stomach tightens the further we get. The suspense presses down on me, almost suffocating me.

The door opens, and when Linebacker One turns around, he's looking right at me. He grabs my arm and jerks me forward. This time, I fight. I pull against his grip and refuse to move my feet, but he digs his fingers in tighter and drags me out of the elevator. My heart thumps against my ribcage and I frantically scan the hall. There has to be something I can do. A way to escape or something I can hit him with. Anything!

There's nothing, though. No hope.

I'm still struggling when he stops in front of room 613 and knocks.

The door opens, and I'm shoved inside before I even have a chance to see who opened it. I stumble forward, tripping over my own feet. The door slams shut as I fall to my knees in the middle of the room. My heart nearly jumps out of my chest when footsteps approach me from behind. Frantically, I crawl forward, trying to get away. I twist around as I scan the room for something I can use as a weapon. My heart stutters and almost stops when my eyes meet his. It's New Guy.

He puts his hands up and takes a step back. "Relax. I'm not going to touch you."

His words have no meaning. I jump to my feet and charge him, slamming my shoulder into his chest. Knocking him to the ground. His arms go around me, and I fall on top of him. My arms get tangled in my T-shirt and I swear, then jerk my body back and forth as I desperately try to free myself. New Guy rolls over, taking me with him. He's on top of me. I thrust my knee up, trying to make contact with his crotch. He curses and pins my legs down with his. I finally get my arms free, but he's ready for it. He grabs my wrists and pins them to the ground. I twist and wiggle, screaming in frustration, but I'm trapped.

"I said I'm not going to hurt you!"

I gasp for breath, and my eyes meet his. Something about the look on his face makes me freeze. His eyes aren't as cold as they were in the car, and there's emotion in his voice. I actually believe him.

He eases up the second I stop squirming, but he doesn't get off of me. "My name is Jon. I'm not one of these sick bastards. I'm just looking for my sister. That's all." His green eyes shimmer, but I can't feel sympathy for this guy. *He* brought me here.

Jon sighs and releases my wrists, then sits back. But he doesn't get up. I glare at him and massage my sore wrists. He doesn't talk.

"What?" I snap. "You want me to thank you for not raping me? Well, fuck you."

"Look, I'm sorry." His voice shakes.

He looks down and blinks like he just noticed he's still sitting on me. Finally, he gets up. I scramble to me feet, taking a few steps back. I want some distance between this asshole and me.

Jon slumps onto the bed. "I needed to gain their trust. It was the only way I had a chance of finding my sister." He doesn't say anything else. He just stares at the floor.

29

The silence between us stretches out, and my heartbeat doesn't slow. Does he want me to say something? To help him? *Do* I help him? I don't want to. He brought me here. As far as I'm concerned, he can go screw himself.

On the other hand, he wants to get his sister out and he obviously needs help. This *could* be the answer I was looking for. Our ticket out of here. But can I trust him? Will he even know what to do to get us out? He doesn't look like it. At the moment, he doesn't look like he could handle a fly, let alone a hotel full of armed men. But maybe he can get word to Axl…

Yes! My heart jumps, and I blurt out, "What's your sister's name?"

Jon swallows, and when he looks up, his eyes are brimming with tears. "Her name's Megan. She has dark hair and green eyes. She's only sixteen." His voice is thick with unshed tears. He clears his throat and looks back down. Like he can't look at me any longer. I'm not sure if he's ashamed of his tears or ashamed of himself for dragging me here, but I don't care.

Megan. The girl with the black eye. Crap. This guy is fragile enough without knowing any of that. Should I tell him? Probably, but first I want some information. I want to know what the hell is going on here, and with the way he's acting, he's liable to fall apart at the first sign of bad news. We need to get some things out in the open before that happens.

"I know who your sister is." His head snaps up, but I shake my head. "First, I want you to tell me what all this is about. None of these bastards will talk, and the girls in the room are all either too scared or too damaged to explain. We're in the dark here, and I don't like it. I need to be prepared, which I can't do without information."

Hope flashes in his eyes, and he jumps to his feet. He takes a step toward me. "You know her? She's okay then?"

I keep my face blank and press my lips together. No way in hell am I going to say another word until he tells me what's going on.

"Shit!" He shakes his head and stares at the floor. When he looks back up, there are more tears in his eyes. He knows it's not good news. "Fine. Sit down and I'll tell you what I know."

I sit on the edge of the bed, and he starts pacing the room, playing with the hem of his shirt. "One man started this whole thing. He got a few people together, armed them, and took over the casino. They cleared out the dead and fortified it so no more zombies could get in. They knew they were safe inside, and as long as they had supplies, they could live here forever. But the stuff in the casino wouldn't last long. The boss didn't want to risk his own ass, so he started recruiting other men. But he needed a way to pay them. Money's worth shit now, and the promise of a room in the casino wasn't enough motivation. There's only one thing these kind of men would be willing to risk their lives for: sex."

I exhale as some of the pieces of the puzzle slowly come together. It makes perfect sense. There are no laws now. No right or wrong. Women have always been easy prey for assholes, so of course something like this would happen.

My throat tightens when I think about all those women up in the suite and all the men down in the lobby. Damn. "So that's why we're here? As payment for the men who bring in supplies."

Jon nods and looks at me apologetically. I want to punch him. "I'm sorry. I really am. I didn't want to help them, but it was the only way to get in and look for my sister. This place is secure and heavily guarded."

My fist tightens. He can shove his sorry up his ass. "How does it work? These payments?"

"They get any woman they can find. Young, old, fat, thin, ugly, pretty—anything goes. The women are separated into three tiers. Tier one is the older, less attractive women. They're payment for smaller scavenges. Things like water bottles from the other casinos or snacks from the vending machines. Anything easy to get and less of a risk. Tier two are the women in better shape. You get them by bringing in bigger hauls of food and supplies. Tier three would be the more attractive girls. They're harder to get. You need to bring in something big. Guns or fuel for the generator. Anything that's a big risk. You and your actress friend are tier three."

"Great," I mutter. "I'm so flattered."

He shakes his head and leans against the dresser. "No, you're lucky. It isn't easy to get a tier three girl, and most guys just settle for tier two. I had to bring in a load of guns to get a night with you. Luckily, I already had them from before Megan was taken. I'd stashed them in a safe place and was waiting until I needed them as leverage."

That makes me relax a little. It's going to take something big for someone to get at Hadley. Hopefully, that will help keep her calm. She's trying, but I have a feeling her breaking point is very close to the surface.

But she's *Hadley Lucas.*

The world may have gone to shit, but when it comes to some things, people have long memories. Americans used to worship movie stars the way Muslims worshiped Allah. How long before someone decides it's worth the risk? We need to get out of here. And fast.

"Now you tell me about my sister," Jon says forcefully.

I bite down on my lip and shake my head. "Promise me one more thing first."

He takes a menacing step forward, but I don't flinch. I can take a lot of abuse, something that's going to come in handy in this new world of madness.

Jon frowns, but he doesn't argue.

"I'll tell you about your sister and help you plan a way to get her out, but next time you bring in a big haul, choose Hadley. Not me."

His frown deepens. He brushes his dark hair behind his ear and narrows his eyes on my face. Like he's waiting for a punchline. Only this is no joke. "You know that will make you more susceptible? You'd sacrifice yourself for her?"

I nod emphatically, trying to look more confident than I feel. It's best not to focus on the consequences of what I'm saying right now. "I can take it, but I'm not sure if Hadley can." Hopefully, it's true.

"Fine," he says impatiently. "Now my sister."

I take a deep breath. This is going to hurt. "She's pretty banged up, but she's alive. Someone said they had a doctor look at her. Anyway, she's supposedly out of rotation until she heals. That's good at least." His eyes fill with tears, and he looks away. Even though I don't want to, I feel bad for him. "I'm sorry."

He nods but doesn't look up. "Thank you."

Jon sits on the edge of the bed and stares down at his hands. His shoulders slouch, and he looks totally defeated. My insides tighten. This is what Axl is going through right now. Only worse. He has no idea where I am.

Now we're both depressed. Neither one of us speaks, and the silence in the room presses down around us, threatening to crush me. I need a distraction. My eyes land on the remote, and I almost stand up. But I stop myself and squeeze my eyes shut. There's no TV in zombie world. I almost laugh. That was the name of that stupid movie Hadley was in. Would she find it funny after everything we've been through? I doubt it.

"So what's your name?" Jon asks, startling me.

I rip my eyes away from the TV and find him watching me. "Vivian."

"Were you at the hospital looking for supplies because someone in your group was hurt?"

Now he wants to make small talk? I almost tell him to shut up, but I need to focus. My mind is turning into Jell-O just sitting here, staring at the carpet.

Those intense green eyes of his don't look away from me, and he doesn't blink. In another time, I would have thought he was sexy. Dark hair and a strong jaw, broad shoulders. Now I just ache for Axl.

I exhale until my lungs are as empty as my life was before all this bullshit happened. Then slowly fill them back up with air. "No, we were just stocking up."

He glances away like looking at me hurts. Maybe he feels guilty. "They get a lot of women that way. They clear out the ER so it seems safe, then wait it out. That's how they got Megan. Only we were in Boulder City. We were with a couple other people, and one of us got injured. We needed something to clean the injury with and just happened to be close to the hospital. It seemed like the safest place to go for that stuff. I was afraid she'd get hurt, so I made her stay in the car. I saw them dragging her out of the car through the window. By the time I got outside, they were already driving away."

Something tugs at my heart when his expression contorts with pain.

No! I refuse to feel bad for this guy. *He* is the reason I'm here. He put my life in danger and ripped me away from one of the only people I've ever loved.

But I don't want to stop talking. If I do, I'll start thinking, and that will only lead to Axl. "How'd you find her?"

He clenches his fist and looks away. "I got in the car and followed them. I left the other people I was with in the hospital. Just jumped in and took off without even looking back. I kept a good

33

distance between us, but they had to have known I was following them. I just don't think they cared because this place is so secure."

He actually feels bad about leaving his friends. I hate how human he's making himself. I don't want to sympathize with him, but I can't help it. "Did you ever go back to check on the others?"

He shakes his head.

We stare at each other for a few minutes in silence. I don't know what to say to this guy. Chatting with him seems pointless. He and I aren't going to be pals. He dragged me to a hotel full of men who are just dying to rape me. It's not exactly the basis for a friendship. On the other hand, we do need to work together if we're going to get out of this alive. And whole.

CHAPTER FOUR

AXL

"Axl, we need to talk."

Winston stops me on the way back to my room. It's gettin' late, and the common room is almost empty. Nathan, Trey, Anne, and the teenager that came in with the last group are all sittin' 'round. I can't think of his name, but I remember he came in handy when we was unloadin' the truck of supplies. Seemed pretty good with a knife.

The only other people in the room are Angus and Darla. They're hangin' all over each other at the bar, and she's got her tongue halfway down his throat. She's trashy-lookin'. Exactly the kinda woman Angus always goes after. I knew he was gonna get in her pants the second he saw her. We never did see eye to eye when it came to women. Darla and Vivian are the perfect example. I always went for the girls who were born trailer trash but didn't quite fit. Angus went for the women that oozed it. They loved their lives and had no intention of ever changin'. Didn't see nothin' wrong with it.

I tear my eyes away from my brother and focus on Winston. I gotta get it together. Angus can do whatever he wants. It don't bother me none. Long as I get Vivian back.

"I'm leavin' first thing in the mornin'," I tell Winston. "Nothin' else to talk 'bout."

Winston presses his lips together. "I understand how you feel, but I think you need to think this through a little more. We don't have a clue where they might be."

I shake my head and try hard to control the rage buildin' inside me. It's like something alive is tryin' to dig its way outta my body. Like an animal is trapped in my chest.

I swallow and try to keep it hidden. I don't wanna lose my cool with Winston. That's an Angus thing. I always looked up to my brother when I was a kid, even if we didn't always see things the same. Angus is the toughest son of a bitch I ever met. He's never done nothin' half-assed in his life, and he's never backed down from a fight. But things are different now. This world we're livin' in has changed. It's changed me. But Angus can't see it, and I'm startin' to worry things ain't never gonna be the same between us after all this. Not unless he can pull his head outta his ass and adjust.

"I ain't gonna just walk away from her," I say between clenched teeth. It comes out rougher than I wanted it to, but Winston don't even blink.

"I'm not talking about walking away. I'm talking about taking a little time to think this through. We have to sit down and talk this over, figure out where to start searching."

He's right. Dammit. But that don't mean it makes me feel better. My neck and shoulders are so tight it feels like they're made of steel. I take a deep breath and work on stayin' calm. "You got any ideas?"

Winston relaxes a little. "We were talking about it just now. Angus told us which direction the van went, so we pulled out a map and Nathan's been helping us brainstorm. He's lived in Vegas his whole life, so he knows the city pretty well. Jhett too."

Jhett. That's the kid's name.

I go over to where they're sittin' so I can get a better look. I wanna know what they're thinkin'. My brain ain't workin', and I got no damn idea where to start. Every time I try to think, all I can see is Vivian's face. Thinkin' 'bout what she might be goin' through right now makes me wanna hurl. I swear to God, if anybody lays a hand on her, I'll rip their heart out.

"What are y'all thinkin'?"

Nathan looks up, and I gotta fight the urge to punch him. He's tryin' to help. I gotta keep that in mind.

"According to your brother, they headed north when they left the hospital. Toward the Strip. Vegas is big and they could be anywhere, but I'd put my money on a casino."

"What about the Monte Carlo?" Darla's voice comes from behind me, and I turn to see her and Angus are walkin' over.

My first impulse is to tell her to shut the hell up. But somewhere deep in my brain, a memory claws its way to the surface. "Didn't you say you saw people outside the Monte Carlo?"

Darla nods, and Angus puts his arm around her waist. "Sure did. Saw a few men going in and out. Thought about heading over there to check it out, but wasn't sure if it was a good idea. Seems like I made the right choice."

I can't help glarin' at her. It pisses me off how little she seems to care that Vivian is gone. Goin' around shovin' her tongue down my brother's throat like a whore. Right in front of everybody. Sure Darla don't know Vivian all that well, but she's still her kid.

"Did you see anything else on the Strip that looked suspicious?" Winston asks. He steps between Darla and me like he knows I wanna punch her right in the goddamn mouth.

Darla's eyebrows pull together and her eyes narrow as she tries to remember. Her face scrunches up so much I think she just might hurt herself. She don't look so much like Vivian when she does that.

"Not sure. I was pretty busy focusing on not getting killed, but seems like the Monte Carlo was the only casino I saw people coming in and out of."

Winston looks over at me and nods. "Might be a good place to start."

Angus grins at Darla like she's some kind of genius, and I look away. What an ass.

I head for the stairs. "Then we'll go in the mornin'."

"Axl, we still need to talk this thing through. Come up with a plan," Winston calls to me.

I shake my head and keep walkin'. I gotta get away from that bitch before I let her have it. "I ain't waitin'. Anybody that wants to come better be here at six. I'm gonna get some sleep."

I take the stairs before Winston can argue, but I've only gotten down one floor when Angus stops me. "You're gonna get yourself killed."

I keep walkin'. "Gotta try. You wouldn't understand."

Angus grabs my arm and turns me 'round to face him. His mouth is all puckered up, and he shakes his head. "Think this thing through, little brother. I ain't tellin' you to leave her, but you can't just run off. You got no plan."

"So you're on Winston's side?"

His face hardens, and he lets go of my arm. He spits on the floor at our feet. I knew that would get to him. "Fuck no."

"Then be ready at six."

I head back down the stairs, and Angus don't argue. And he don't follow me. I'm glad. I need some time to myself. To think.

Vivian and Hadley's condo is quiet. Almost too quiet. I strip down to my boxers and climb in bed, buryin' my face in the pillow. It smells like Vivian's hair. Some kind of flower or fruit or some shit. Whatever it is, it makes my throat feel like somebody has their hands wrapped around it. Like they're squeezin' the life outta me.

I try to relax. To get some sleep. As usual, it ain't workin'. I haven't gotten a real good night's sleep in years. Back before my mom died. It used to be nightmares that kept me awake, but now it's more like habit. My body's used to gettin' just a few hours of sleep at a time. Although the dreams still come from time to time.

After a couple hours of starin' at nothin', I get up an' start pacin' the room. Thinkin' 'bout tomorrow mornin' and what I'm gonna need. Weapons. That's 'bout all. I don't need to take no clothes or food. Clothes are a luxury I don't need on a rescue mission, and food is easy to come by if you know where to look. I do.

So all I gotta do in the mornin' is stuff a bag full of weapons and go.

The thought should help me relax. But it don't. The hours go by, and I pace back and forth in the condo, walkin' in circles. Tryin' to get my brain to stop thinkin' 'bout Vivian. It don't work.

'Bout three in the mornin' I finally give up and throw on some clothes. My body ain't relaxed even a little bit since I saw Vivian get pulled into that van. I can sleep after I get her back. And I *will* get her back.

I've got all the weapons and supplies we need packed by five o'clock. Now all I gotta do is wait. I'd leave now if I could, but I need the others. I need the help. Much as I hate to admit it.

Trey comes staggerin' in 'round five thirty, carryin' a cup of coffee and lookin' groggy. "Morning," he says, barely lookin' up.

I nod but can't seem to get any words out. I've spent the last several hours goin' over the plan in my head, thinkin' 'bout everything that can go wrong. 'Bout the things Vivian might be goin' through right now. It's weighin' on me.

"You doing okay?" Trey asks.

He's studyin' me like if he looks hard enough, he'll be able to read my mind. I just shrug. I ain't okay, but I was never one to bother other people with my problems. Probably 'cause I learned at an early age that people usually just don't give a shit. Nobody cared when I was little and my mama slapped me 'round. Nobody cared when I got older and I showed up at school with cuts and bruises. Just the way it is.

Trey frowns like he knows how I'm feelin'. Probably does. He and Parvarti seem to be all hot and heavy now. Guess he'd be feelin' 'bout the same way if she was the one missin'.

It hits me for the first time what he might be givin' up to save Vivian. I hadn't thought 'bout what the others were riskin' before now, but I suddenly realize it ain't exactly fair of me to ask them to do this.

"You don't gotta go," I say. "I know it's a risk."

Trey don't even look up from his coffee. "I'm going. Vivian stuck her neck out for Parv and me. I can't forget that. And you'd do the same for me. If Parv was the one missing, you'd go after her. You're a good guy."

He's right. And Vivian would be right there next to me. Still don't feel fair, though. "I just wanna let you know that I wouldn't blame you if you didn't go."

Trey takes a deep breath and looks up. His hands squeeze the coffee cup like he's tryin' to crush it. "I'm going. There's nothing else to talk about." He's quiet for a minute, drinkin' his coffee. Then he says, "I want you to know how grateful I am that you guys let Parv and me tag along. I don't know what we would have done if you hadn't."

"You woulda been fine."

"I don't know. I wasn't really exposed to any of this stuff growing up. My parents had money and they tried to give us everything they never had. That meant an easy life for me and my brother. We were handed everything. I never had to work a day in my life. I'm sure my parents thought it was the best thing for me, and if things hadn't changed it probably would have been fine. But in this world, I would have been pretty useless."

I press my lips together and shake my head. "You sound jealous." That's a new one. I ain't never had somebody be jealous of me. Never been a reason to.

Trey shrugs and chuckles like he can't believe it neither. "Guess I am. You know who you are and where you fit in. I'd be lost in all this if it wasn't for the things you taught me. I owe you."

I got nothin' to say to all that. It's an uncomfortable feelin', havin' somebody think I'm better than them. Never happened before. Except maybe back when I played high school football, and all that was bullshit. It weren't real like this.

I say the first thing that pops into my head. "I didn't wanna go get you. Vivian and the doc did all that. I was on Angus's side."

Trey laughs, which is nuts. He should be pissed. "That's what I like about you, Axl. You always tell the truth. I never have to worry about what's going on inside your head."

"Never saw a reason to keep my thoughts to myself. It ain't like they're all that deep or nothing."

Trey lets out another laugh just as Winston walks into the room. He looks me over in a way that makes my scalp tingle. He scratches at his beard and shakes his head. "You look like shit. You get any sleep?"

"I'll sleep when Vivian's safe."

Winston frowns even more. "You're not going to be much use to Vivian if you don't get some rest."

"I'll be fine," I snap, then press my lips together even harder. That sounded too much like Angus. Shit.

Winston don't seem to care. He just shakes his head and gets busy gatherin' his stuff. Gettin' ready to go.

Angus and Darla walk in a few minutes later, and by then I can't hold still. I'm ready to go. They're draped all over each other just like last night, and Darla's dressed like she's plannin' on comin' with us. I try not to glare at her, but it ain't easy. I don't know why she'd want to come. Vivian don't mean nothin' to her.

Angus catches my eye and puckers his lips. "You got a plan?" He's choosin' to ignore the fact that I'm glarin' at Darla. Figures.

I nod because I do have a plan. That's what happens when you don't waste time with sleep. You're ready for anything. "Been up all night thinkin'. Best thing may be to head on back to Paris where Vivian and me spent the night. We could see a lot of the Strip from up on that roof. The Monte Carlo ain't that far, we should be able to get a good look at it."

"So you want to just drive up the Strip and walk into the casino?" Trey says doubtfully. "We could hardly get down the Strip before."

"We'll have to create another diversion," Winston says.

"What if they don't go for it?" Trey don't look very confident. Damn. I wish he'd stay behind. He's useful, but I don't wanna see somebody else get hurt.

"We'll work it out," I say. "We gotta."

Trey nods, but the expression on his face don't change.

I ignore it and turn to Winston. "We all that's comin'?"

"Nathan said he was going to come. Let's just wait a few minutes to see if he shows up."

I nod even though I ain't too happy 'bout Nathan comin'. Every man helps, but I'm still pissed at him for makin' Vivian strip. I guess he's probably tryin' to make it up to us. It's gonna take a lot.

A few minutes before six, Nathan comes walkin' in with his wife clingin' to him. I can't remember her name. She don't look like she's very happy to see him go. It reminds me of when we was in Sam's Club and she freaked out just 'cause he was goin' to the front of the store without her. I didn't really get it at the time, but I kinda do now. Not sure I'm ever gonna let Vivian outta my sight when I finally get her back.

And I will get her back.

There's nobody 'round to back us up when we go outside this time, so Angus and me head on over to the fence while everybody else climbs in the car. The zombies come chargin'. They're pretty rotted, but they ain't slowin' down like you'd think they would. It ain't gonna be easy to get out.

Angus pulls the gate open as soon as Winston's ready. Every muscle in my body tenses when the zombies head toward us. I got my knife in one hand and my gun in the other, but I don't do a thing 'til they're closer. Winston pulls through, runnin' over a handful on his way out. I hack away at the nearest zombies, takin' out the two bodies that managed to make it inside the fence before runnin' out after the car. Angus shuts the gate, then comes over to help, and we fight our way to the Explorer. It's surrounded, and Trey has to roll down the back window so he can take a couple out from inside.

A zombie in camo grabs my arm with his bony fingers and pulls me closer. His grip is strong, and I gotta fight to break free. But I stumble on a lifeless body at my feet and slam back against the car. The zombie's rotten mouth is only inches from takin' a bite outta my arm when Angus stabs him in the head.

He grabs my shirt and jerks me into the car. I climb in, rubbin' the place on my arm where the bastard's fingers dug in as Angus gets in behind me.

"You get scratched?" Angus growls once we're both safely inside and Winston is on his way.

I shake my head but flip on the overhead light to get a closer look anyways. Nothing.

I let out a big breath. "I'm okay. You saved my ass, though." My voice shakes. Damn zombies.

Angus nods and looks the other way, pretendin' he's starin' at Darla's tits. But I know him better than that. Things are gonna get pretty bad for everybody in the shelter if something happens to me.

CHAPTER FIVE

VIVIAN

"Tell me you have a plan for getting us out of here." The silence is starting to be too much. Jon dragged me into this. Now I want to know what he plans to do to get me *out*.

Jon shakes his head and stares at the carpet like it will somehow give him the answers. "No. I needed to figure out where my sister was first."

I suck in a deep breath and hold back the dozens of names I want to scream at him. "Nothing? No plan at all?"

Did this guy seriously drag Hadley and me into this without even a thought as to how we were going to get out? What little bit of sympathy I had for him and his sister disappears. This guy put me in danger. I don't have to feel bad for him.

Jon shakes his head again and starts pacing the room. After a few minutes, he stops and rubs the back of his neck. He's clueless. I can see it written in every move he makes.

Which leaves it up to me to get us out of this mess.

There's a raw spot on the inside of my cheek like I bit it while I was sleeping. It stings when I gnaw on it, and the sharp coppery taste of blood fills my mouth. I chew harder as I think. If I'm not careful, I'll end up with a big, gaping hole where my face used to be. Then I'll fit right in. I'll be able to walk down the Strip and the zombies will think I'm one of them. *There's* my way out.

I grind my teeth and push the ridiculous thought out of my head. I need to get my shit together. It's going to be up to me to save our asses. If I wait for this guy to figure it out, we're all screwed.

So what are my options? I could tell him where to find the others, but that would mean telling him where the shelter is. How much can I really trust him? He didn't rape me, but he did help kidnap Hadley and me. Obviously, he's willing to do anything to make sure his sister is safe.

So what other choice do I have? There's no way we're going to be able to break out of this casino on our own. Megan is too damaged to be of much help, and Jon seems pretty useless. He acted like a tough guy in the van, but that person has vanished. Now he just looks lost. Lost and confused. Hadley and I are only two people. We don't stand a chance against this hotel full of men. I *need* Axl.

Even if I did tell Jon where the shelter is, I'm not sure it would matter. Axl definitely went back to the shelter for backup—he'd be stupid not to—but there's no way he'd stay there long. He's on his way back to Vegas now or will be soon. Either way, that means two things. One, I don't have to reveal the location of the shelter. And two, I have to think like Axl so I can figure out where they'll be.

"What?" Jon's eyes narrow on my face. He knows I'm coming up with something.

"I have friends," I say. "They can help you."

He jumps to his feet. "Where are they?"

I shake my head and stare at the carpet. "I'm not sure, that's the problem."

I flip through the memories in mind, thinking about all the places Axl and I have been in Vegas. He'd want to go somewhere familiar so I could find him if I got away. I'm sure of it. So there's really only one place that really makes sense.

"Paris," I whisper. My head snaps up, and I get to my feet. I twist a strand of blonde hair around my finger and pace. "Can you see the Paris casino from the Monte Carlo?"

"Yeah, it's across the street a few casinos down, but it's not far."

Now I'm even more certain that's where he'll go. "That's where they'll be. He'll want to be able to stake the place out until he can come up with a plan. Axl isn't impulsive."

I say the last part with less certainty. Usually he isn't impulsive, but who knows how he'll react to this situation. He could have lost it. Lord knows it's in his blood. Look at Angus.

Jon frowns and takes a step back. "What do you want me to do? Just stroll in there and tell them I'm the guy who kidnapped you? Sounds like a good way to get myself killed."

"Axl won't kill you. The most he'd do is beat the shit out of you. If he killed you, he'd never find me."

Jon rolls his eyes and rubs the back of his neck again. He looks nervous. Good. I want him to be.

"Still doesn't sound good for me," he says.

I press my lips together and suck in a deep breath. Is this guy kidding me? My face heats up as I take a menacing step toward him. "I don't give a shit. You brought me here, and it's not like you have a plan. You do this or we're all screwed!" He still doesn't look convinced, so I take a step closer and lower my voice. "They're not going to let your sister just lay around forever, you know. Eventually, she's going to have to earn her way."

He glares at me, but I meet his stare with a vicious one of my own. This guy will do whatever it takes to get us out of here or he'll be sorry.

"You do it or I tell the men in charge what you're really doing here. What do you think they'll do to you? To your sister?"

His eyes flash. "You wouldn't."

"I didn't survive a zombie apocalypse just to live out the rest of my life as a whore."

Jon's face hardens, and he looks away. I don't say anything. I want to give my words time to sink in. He needs to know who he's dealing with. That I won't just roll over and die. I'm a survivor. Always have been. Maybe that makes me better equipped to deal with this situation or maybe not. I don't know. All I know is nothing brought me down before zombies showed up, and there's no way in hell I'm ready to give up now.

"Fine," Jon finally says, looking up. His eyes aren't hard or angry, just resigned. "Tell me what to do and I'll do it."

I swallow and nod, trying to keep the hope swirling around

inside me down. Letting it out now would be pointless. There's still a long road ahead of us, and getting out of this isn't going to happen overnight. As much as I hate to admit it, we could be here for a few days.

"Go to Paris. To the pool on the roof. That's where they'll be. Ask for Axl James."

"Axl? Who is he?"

I bite down on my bottom lip and struggle to come up with a word for who Axl is. Boyfriend? That seems too childish. Lover? Too casual. Axl's mine. That's the only way I know how to describe it. But Jon wouldn't understand.

"We're together," I finally say. "It doesn't matter. All you need to do is find my friends."

"What then?"

I don't have a clue, but I'm more than confident Axl and Winston will be able to come up with something. Hell, I wouldn't put it past Angus to be able to find a way out of this. He's a racist moron, but he's resourceful. "Come up with a plan."

Jon scoffs and squeezes his head between his hands like he's trying to crush his own skull. "You might be underestimating the men running this place just a little."

"Whatever. Just get there." I don't want a debate. I just want him to get over to the casino so Axl knows I'm alive. "Just get there."

Jon sits on the bed, and I want to scream. "What are you doing? Go!"

He shakes his head and leans back. Like he's ready for a nap or something. "Can't. It would be pretty suspicious if I ran out of here in the middle of the night, especially when I have you here."

His eyes move down my body, and I'm suddenly very self-conscious. I'm not exactly dressed, plus I trust this guy about as far as I can throw him. I squirm on the bed, trying to scoot further away from him.

One corner of his mouth turns up. "You don't trust me? I haven't even tried to touch you."

"How could I trust you? You dragged me and my friend here." I roll my eyes. Why do we even need to have this conversation?

He nods but doesn't look the least bit guilty. "I'm sorry, but I didn't have a choice. I was told to go out with those guys. I didn't volunteer. I had to prove my loyalty or they would have thrown me out. My sister's just a kid."

I probably should feel bad for him. Megan is young, and they didn't ask to be in this situation. But I can't. Sacrificing me for his sister doesn't exactly make him the most sympathetic person.

"Well, don't expect me to get over it anytime soon."

Jon gets up and walks to the other side of the room. He dramatically lowers himself into a chair. "Better?"

I give him the finger. What an ass. The sooner I can get out of here and he can be on his way the better.

I glance toward the clock on the bedside table. It isn't even nine! We probably have a good twelve hours to kill before the linebackers show up to get me. Then he can go. If he can get away undetected, that is. What if something happens and he can't get there right away?

I tug on the hem of my ridiculously long shirt. "You going to head over to the casino in the morning?"

Jon leans back and crosses his arms over his chest. "I'll wait until after dark. I don't want to risk anyone seeing me. Plus, the zombies seem to be a little less active at night."

That's news to me. Doesn't make much of a difference as far as I can tell, though. There are so many zombies out there that "a little less active" is as reassuring as telling a diver there are only fifty sharks instead of a hundred.

We sit in silence for a while, but Jon can't stay still. He gets up and paces for a few minutes before sitting back down, only to start pacing again. He's making me nervous.

"So what'd you do before all this?" I finally ask, just to break the silence.

Jon throws himself on the bed. He's far away from me since it's a king size mattress, but it still makes my stomach lurch painfully. I stand up and lean awkwardly against the small desk.

"Pilot," he says. "I flew helicopter tours over Vegas and the Grand Canyon."

I cross my arms over my chest, tapping my toe nervously on the floor. I want to get out of this room, but I'm stuck here all night. "Family? Other than your sister, I mean."

Jon turns his head toward me but doesn't stand up. "Yeah. Wife and a baby." He swallows, and I suddenly feel bad for him despite how much I don't want to.

"I'm sorry," I whisper.

He turns his gaze toward the ceiling. I look away when a tear escapes the corner of his eye and slides down his cheek. Emily's face flashes through my mind, and I squeeze my eyes shut, trying to block it out.

Instead, I focus on Axl, remembering his lips on my skin, the way his calloused hands felt on my body. How amazing that night on top of Paris was. Being left behind was horrible, but being up there, away from the Strip, we were able to pretend it was just us. That there was nothing in this world to fear and all we had was each other. I've never felt as safe as I did that night.

Even those memories aren't a comfort, though. It hurts because I don't know if I'll ever see him again.

"What about you?" Jon asks, startling me.

I open my eyes and find him watching me. His eyes are red, and for the first time since I stepped into this room, he looks slightly guilty.

"I was a stripper. Had a daughter."

"This Axl guy, he was the dad?"

I shake my head and tap my toe even faster. "No. We met after all this started."

He nods and goes back to studying me silently. The longer he looks at me, the more the hair on my scalp tingles.

"You can trust me," he finally says. "I swear I won't hurt you. And I promise to do whatever it takes to get you out of this."

I shake my head. "I don't trust anyone."

The response is automatic. It's how I've felt my whole life, but it's not how I feel anymore. I do have people I trust now. I'd trust Axl with my life. And almost everyone else back at the shelter. Maybe even Angus. We're a family now. A new kind of family created by this mad world we live in.

"You can trust me," Jon says again.

"We'll see."

CHAPTER SIX

AXL

It takes three tries to find a car with an alarm. Soon as it goes off, the zombies come runnin'. We're only one street away from the Strip, but this time we're behind Paris. We're gonna get in through the back door.

Winston speeds away from the shriekin' alarm and heads toward the Paris hotel. The fake Eiffel Tower is right in front of us. I stare out the window as it gets closer, searchin' for an alley or some other way to get in the back. There's gotta be an employee entrance or something.

"There!" Trey yells from behind me.

Winston slams on the breaks, and I almost hit my head on the back of his seat. I woulda missed it if Trey hadn't pointed it out. The street is mostly blocked by a burnt-out car.

The alley leads to a narrow street that runs behind the casinos. We turn the corner, and the employee parkin' lot for Paris is right in front of us. There are zombies back here, but it ain't nothin' like out on the Strip.

"Can't be more than thirty of 'em," Angus says.

"Better than the Strip," Nathan says from the passenger seat.

"I told you there was a back road," Darla calls from the behind. She's grinnin' so big I wouldn't be surprised if she patted herself on the back.

Angus gives her one of his stupid-lookin' monkey smiles. His lips all puckered and his jaw tight. I look away. Makes me sick to my stomach. But Angus don't know she's Vivian's mom, and I try to convince myself he'd care if he did. It don't really work.

Winston parks the car and looks back at us. "Everyone ready? It's going to be rough."

I grab the duffel bag off the seat next to me and hop out without waitin' for anybody else. We're only 'bout ten feet from the back door, but I doubt it's unlocked. And it's metal. It ain't like we're just gonna be able to break the glass or nothin'.

I run up to the door, stabbin' two zombies in the head as I pass 'em. First I try the handle, but it don't budge. "Fuck," I mutter, tossin' the duffel to the ground and rummagin' 'round 'til I find the crowbar I brought. I can hear the others behind me, so I don't even bother lookin' over my shoulder. Angus'll have my back.

It only takes a few minutes of pryin' at the door to get it open. It comes loose with a crack that vibrates through my body. I shove the crowbar back in the duffel and get to my feet.

"Got it!"

I don't even look back before I rip the door open. Thankfully, I'm ready. A zombie with almost no skin on his face is just inside the door. Chunks of flesh are missin' from its arms and legs, and most of its clothes have been ripped off. Looks like a lot of the damage was done when it was still human. It moves slow, draggin' a broken ankle behind it. I slash my knife deep into its brain just as the others run inside.

I move further in, motionin' for everybody to follow. Never been in this part of the casino, so I ain't sure where to go, but it don't take me long to find the stairs that lead to the pool. The stairwell is empty, just like the last time I was here. So I charge up, not restin' 'til I'm out on the roof.

I hafta stop an' catch my breath when I reach the top. The sun's bright on the roof, reflectin' off the pool. The rocks in my stomach get heavier when I think 'bout the last time I was here. With Vivian. Her naked body. Damn.

I gotta get her back.

50

I toss my duffel aside while I wait for the others. They're all huffin' and puffin' when they reach the top. Angus looks pretty pissed off.

"We gotta block the door," I say, ignorin' the dirty looks from my brother.

He's bent over tryin' to catch his breath. Breathin' harder than anybody else. He ain't used to physical activity. I played football in high school and worked construction, so I've always been in shape. Angus ain't done nothin' but sit on his ass his whole life. Shoulda taken better care of himself.

Trey recovers faster than the others, then helps me pull chairs and tables over to stack in front of the door. It ain't much, but it's all we got.

"Now what?" Nathan asks.

"We can see out onto the Strip from behind them cabanas. It's a tight squeeze, but Vivian and me did it last time we was up here."

He nods and heads that way. "Let's check it out."

I follow even though I ain't real happy 'bout workin' with him. But he's willin', and I need an extra set of eyes. The Monte Carlo ain't close, and with all the bodies walkin' 'round down on Nathan asks as he squeezes in between the cabanas.

"Yup."

He glances back and frowns. "You ever going to stop hating me?"

I shrug and find myself puckerin' my lips. Just like Angus. I hate it when he does that. "Maybe, if you help me get Vivian back."

"I get it," he says over his shoulder.

There ain't much room behind the cabanas, and it's hard to get close to the edge with all the bushes planted back here. Nathan tries to push his way closer, but it don't work. After a couple minutes strugglin', he grabs a bush and jerks it up, then tosses it over the rail. He pulls a few more up 'til there's enough room for us to squeeze behind the building.

I climb on back next to him and look through the binoculars, studyin' the Strip 'til I find the Monte Carlo. It don't look no different from the other casinos. There are just as many of the dead in front of it as every other hotel.

"See anything?"

I shake my head. "Fuckin' zombies."

I move the binoculars up and down, studyin' the whole

building. The sun's up, so it's impossible to tell if the electricity is on inside. We may be able to get a better look at things after dark.

Angus squeezes in behind us and stands next to me. "What'd you find?"

"Nothin'," I say. "Not a damn thing."

The three of us stand there in silence for a few minutes, passin' the binoculars back and forth. I'm startin' to think this might be a waste of time. I'm gonna hafta go in.

"I gotta get in there."

Angus frowns and puckers his lips. "No way. You don't know what's goin' on in there."

I yank the binoculars outta his hand and look back down at the Monte Carlo, studyin' the sidewalk in front of the casino. The only thing that looks even slightly outta place is the van parked in front. But that don't mean nothin'. Somebody coulda broke down there before the dead took over the city.

"So now what?" Nathan asks.

"We wait. We watch the place and come up with a plan," I say, but I know exactly what I'm gonna end up doin'. No matter what Angus says, I gotta get in there.

Angus puckers his lips again. He looks even dumber in this light than usual. More like a monkey tryin' to figure something out.

"You ain't gonna run off half-cocked. You're smarter than that, little brother." I shake my head, but he don't let me get a word out. "She's gotten in your head and you ain't thinkin' straight."

My shoulders tighten. We've had this conversation already. I told him I loved her. Guess I shouldn't expect him to understand. Angus don't love nobody. Probably not even Angus.

"I won't leave her there, Angus."

He swears and spits over the side of the building, wipin' his mouth with his hand. "I ain't tellin' you to. I just wanna be sure you don't run off and ditch us. You can't do this alone."

"You got any ideas?" I spit at him.

"I'm workin' on it. Just give me some time. Have I ever steered you wrong? I always been there for you. Always." Nathan clears his throat behind us and shuffles around like he wants to get out, but Angus is blockin' the way. "You and me against the world. That's what we always said. You think I forgot it just 'cause you did? Just 'cause you're gonna choose a pair a tits over me don't mean that's what I'm gonna do."

My jaw tightens, and I cringe when my teeth scrape together. Angus has steered me wrong lots of times, only he can't see that. All that hatin' people and tellin' me that trailer trash was all I could ever be. He held me back. Not that it matters none now. I'd still be screwed if I'd gone to college. Zombies don't care if you got an education. But I am worth something. Vivian taught me that.

"You still gonna do it, ain't ya?" Angus spits again, and it comes awful close to landin' on Nathan's shoe. He makes a face but don't say nothin'.

"I ain't promisin' you a think," I say. "She's in danger, and I won't just walk away."

the Strip, it could be pretty hard to check things out.

"You have those binoculars?"

CHAPTER SEVEN

VIVIAN

I wake up in a nice, warm bed with a warm body pressed up against me. My hand moves across the sheets, reaching for Axl. Just as my fingers touch his chest, everything that happened yesterday comes screaming back, and my eyes fly open. It's Jon sleeping next to me, not Axl. A sob forces its way out of my mouth, and I roll away. I don't remember falling asleep in the same bed with him.

His green eyes flutter open, and he tilts his head my way. His mouth turns up into a tentative smile. "Sorry. I didn't want to sleep on the floor."

I nod and scoot further away, very aware of the fact that I'm not wearing pants.

Jon moves to the other side of the mattress, but he doesn't get up. He yawns and stretches. Acts like being in bed with me is the most natural thing in the world. I pull the sheet up to my chin.

He rolls his eyes and cracks his knuckles. "So tell me about your group. Where have you been staying? How many people do you have?"

I take a deep breath. How much do I tell him? I'm still not sure about this guy. I made it through the night without being attacked, but I can't forget how I got here. I don't trust him completely. Not yet. Maybe not ever.

"We have a safe place outside the city." I meet his gaze, but there's no way he'll be able to miss how elusive that answer is. "There will probably be four or five of our people at Paris."

He narrows his eyes. "Okay. So who will be there? Other than this Axl guy."

Who will be there? That's a good question. "Axl's brother, Angus, for sure." He isn't really a big fan of me, but he'd never let Axl go without him.

Jon frowns. "Angus and Axl? How white trash are these guys?"

My shoulders tense, and I sit up. Axl may be trailer trash, but that doesn't mean I'm going to let someone else put him down. Especially this guy. Angus I don't give a shit about. "Watch it. Axl may not have grown up with much, but he's smart and resourceful."

Jon smiles, and I have the sudden urge to punch him. "You're not going to stick up for Angus?"

I shrug and lean back against the headboard. "Angus is an ass and he's trash all the way through, but he has his uses. And Axl loves him. I wouldn't put up with him for anyone else. But for Axl…" Tears sting at the back of my eyes, and I have to look away.

"I get it."

I clear my throat and swipe the back of my hand across my eyes. "Anyway, Winston and Trey will probably be there too. We picked Trey up on Route 66. He and his girlfriend were headed west after New York fell. We found Winston up in San Francisco along with another group." I bite my lower lip and consider who else might be there. Anne? Probably not, she has Jake. Would Moira let Nathan out of her sight? It's hard to say since I don't know them very well, but it's possible. He was the leader of their group. "Probably Nathan," I say hesitantly. "We just found him a few days ago." Has it really been only a few days since we went to Sam's Club? It feels like years.

Jon nods and lets out a sigh. "I'm really sorry for getting you into this."

He doesn't sound too sorry, more like he's only saying it to make me feel better. He'd probably slit my throat if it meant getting his sister back. Not that I can really blame him that much. I'd slit his throat if Axl were in danger and it would somehow save him. That's the kind of world we live in now. Kill or be killed. Not a pleasant thought. Thinking about how much the world has changed in such a short time makes me nauseous.

"Let's focus on something else," I say.

He nods and climbs out of bed. He's wearing nothing but a pair of boxer briefs, and I pull the covers up to my chin, feeling even more vulnerable than before.

His green eyes meet mine, and he grabs a pair of pants, shaking his head. "I'm not going to touch you."

"I think you would," I say. "If you had to do it to save Megan."

Jon stops mid-zip and presses his lips together. "How would raping you save Megan?"

My throat tightens just hearing him say the word. He's not going to do it, though. I'm safe with him. Hopefully. "I'm not saying it would. I'm just pointing out that you would do it if you had to."

He looks down at the floor and swallows, but eventually nods. "You're probably right. She's all I have left."

Panic builds in my chest. Even though I knew it was true, hearing him acknowledge it is terrifying. But it's a stupid thing to worry about. There's no way it would ever come to that. It doesn't even make sense. Then again, neither did zombies a few weeks ago. Anything can happen these days.

Jon zips his pants and pulls a shirt over his head. Now that he's dressed, my chest isn't quite as tight. "They'll be back to get you in a bit. Do you want to take a shower before you go?"

"Yeah," I say, stepping out of bed on shaky legs. He looks away. Probably to make me feel better. "Thanks." I hate to thank him for anything, but in the suite there are two showers for about thirty women. It would be nice not to have to fight for my turn.

I make it quick. The warm water feels fantastic, but I'm not comfortable being naked in this hotel room with Jon. And it's not just him. They could come back for me at any moment. Who's to say they won't rip me out of this shower and make me walk back to the suite naked? I wouldn't put anything past these men.

Jon's laying on the bed when I come out. Cool air from the AC whooshes across the room and goose bumps form on my arms and legs. I wish I had more clothes on. Jon is just staring at me, and even though it isn't sexual, it makes me squirm. I cross my arms over my chest as if that will cover up the fact that I'm not wearing a bra. It won't, of course. Not for the first time, I realize how much of a liability these double D's might be in this new reality I'm living in.

I can't focus on all that right now. They'll be here to get me any minute, and we still need to nail down a few details. "So what are you thinking? How will you get word to me after you meet with Axl?"

Jon sits up and runs his hand down his face. He looks exhausted. Like he hasn't slept in months. We probably all look like that nowadays. "I'll figure out a way. Get you or Hadley for a night."

"Hadley," I say firmly.

He shakes his head and frowns like he thinks I'm stupid. "I don't know if you're really thinking this through. Are you willing to sacrifice yourself for her?"

"I am." I look down so he doesn't see the uncertainty on my face.

"Alright then, if you that's what you want."

"It is." It isn't, but I know I could recover. I don't know if Hadley could.

"What if I can't find your friends? What should I do if they aren't at Paris?"

"They will be." But he has a point. What then? I sigh and shake my head. "If they aren't there, I guess I'll have to tell you where our shelter is. But for now you need to get to Paris."

Someone pounds on the door, and I almost jump out of my too-big T-shirt. Jon gets to his feet, giving me a sympathetic look as he crosses the room. My heart pounds when he opens the door, revealing the now familiar face of Linebacker One.

"Time's up."

Jon squares his shoulders and turns to me, then tilts his head toward the door. "Go on." His voice is cold, just like it was in the van.

I do as I'm told and walk toward the door. The linebacker grabs my forearm, jerking it so hard I'm forced to uncross my arms.

He puckers his lips and nods, looking me over before turning back to Jon. "She a good fuck?"

I shudder and look up to see Jon smiling. "Oh yeah."

The linebacker doesn't respond. He drags me down the hall, looking me over as we go. "Gonna have to go out on a run," he mumbles to himself as we wait for the elevator to open. "Get you on a free night. You already got somebody tonight, though." He smiles and raises his eyebrows as he jerks me forward again, stepping into the elevator. "You're gonna be a popular one."

I swallow as my body starts to tremble. Someone has already requested me for the night? It can't be Jon, so that means I'm in trouble.

I *can* handle it. I've been through worse.

The words go through my head over and over again while we walk. Thinking them doesn't make them true, though. My dad beat the shit out of me more times than I can count, but I've never been raped. Never.

When I get back to the suite, I find Hadley sitting in the exact same place she was when I left. Her eyes meet mine as I head her way, and her face crumples.

Yes, I've made the right decision. If I can protect her, I will.

I lower myself onto the floor next to her, and she puts her hand on my leg. "Are you okay?"

I nod and glance across the room. Megan hasn't moved either, and I can barely see her face. If anything, she's even more covered by blankets than she was yesterday.

"He didn't touch me," I whisper.

Hadley's eyes get huge, and she opens her mouth to say something. Probably ask questions. But I shake my head. I don't want anyone to hear. Who knows if these women would turn us in?

I lean so close to Hadley that my lips almost touch her ear, then tell her what happened with Jon. She grabs my leg, and the longer I talk, the harder she squeezes. By the time I'm done, she's shaking with excitement and hope.

"We're going to be okay?" she whispers.

I bite down on my lip and swallow. "Yes. Eventually." My insides constrict. Eventually. But first I have to get through tonight. Hopefully, no one comes looking for her.

Hadley glances toward the battered girl across the room. "We need to talk to her."

I look around, but no one seems to be paying attention to us. Still, I don't want them to start. Drawing attention to ourselves right now would be bad. "Let's wait a bit. Try not to make it

59

obvious that we're seeking her out."

Hadley nods and we go back to sitting in silence. There isn't much else to do. The other women in the room do the same, talking to one another occasionally in hushed tones, but mostly they just sleep or stare off into space. As a whole they're a pretty defeated bunch.

And we're going to be leaving them behind. My insides tighten even more, and I clench my fists. We don't have a choice, but it doesn't make me feel any better. These women are going to spend the rest of their days like this. It's almost too much to bear.

MY STOMACH IS GROWLING WHEN THE DOOR OPENS AND one of the linebackers brings in a box of food for lunch. More vending machine junk, but still food. Just like yesterday, they dump it in the middle of the floor. The women go crazy. Hadley and I are all the way across the room, so there's a crowd already fighting for the food by the time we get there. We have to push our way through. By the looks of it, there's even less to choose from than there was last night.

I do my best not to feel guilty as I elbow my way through the crowd. These women may be starving, but I have to keep my strength up if I want to make it out of this alive. I get my hands on one bag, but go in for another. Megan needs something.

Just as my fingers wrap around a second one, somebody shoves me back. A red-faced, smelly blonde woman in her thirties snarls at me like a rabid dog. "Move!"

I stumble back with my food clutched to my chest and watch as the blonde woman wrestles someone for a Twinkie. She was probably attractive once, but she's clearly stopped trying. Her hair is filthy and matted to her head. She smells like death and body odor mingled with just a hint of piss. She's probably doing it on purpose. Trying to make herself less appealing. I wonder if it works.

I won't be around long enough to try out her approach, though. Not if I have anything to say about it.

"What'd you get?" Hadley asks as we walk back toward our pillow.

"Cheez-Its and animal crackers. You?"

"Strawberry Pop-Tarts."

I stop when we reach Megan and tilt my head toward the sleeping girl, holding up the bag of animal crackers. "Now's our chance."

Hadley looks around and nods. No one is paying attention to us. They're too busy eating. Tearing into the packages of processed food like animals. They're starving, so I try not to judge. Maybe I'll be the same way if I'm still here in a few weeks. I'd like to think I'd be able to hold it together a little better, but no matter how strong a person is, everyone has their breaking point.

I kneel down next to Megan and gently tap her shoulder. She flinches, and her eyes fly open. Wide with terror. They look exactly like her brother's. Green and intense, swimming with the pain and loss they've endured. Her face is spotted with bruises, but a lot of them have faded and turned into an ugly yellowish color. Her eye is still pretty swollen though, and her lip is split. It's going to be a while before she's completely healed. If ever.

"It's okay." I try to sound as gentle and reassuring as possible, but she doesn't relax. I sit down next to her and brush the hair from her face. "It's okay. Jon sent me."

A sob shakes her body, and her eyes fill with tears. She trembles and opens her mouth, letting out a strangled sound that could only be her brother's name. It sounds more like a wail.

I hold the bag of cookies out to her. "I brought you some food. Why don't you sit up?" She hesitates, and I decide not to give her a choice. I grab her by the arm and pull her up to a sitting position. She winces but doesn't lay back down.

"Here." I hand her the open bag of animal crackers. "You need to eat something."

She takes the bag with shaky hands and slowly starts eating. The movement doesn't seem to register, though. It looks automatic. Cracker in the mouth, chew, swallow. Repeat. I'm not even sure she realizes she's doing it.

I glance around to be sure no one is paying attention, and my gaze meets the stinky blonde woman's. Her blue eyes pierce mine. She's very interested in what we're doing.

I look at Hadley and shake my head. "Let's just eat for now."

We split the bags of food between us, eating in silence. I eat half my Pop-Tart before passing the rest to Megan. She needs it more than I do. Hadley doesn't share, and I don't suggest it. She can't really afford to lose any weight. She's skin and bones as it.

"God, I'm a fool," she says when she's done eating. She picks up the Cheez-It bag and shakes the crumbs into her mouth. "All those years I spent starving myself so I could compete in Hollywood. What I wouldn't give to have a few extra pounds to spare right now. Look at me! How long do you think I'm going to make it on this diet?" She shakes her head and sighs.

I put my arm around her. "We'll make it out of here, don't worry."

Megan watches us. Her green eyes are full of so many emotions I can't even begin to describe them all. She's filthy and smells almost as bad as the blonde woman. Who still hasn't stopped watching us.

I bite my lip and look around. We can't talk here. Not with that chick staring us down. The bathroom might be safe, though. "Megan," I say, leaning forward to touch her arm. "How about I help you get cleaned up? How long has it been since you took a shower?"

Hadley gets to her feet. "I'll help, too."

Megan doesn't argue, and she even lets us help her up. But she doesn't talk as we lead her to the bathroom. There's a line, of course. Megan stares off into space while we wait. She isn't good. She's more like a zombie than some of the bodies walking around on the Strip.

When it's finally our turn, Hadley and I pull the girl inside and lock the door behind us. I sit Megan on the toilet and kneel down in front of her while Hadley starts the bath. Megan doesn't look at me. She doesn't look at anything. I hold her hands in mine and whisper her name, trying to get her attention. She blinks and her eyes squint like she's trying to focus on my face. After a few seconds, they seem a little clearer.

"Jon is here. He came for you." She nods but doesn't smile, so I'm not sure if she understands what I'm saying. "He's going to meet with some of my friends tonight. They're going to get us out."

She just keeps nodding.

I exhale and stand up. "She's bad off."

"Can you blame her?" Hadley says.

She helps the girl to her feet and whispers reassuring words while she removes her filthy clothes, then urges her into the bathtub. Megan's body is just as battered as her face, and I have to look away. My heart constricts, and all the bitterness I felt toward

Jon is suddenly gone. He was right to try. Even if it means putting Hadley and me in danger, he couldn't walk away from this girl. I know that now, as much as I hate to admit it.

Once she's clean, Hadley helps Megan out, and I wrap her in a damp towel before leading her out of the bathroom. The blonde woman is standing against the wall with her arms crossed over her chest. She glares at me when we walk out. She isn't waiting for a turn. She's waiting for us.

"I'll get some clothes," I tell Hadley.

Hadley leads Megan back across the room, and I head to the pile of shirts and underwear laying on the floor. At least they give us clean clothes. How generous of them.

Dirty Blonde follows me.

I try to ignore her while I dig through the shirts. They're all different sizes, and I want to finds something big. Something that will cover as much of this poor girl as possible. Dirty Blonde is behind me the whole time, though. I can smell her. The overpowering scent of sweat and filth makes my nose wrinkle. I try to ignore her. To breathe out of my mouth. It doesn't work. She's breathing down my neck, and her breath is as foul as the rest of her.

There are a few other women around, but no one pays attention to us. I can't take it anymore. I spin around to face the stinking woman. "You got something to say to me?"

Dirty Blonde sneers and crosses her arms over her chest. Her breasts are large and round. Like mine. Fake, I bet. "Why you being so nice to that girl?"

"Because it's the decent thing to do."

"Decency doesn't exist anymore," she says, rolling her eyes. "I saw you come back into the room this morning. Didn't look like you had such an awful night. All clean. No tears. Not the usual walk of shame we're used to 'round here."

Shit. She's right. That was a dumb move. I should have played it up more.

I lick my lips and glance around. The other women still aren't paying attention. When I look back, the blonde's icy eyes are as sharp as knives.

"Maybe I'm just a strong person."

"Ain't no such thing in this place, sweetie. Even the strong women walk away with scars."

"I've got plenty of scars," I mutter, turning away from her.

She grabs my arm and forces me to turn back around, getting right in my face. "I'm watching you, girlie."

Her stinking breath and foul odor make my stomach turn inside out. She grins, probably mistaking my disgust for fear, then releases me and walks away.

I rub my forearm where her fingers dug into my skin. Right on top of the bruises left by the linebackers. Guess I'm going to have to get used to having bruises there. At least for the time being.

CHAPTER EIGHT
AXL

Smoke, it always starts with smoke. It's dark and I'm back in my old room in the trailer — if you can call it a room — and I stumble outta my bed. My heart's poundin' and I'm sweatin' even though I know it's just a dream. My hand shakes when I reach for the doorknob.

I gotta get her.

That's the thought that always goes through my mind. Even though I know this ain't real and I know I can't do nothin' to change the past. I still try.

I can feel the heat before I open the door. Flames. The whole goddamn trailer is covered in flames. I cough just like I did that night, and the smoke burns my lungs. I ain't never forgot that feelin'. Never will. I want to get her, but I can't. There ain't nothin' I can do—

I jerk awake, coughin'. My eyes are wet, just like they always are after I have that goddamn dream. And I'm covered in sweat. I inhale slowly and wipe the tears away before Angus sees 'em. Why the hell did the dream come back? It's been years. Stress, maybe.

"Who the fuck are you?" Angus yells from the other side of the roof.

I jump up, stumblin' over my feet and almost fallin' on my face.

My heart's poundin', and I'm wide awake the second I hear my brother's voice. The long, hot day of sittin' on the roof watchin' the Monte Carlo comes back to me, and I curse myself for fallin' asleep. It's dark. Now's the time I should be watchin' the casino.

More yellin'. Angus is really worked up 'bout something. I pull my gun out and run toward the voices. There ain't no lights up here, but the moon's full. I can just make out the shapes of a few people on the other side of the roof. Right by the door.

"I'm looking for Axl James."

My heart almost stops beatin' at the sound of my name. I don't recognize the voice, but I'd be willin' to bet my right nut he's here 'bout Vivian.

I push my way through the group of people gathered 'round 'til I find a face I don't recognize. He's a preppy-lookin' bastard. Older than me, but probably not more than thirty. He's clean. Obviously he ain't been sleepin' in no abandoned buildings, which means he's with the bastards that took Vivian and Hadley.

I slam him against the wall and push the barrel of my gun right between his eyes, pressin' it into his skull. "Where the hell is she?"

The guy swallows. His eyes are so big they look like they're gonna pop outta his head. "You shoot me and you'll never know," he says in a surprisingly calm voice.

My entire body shakes, and my finger's just itchn' to pull the trigger. But he's right. I can't shoot him. Not if I wanna find Vivian.

But I could shoot his balls off.

I jam my arm against his throat and press as hard as I can before movin' my gun to his crotch. "I ain't gonna kill you, but if you don't tell me where she is, I guarantee that by the time I'm done with you, you'll wish you had."

"The Monte Carlo! The Monte Carlo!" His voice ain't calm no more.

"I told ya!" Darla's shrill voice screams out behind me.

"Shut the fuck up," I say, not takin' my eyes off the tremblin' guy in front of me. "She better be okay."

He nods as hard as he can with my arm pressed against his throat. "She's fine. So is Hadley."

I wince. Damn. I shoulda asked 'bout Hadley.

Winston steps forward and puts his hand on my back. "Let him go, Axl. We need to let him talk if we're going to figure out what's going on."

The muscles in my neck are stretched tight, and my arm twitches as I press it against the guy's neck. I don't wanna let him go. I wanna bash his damn face in.

But Winston's right. Even in my rage I know he is.

I press my arm harder against the guy's throat, makin' him gag a little before takin' a step back. My jaw is clenched, and I can't loosen it enough to talk. I nod at Winston, givin' him permission to take over. He'll do what's gotta be done.

"Why don't you tell us what you're doing here," Winston says.

The guy rubs his throat and glares at me. I spit on the ground at his feet.

"My name's Jon. My sister was taken by the same men who grabbed Vivian and Hadley."

He keeps rubbin' his neck, and his voice is hoarse. Maybe I was a little too rough. Don't wanna do no permanent damage 'til I know Vivian's okay. Then I can kill the asshole.

He clears his throat before goin' on. "Vivian's tough. I knew she could help me."

"How'd you find us?" Angus asks.

I can't look at him. We've hardly talked, and I know he's pissed. It's like Lilly all over again to him. But I don't give a shit. Angus has always looked out for me, but things are different now and I ain't gonna let him tear this thing apart. Not again.

Jon narrows his eyes at my brother. "Vivian. She knew Axl would be here."

My eyes sting, and I gotta look away. The animal trapped inside me starts tryin' to claw its way out again. I can't even think 'bout what's goin' on over there. There's no law these days, and I know how sick men can be.

"They got a lot of women over there?" Angus asks.

My eyes snap his way. Why's he askin' that? He thinkin' 'bout goin' over there to join 'em? No. His lips are puckered and he's starin' at Jon. Somethings up.

Jon squirms a little. "Um...I'm not totally sure. More than twenty."

Angus rubs his jaw, and everybody else is watchin' him. It's like they're all holdin' their breath, waitin' to see what he's got to say. I ain't never seen anybody hang on Angus's words before.

"So outta all these chicks, you just happened to pick Blondie out? How'd you choose her to help you?"

My jaw tightens, and my hand moves toward my knife. Now I get what he's thinkin'. It shoulda been obvious to me, too. This is the prick that took her. He was there, at the hospital. I remember now. The guy in the passenger seat who was a shitty shot. That was Jon.

I take a step forward, and Jon backs up. Too bad he don't got nowhere to go. He bumps into the wall, and he puts his hands up. "Look, I had to do it. I did! She's my sister!"

Hell. No.

My fist slams into his jaw, cuttin' off anything else he was gonna say. Pain rips through my knuckles, and Jon barely reacts. I forgot my hand was broken. It probably didn't even hurt him. But it hurt me a hell of a lot. My hand throbs, but it only makes me madder, so I reach for my knife.

I'm gonna kill him.

Before I can get it, Angus is on me, pullin' me back. I fight him, but Angus is stronger than that beer belly makes him look. He's got me back and Winston steps between me and that bastard. I'm breathin' heavy and my fists are clenched. I'd be happy to beat the shit outta this guy right now.

"Axl," Winston says calmly. "I understand how you feel, but you don't want to do this. Not now. Not while Vivian's in trouble. We need this guy to help us."

Everybody's starin' at me. Waitin' to see what I'm gonna do. That animal starts eatin' at my insides again, but I stop fightin' Angus. He relaxes his grip on me, and I shove him back.

"I'm good," I mutter, starin' at the ground. I can't look at that bastard standin' in front of me or I'll kill him. I swear to God, I'll cut his guts out and shove them down his throat.

"Why don't you tell us what happened?" Winston says.

Jon starts talkin', and I squeeze my hands into even tighter fists. He took her from the hospital and brought her here. Then picked her out as some kind of sick payment for guns. He ain't no better than them other men.

"You helped arm these guys?" Nathan asks.

He sounds as pissed off as I feel, and I can't help lookin' at him.

Mr. Nice Guy is gone and that prick we met in Sam's Club is back. He looks like he's ready to kill Jon, too. Guess he'd be feelin' just like me if it'd been his wife instead of Vivian.

"I had to!" Jon yells. His voice echoes across the empty roof.

If he says that one more time, I won't be able to control myself. I'm already close to throwin' him off the damn roof as it is.

"You got a plan?" I glare at him, and he 'bout pisses in his pants.

Jon shakes his head. "No. That's why I'm here. I can't get them out alone. There are too many men on the inside. I need help."

The animal inside me starts clawin' harder, and it feels like it's gonna rip right through me. My insides are bein' torn to shreds. I'm havin' a hard time focusin'. All I can think 'bout is Vivian. He took her there, and he didn't even have a plan to get her out. The dumb shit.

"Anybody put their hands on her?" My teeth are clenched so tight I can hardly get the words out.

Everybody stares at Jon, and it feels like they're all holdin' their breath. I don't wanna know, but I gotta. Before we go any further, I gotta know who I'm gonna kill.

Jon shakes his head, and I try to relax. I swear I do. I just can't.

"Not that I know of. She's only been there one night and she was with me." Every muscle in my face tenses. Jon puts his hands up and takes a step back. "I didn't put a finger on her. We just talked."

I nod, but I still can't seem to get my jaw to relax enough to get any words out.

"Is there a back way into the casino?" Winston asks.

"Employee entrance is at the rear of the building. There aren't as many zombies back there."

"You gotta get me inside. I gotta see Vivian."

Jon frowns my way. Like he thinks I can't handle it or something. "Not sure if that's a good idea. Once you're in, you've lost the element of surprise. Not to mention the fact that you can't just waltz in and get a night with a number three. You'd have to bring in some serious supplies. You have any guns or diesel you'd be willing to give up? That's what it would take."

A light bulb goes off in my head just like a goddamn cartoon. The second tanker truck in Boulder City. We went out there to get some fuel, but we could only take the one truck. We had to leave the other one. "I got diesel."

Angus puckers his lips and shakes his head. "You ain't goin' in there. It ain't a good idea."

"Screw you, Angus. I ain't walkin' away from Vivian. We already talked 'bout this, and I ain't changed my mind. I'd rather die tryin' than just sit back and do nothin'."

Angus glares at me before lettin' off a string of curses that echoes across the dark night. The damn zombies down the Strip can probably hear him. He shakes his head and turns back to face me. "Well, you ain't givin' them that tanker of diesel neither. I know what you're thinkin', and we can't give them a truckload of fuel. We need it."

I'm 'bout to argue when Jon steps in front of me. My jaw twitches, and I clench my fist, fightin' the urge to punch him in his stupid, preppy face again. Harder. I'd love to see his nose broken and his face covered in blood. When I'm done with him, he won't be nearly as pretty as he is now.

"It wouldn't even take the whole truck. A couple gallons would do it," Jon says.

Winston scratches at his beard and turns to look at me. "That what you want to do?"

"I ain't gonna leave her."

"Nobody's expecting you to. I just want to make sure there isn't another way. I don't want to see you get yourself killed if we can do this right and get you all out alive. Plus, I don't love the idea of handing these animals more fuel when it's only going to help them keep going."

He's got a point, but I don't know another way. "We gotta."

"If you did go in, what next?" Nathan asks.

"Meet with Vivian." It sounds stupid, and I know it. I need more of a plan than that, but I can't seem to get my brain to think of another one. Vivian is all I can focus on.

Angus curses and walks away, kickin' a chair as he heads toward the pool.

"We need more of a plan than that, Axl," Trey says. His voice is low, almost cautious.

He ain't scared of me, so I ain't sure why 'til I look over at him. He's worried. Just like Angus. Worried I'm gonna get myself killed. It's a goddamn messed-up world we're livin' in.

"We stake the place out, figure a good way, and meet up with y'all after. We'll get a plan together and bust 'em out." No one looks very happy 'bout it. "I gotta see what's goin' on inside before we do anything else. You gotta know that."

"I hate to say it," Nathan says, "but he's right. We don't know what's happening in there."

"It's not like anyone's going to be suspicious of *him*," Jon says.

I glare at him and he takes another step back, bumpin' into the wall again. I hope he hits his head and knocks himself out.

When he talks again, he looks like he's 'bout to piss his pants. "No offense, but he'll fit right in. I mean, these aren't the classiest bunch of men you've ever met in your life."

"So you're sayin' I'm trash, is that it?" I don't give a shit, I just wanna scare the guy.

Jon shakes his head and stumbles all over himself tryin' to find a way to pull his head outta his own ass. "No. I just...You fit a certain..."

"Shut the hell up," I mutter, turnin' back to Winston. "I gotta get that fuel."

"I know. We shouldn't all go though, just in case you don't come back."

The animal inside me finds its way to my heart and takes a big, fuckin' bite outta it. "You'd still get her? If I didn't make it back?"

Winston puts his hand on my shoulder. "I'd try."

"You two pussies gonna make out now?" Angus growls.

Winston drops his hand.

"I ain't lettin' you go alone," Angus says. "I'll go in with ya. Maybe get me a night with that Hollywood chick."

He wiggles his eyebrows, and I gotta turn away before I beat the shit outta him. I ain't never punched Angus, but I'm 'fraid that by the time I get Vivian back, it's gonna happen. He's pissin' me off.

I turn to face Jon, glarin' at him for a few seconds before talkin'. "First thing we gotta do is head out to Boulder City and get us that fuel. Unless you know of a place 'round here that ain't been hit?"

Jon shakes his head, but he's too scared to actually look at me. Good. "Most places ran out of fuel before the zombies even popped up. Every station I've hit has been bone dry."

"Figured," I mutter, turnin' away from the prick. "Who's goin'?"

Winston tilts his head toward Angus. I know what's he's sayin'.

When I turn toward Nathan, I find I'm suddenly not as pissed at him. Not with Jon standin' on the other side of me. "You wanna head on over there with Angus, Jon, and me?"

Nathan nods slowly. Like he ain't too thrilled 'bout it. Guess we ain't the best company.

"Alright, then. We'll head out now. Run on over to Boulder City and get us a few cans full of diesel. We'll drop Nathan off here before the three of us head into the Monte Carlo, that way you know we made it safe."

Winston nods and holds his hand out. I take it in mine, ignorin' the way Angus is eyeballin' us. I don't give a shit what he thinks. I told him before, things are changed. He's gotta learn. All that racist bullshit he's got goin' on in his head don't mean nothin' no more. Probably never did.

"Be careful," Winston says.

I nod, slap him on the back, and head toward the stairs. "I ain't plannin' on dyin' today."

CHAPTER NINE

VIVIAN

Dinner is pretty much exactly the same as lunch. Only this time, Hadley and I get our hands on a Snickers bar, a bag of chips, some chocolate chip cookies, *and* a bag of fruit snacks. Not exactly the healthiest meal, but I'm satisfied. We split it between the three of us before digging in, and I try my best to avoid the glares Dirty Blonde throws my way.

Our dinner of vending machine cast-offs is followed closely by the reappearance of the linebackers. Not a surprise, but it still makes my body start to shake the second they open the door.

They walk around the room, yanking women to their feet and shoving them toward the door. Kicking anyone who gets in their way. I shrink down. Like it will make me invisible. Right. No such luck. Of course, luck has never really been on my side. Zombies can't change that. Maybe whoever requested me changed their mind? I can only hope.

It's no surprise when Linebacker One stops in front of me. A sickening smile lights up his broad face. He reaches down, and I gasp when his fingers dig into my forearm. He jerks me to my feet, and my heart pounds so hard it vibrates against my ribs. It isn't until I see him jerk Hadley to her feet too that I almost throw up.

"Both you girls have dates for the evening," he sneers. He takes way too much enjoyment in his job.

Hadley lets out a little sound that's somewhere between a whimper and a scream, and I throw myself in front of her. There has to be way out of this. At least for Hadley.

"Who wants her?"

Linebacker One rolls his eyes and pushes me aside. He grabs Hadley and pulls her forward. "We've got guys dying out there on the Strip for a chance to get with Hadley Lucas. She's going to be very popular."

He yanks us toward the door. Each one of his meaty hands gripping an arm. He moves fast like he can't wait to deliver us to whatever form of hell these men have created in this hotel. I try to keep up, but it isn't easy. My feet stumble over the blankets and pillows spread out on the floor. Hadley has a difficult time, too. And she's crying. I can tell she's trying to be quiet about it, but it isn't working. The sound of her sobbing squeezes my heart, and I desperately try to think of a way out of this. But there's nothing I can do. We are screwed.

A short, round, balding man stands in the hallway when we step out. His face lights up, and he hops around on his toes like a little kid. My stomach lurches.

"I told you we'd bring her down," Linebacker One snaps. He shoves women toward the elevator where Linebacker Two waits.

The bald man smiles and looks Hadley up and down. He acts like he's won the damn lottery. I just can't wrap my mind around what's about to happen. He looks so average. Like an accountant or an elementary school principal. A dad. Not a rapist. Not someone who's so freaking happy to be a rapist.

"I couldn't wait," he gushes.

My stomach twists inside out.

The linebacker shoves Hadley toward him. "You can handle her?"

The man nods and pulls her toward the elevator. "Oh, I can't wait to handle her."

Hadley turns her tear-stained face toward me like I can do something to save her. I can't. God, I wish I could. I do my best to put on brave face. It's fake. There isn't a brave bone in my body right now. My legs are like Jell-O, and the Snickers bar has turned into a rock, churning the contents of my stomach as I walk.

The elevator is crowded tonight. The linebackers, seven other women, me, Hadley, and the bald man. He shoves Hadley against the wall the second we're in and starts groping her. Kissing her. He runs his tongue across her face, and I gag. She struggles, but he presses his body up against her and pins her hands to her sides. He's stronger than he looks.

I can't watch, so I turn away.

The elevator opens on eight, and the linebacker pulls me forward, laughing. Like this is a carnival or a comedy club or Disneyland. He's lucky I'm not armed. I'd happily chop his head off. Then spit in the stump.

I squeeze my eyes shut and allow the chuckling linebacker to drag me down the hall. Please let it be Jon. Please. Or another desperate person. Surely there's someone else in the hotel who wants me to help him rescue a family member. Wouldn't that be funny? Men lining up to get me to help formulate an escape plan. Like I'm a secret agent, not an ex-stripper.

Linebacker One comes to an abrupt stop, and the click of a door makes me open my eyes. He hasn't even knocked yet. Tat stands in the open doorway with an evil smile curling up his lips.

My legs wobble, and I stagger back. Tat grabs my arm and jerks me into the hotel room. I fall to my knees. The door slams behind me, and I scramble to my feet. My heart pounds harder. Faster. Trying to escape my body. Escape. I need to escape. I frantically look around. There has to be a way out. Some way to get free. I'm panicked. More terrified than I've ever been in my entire life. It makes my body shake. I can't control it.

Tat chuckles, and I spin around to face him. His hand makes contact with my cheek, and my head jerks back. My face stings and my eye throbs where his fingertips smacked against it, but it brings me back to the present. To who I am. Tat isn't any scarier than my dad was. Not really. I put up with Roger's rage for years. I can take this.

I can.

Tat's eyes cloud over and he takes a menacing step forward, but I don't flinch. I keep my head up. I know his kind. He lives for fear. Wants to hear me cry. Wants me to beg for mercy. I won't give him the satisfaction.

"You think you're tough?" That same sadistic smile that made me want to throw up when he first opened the door curls his lips. "You aren't."

His fist slams into my cheek. I cry out and stumble back. Intense pain radiates across my face. There's nothing worse than the feeling of bone on bone. It makes me think of my father. My eyes tear up, and I take a step back. I rub my face and do my best not to think about that bastard. Having Roger's ghost in the room with us will only make all of this harder to deal with.

Tat takes a step closer, smiling wickedly. My eyes dart around the room. I need a weapon or a place to hide. But there's nowhere to go. Nothing that can help me. He knows it.

Two quick steps, and his fist makes contact with my face for the second time. This time he gets my left eye. Stars burst across my vision like it's the Fourth of July. I stumble again and end up slamming into the desk, knocking over a lamp. It crashes to the floor, shattering.

I've barely had time to recover when Tat grabs a handful of my hair. He jerks me forward, and I scream. I try to slap his hands away. He just pulls harder. My scalp stings and I'm sure I'm about to lose a chunk of hair.

He slaps me across the face, and I hit the floor. My lungs sting as much as my face throbs. I gasp and try to get a mouthful of air. Tat steps closer. He's going to kill me.

Someone pounds on the door, and Tat freezes. My head pulsates. Like there's a drum pounding inside my skull. Tat glares down at me. There's another knock, and he blows air out through his nose like a bull. Tat crosses the room and jerks the door open. Linebacker One stands in the hall.

He looks past Tat to where I'm sprawled out on the floor. Blood trickles from my nose, and my eye throbs in a way that I know means it's getting ready to swell shut. I probably look pretty messed up.

The linebacker shakes his head. He doesn't look apologetic or concerned, just annoyed. "You can't leave a mark on the merchandise. You've been told."

Tat scowls and glances at me. His eyes burn with rage. "She's my payment. I should be able to do whatever I want with her."

"The last girl you did whatever you wanted with is still recovering. The boss wants to make sure you don't damage this one. He won't put up with it." The linebacker's voice is firm. Hard despite the high octave. There's a definite threat in his words, and Tat knows it.

Tat curls his upper lip. He shoots daggers at the linebacker with his eyes, but all he does is shrug. "Fine."

He slams the door in the linebacker's face, and I hold my breath while I wait to find out what's going to happen. Tat's back is to me. He clenches his fist, then spins around and slams it into the wall. He throws what can only be described as a temper tantrum. Pulling pictures off the walls and smashing the television with a lamp. He rips the sheets off the bed and lets out a scream of fury while I cower on the floor. Doing my best to stay out of his way. He keeps looking at me, pacing back and forth. Throwing things.

Even after all my years with Roger and all the zombies I've encountered, this is the most terrifying moment of my life. Waiting to find out what Tat is going to do.

Finally, he yanks me off the floor and throws me on the bed. I kick and twist. His face is red and sweaty, and he's focused on only one thing. Rage. He grabs my shirt, and it comes off my body in one terrifying rip. He straddles me. My legs are pinned down. I slap at his face, but he grips my wrists in one of his hands and pins them down as well. There's nothing to protect me now but a skimpy thong. I twist and squirm. Scream and thrash. Tat is too strong.

My bare skin is his to torture. He gropes and squeezes and bites. I howl in pain. Like a wild animal caught in a trap. There's no escape. No matter which way I twist, his teeth or hands are there to torment me. There's nothing I can do, and staring at his face only makes it so much more painful. The evilness in his eyes seeps inside me.

I turn my face away from him and close my eyes. Blocking him out is my only defense.

He rips the underwear from my body, and I squeeze my eyes tighter. The sound of his zipper makes me shake, and I do my best to leave my body as he wiggles out of his pants. His skin is warm against mine. He rubs against me while his hands do their worst. I don't move. Don't fight. There's no point.

Minutes go by with him on top of me. Squirming. Groping. Rubbing. Nothing else happens. He moves faster and makes frustrated noises. Then starts to curse. He's furious. Cussing. Growling. Still, nothing happens. Nothing. I finally open my eyes.

Tat's face is bright red and his jaw is clenched. His eyes are closed like he's concentrating. But there's still no progress. He can't get it up.

I let out a bitter laugh. I can't hold it in.

Tat flinches, and his eyes fly open. He turns them on me, and they burn with hate. "What the fuck are you laughing about?"

"You having a little trouble?" I know I shouldn't make him angry, but I can't help it. He's so pathetic-looking. Desperately trying to get off. But he can't, not without the violence.

Tat lets go of my hands and jumps up. He screams in frustration. Then pulls his arm back. I shrink down and wait for the blow. But he obviously thinks better of it, because he turns around and slams his fist into the wall. Leaving behind little splatters of blood.

"Shit!" He starts pacing the room. Throwing and kicking things like a three-year-old. "Fucking zombies!"

He stops and glares at me. I pull the sheet up to my chin, feeling more naked than ever under his angry gaze. But deep down I know he's not going to do anything. He isn't stupid. If he beats the shit of me, he'll be out on his ass. On the Strip. Which means he'll be zombie food.

He takes a menacing step toward me. "You're lucky."

I almost roll my eyes. I feel real lucky. "Fuck you."

"Don't piss me off," he growls.

I clamp my mouth shut. Pushing him right now would be a very bad idea.

He puts his pants back on, saving me from the torture of having to look at his useless dick, then goes back to pacing the room. He pauses every now and then to look at me. My heart pounds harder with every glare he throws my way. After a few minutes, he crosses the room and grabs me by the hair. He jerks me off the bed and drags me to the door.

I'm naked, but he doesn't seem to care. He leads me out of the room and down the hall toward the elevator, gripping my hair tightly. The skin on my scalp throbs. I can only imagine the bald spot I'm going to have after this. We pass a few men in the hall who stop to leer at me, but Tat doesn't slow.

He shoves me into the elevator when the door opens, and I lean against the wall, gasping for breath while I do my best to cover myself. My face and head throb. My eye feels like it's on the verge of swelling shut. I'm going to be black and blue. But it isn't the worst thing that could have happened to me, so I can't really complain.

Especially when I think about Hadley.

Tat is so angry when he steps into the elevator his body shakes. Two men follow us in. They stand across from me. Ogling. I doubt they have anywhere to go. They probably just wanted to stare. I give them the finger.

The elevator opens, and the stench of rotten flesh hits me like a slap in the face. He's taking me back. Did he really give up so easily?

Tat shoves me out of the elevator, and I slam into Linebacker One. His arms go around me, and he does his best to pretend he's trying to keep me from falling. Right. Like he needs to squeeze my tits to be sure I don't fall on my ass. I shove him away, but he's too busy staring at Tat with his mouth hanging open to slap me.

"What are you doing?" the linebacker asks in his Mike Tyson voice. He sounds like he sucked in a mouthful of helium.

"I'm finished with this bitch. Don't want her in my room," Tat says.

The linebacker looks me up and down, and I cross my arms over my chest. He shakes his head at. "That's a first. Whatever, it's your time."

Tat glares at me one more time before turning back to the elevator. Finally, I allow myself to relax. I made it one more night.

But I can't be too happy. Hadley didn't.

MEGAN AND I ARE HUDDLED TOGETHER ON THE FLOOR when the door of the suite flies open. Hadley stumbles in. She's pale, and her face is red and puffy. Our eyes meet as she walks across the room, and a rage so thick and volatile comes over me that I swear I'd be able to rip a man apart with my bare hands. She gingerly lowers herself to the floor next to me like her whole body aches. It's impossible to tell whether the pain is physical or emotional, though.

I wrap my arms around her and pull her shaky body to mine. "You okay?"

She shakes her head. She won't look at me.

If I ever see that bald bastard again, I'll castrate him.

"We'll get out of this. Axl will get us out of this."

Hadley pulls her legs up to her chest and rests her forehead against her knees. Her shoulders shake. I have no idea what to do. How do you comfort someone who's been through something like this? I'm not even sure if it's possible.

CHAPTER TEN
AXL

"Vivian said you guys met after all this started," Jon says.

My hands tighten on the steerin' wheel like it's that asshole's neck. How the hell he ended up in the passenger seat is a damn puzzle. I grind my teeth and look in the review mirror at Angus and Nathan in the back. They don't seem to be enjoyin' the ride any more than I am. Jon keeps tryin' to get me to talk, but I ain't interested in bein' his buddy. He sighs when I don't answer, and I grip the steerin' wheel tighter. Only way I'll be able to keep from hittin' him. When this is all over, I'm gonna beat the shit outta that guy.

"So we just walk in with a couple gallons of diesel and they'll hand us a chick?" Angus says from the back.

He keeps askin' how it all works like he'd be more than happy to head on over there and set up camp. Probably would if it weren't for me. I thought my brother was better than that. Guess you really never know a person.

Jon turns to face the back and studies Angus, glarin' at him. "That's pretty much how it works, yeah."

Angus grunts, and my broken hand throbs when my fingers tighten. Punchin' Jon made the damn thing worse. 'Course, if Angus don't cool it, I'm gonna kick his ass when we get outta this car. I don't gotta wait 'til Vivian's back for that.

"How much farther do we have to go?" Nathan asks.

I'd be pissed, but I'm sure he's just ready to get the hell away from Angus. "'Bout fifteen minutes. Let's just hope nobody found that truck."

There ain't a lot of talk as we get close to the truck yard. It's still dark, but the sky's gettin' orange in the distance. Zombies stumble across the street, and I run right into 'em. The car bounces when the tires thump over their bodies.

"You got that key?" I yell back to Angus. Didn't even think to ask 'bout it 'til now. Don't matter. I'll jump the fence and run the truck right through it if I gotta.

"Brought all the keys," Angus says.

My hand tightens on the steerin' wheel, and I pucker my lips. Again. "You mean you brought the keys for the cars too?"

"Sure did. And the Sam's truck. That asshole's still got the keys to the fuel truck, though."

Bastard. With Vivian missin', I forgot all 'bout Angus's temper tantrum. We're gonna have to deal with that once all this is over. I ain't lookin' forward to it. Angus is a stubborn bastard, and he ain't really one for adjustin' his way of thinkin'.

The truck yard comes into view, and I slow to a stop. Angus hops out to unlock the gate, and Nathan follows him. There're only a few zombies 'round. Nathan's only gotta take out two before the gate's open. Soon as Angus is outta the way, I hit the gas. Jon lurches forward, and I have the urge to hit the brakes. I'd love to see his face slam into the dash.

I drive to the back and park right in front of the fuel truck. It's still here.

I leave the lights on and shove the door open. Then hop down. "Grab them gas cans," I call over my shoulder. I don't even look at Jon.

Angus comes joggin' up, and my jaw tightens. Things ain't ever been this tense between Angus and me before. Not since Lilly, anyways. Not sure why he's so threatened by me and women. Like I'm gonna forget him or something.

Nathan comes up behind Angus, keepin' a safe distance.

Angus puckers his lips. "What's your problem anyways? You've got your panties in a bunch 'bout something. You gotta problem that ain't got nothin' to do with Vivian." He narrows his eyes. "It's 'bout me, ain't it?"

Screw Angus. Everything's always 'bout him. "This ain't the time."

I follow Jon to the back of the fuel truck. The Nissan's lights are bright, but only comin' from one direction like that ain't helpin' me see. Least we got flashlights.

Jon is starin' at the valve. "You know what to do?"

I shove him aside. "Pretty sure I can figure it out."

I aim the flashlight at the valve and fool with it for a few seconds. Seems pretty simple, but I'm gonna need two hands. "Hold this," I say, thrustin' the flashlight at Jon.

He grunts, and my jaw tightens. I turn to face him. "You want me to beat the shit outta you?" He shakes his head, and I turn back around. "Then shut the hell up and do what you're told."

Less than ten minutes later we got two full cans of diesel.

"Told you I could do it," I mutter as I screw the lid on.

"I never said you couldn't."

I get to my feet and take a step closer to Jon.

He puts his hands up. "Look, I'm sorry. Okay?"

My jaw tightens. I clench my fist and wince when pain shoots up my hand. Dammit. I keep forgettin' I hurt it. "No. It ain't okay," I say through gritted teeth.

Jon swipes his hand across his eyes and shakes his head. "I had to save my sister. Come on! You have a brother. What would you do if he was in danger? Would you risk the life of a stranger?"

I flinch and take a step back. Shit. Angus can be a prick, but he's blood.

"Shit." I rake my hand through my hair and look down.

"Yeah," Jon says.

I look up and glare at him. "I still don't like you."

"I'm not asking you to."

I grab a gas can and turn 'round. "Good."

Angus and Nathan are waitin' by the car. On opposite sides.

Angus spits when he sees me. "We good?"

I nod and walk by him, puttin' the can in the back. Jon hoists his in and heads to the passenger side, leavin' me and Angus alone.

"This 'bout Darla?" Angus asks.

Among other things. Like him bein' an unreasonable, racist asshole. "Something like that."

"What's the deal? I know Blondie don't like her. That why you're bein' such a dick?"

I swear and look away. There's no time to deal with this bullshit. I gotta get to Vivian. Plus, this Darla thing is...complicated. Not sure if I should tell him, though. Vivian wouldn't like it.

Angus huffs. "Just tell me what the hell is goin' on."

"Darla's Vivian's mom." I wince and feel like hittin' myself in the head. Shouldn't have said it.

Angus narrows his eyes 'til they almost disappear. "You're shittin' me."

"Nope." Can't do nothin' 'bout it now, so's I might as well just tell him the whole truth. Maybe Angus will surprise me and turn out not to be such a prick. Maybe. "Darla's the bitch who left Vivian. Left her with an asshole dad who beat the shit outta her. That's who you're screwin'."

Angus puckers his lips and clenches his fist. "Son of a bitch! That bitch told me she was sterile."

Of course that's all he can think 'bout. Not that she left her only child with a man who beat the shit outta her. Not that Vivian's missin' and Darla don't give a damn. Just Angus. I've known for a long time that Angus was a selfish bastard, but this is just too damn much. The only thing Angus cares about is Angus, and it's pissin' me off.

I clench my jaw and pucker my lips again. Dammit! I take a step away from Angus and do my best to relax. It ain't easy. There's too much goin' on. "Let's get the hell outta here."

I can't look at him. He's still swearin' and mumblin' under his breath as he walks to the front of the Nissan. He hops in, and I stand by the driver's side door for a few seconds, tryin' to get my shit together. It's no use. That animal inside me is awake. Pretty soon it's gonna win and rip right through me, then everybody's gonna be in some big, fuckin' trouble.

The horn blares, and I jump. My jaw tenses all over again, and I rip the door open.

Angus glares at me. "We goin' or what?"

"Yeah," I mutter. "We're goin'."

I SLOW THE NISSAN WHEN WE GET CLOSE TO THE MONTE Carlo, and right away the zombie bastards on the Strip go nuts. They bang on the outside so hard it shakes the whole damn thing. There're two other cars in front of the casino. A black truck and a white van that looks a hell of a lot like the one from the hospital. Its two front tires are up on the sidewalk.

"So we're just gonna waltz in there with them gas cans?" Angus asks. He sounds scared as shit. Good. It's good for him to show some damn human emotions every now and then. He turns 'round and looks at Jon in the backseat. The gas cans are on the seat next to him.

"That's what we're going to do," Jon says.

"Dumbest goddamn idea I ever heard," Angus mutters.

I slam the car in park and grab my knife. "Shut the hell up, Angus."

When I hop out, the Vegas sun blinds me, and the smell of death makes me wanna hurl. It's hotter than the pits of hell, and I can almost hear the rottin' skin on these poor bastards sizzlin' under the sun. Flies buzz through the air, and the zombies charge at me. But I can outrun 'em.

I slash my knife at the nearest one and shove my foot against his chest. His motionless body flies into a few other dead bastards, knockin' 'em down. I take off runnin'. Angus and Jon are already headin' toward the casino, and they each got a gas can. The zombies chase me, but we only gotta make it to the overhang of the hotel. There's a barrier set up, and armed men. They see us comin' and fire into the bodies before we're even halfway there.

We charge into the casino, and a blast of cool air hits me in the face. I'm breathin' hard, so it takes a few seconds for me to register what's goin' on. Soon as I do, I wanna pull my knife back out. The air is clear and they've got electricity. There are men everywhere. Clean and safe. Usin' women like toys...

"Here he comes," Jon says, breakin' through my thoughts.

I take a deep breath. My face is hot, and something inside me is threatenin' to explode. Jon puts the gas can down at my feet as a man wearin' a suit walks up. Actin' all important. Right. I size him up when he stops in front of me. He's short and round. Bald. I could take him.

"You pick up a few new people?" The man eyes me and

Angus, and I clench my jaw so tight my teeth grind together.

"Yeah. Found these guys in Boulder City," Jon says. He sounds different. He's standin' taller and his face is hard. His eyes cold. It makes my shoulders stiffen.

The man nods, and his eyes go down. To the gas cans.

Angus clears his throat. "Jon told us 'bout the set-up you got here. Sounds like you got a good thing goin'. It's hell livin' out there. We brought you some diesel. Wanted to show you that we was team players."

"Where'd you find it? My men haven't been able to locate any for a while." He looks at me.

I should say something, but I'm too tense. I can't even get my jaw to loosen.

"Had it in my garage. When things started gettin' bad, I stocked up. Bought me a small generator just in case. This is all I got left." Angus's voice is smooth. He's a good liar. Always has been.

The bald man nods. He's still lookin' at me. "What's your story?"

I swallow and pry my jaw open. It hurts. "We're brothers." My throat is tight, and my voice comes out soundin' funny.

The bald dude don't seem to notice, though. He nods for a few seconds, then smiles. "Okay! This diesel will be enough to get you two a couple of threes. Not a bad way to start your time off here." He turns and motions for us to follow. "Come on over. I'm assuming Jon told you how it all works?"

"Yup," I manage to get out.

"Good. I'll get you some receipts. Go ahead and check out what we have. Not a bad selection, if I say so myself. I think you'll be pleased."

He jerks his head toward the wall, and I freeze. My blood gets hot, and I grind my teeth together even harder. There are dozens of pictures of women. All naked. I scan the pictures under the number three, and when I find her, I almost lose it. My stomach jumps to my throat and almost dumps the food I ate this mornin' all over the floor. And that animal is back. It's clawin' and bitin' my insides harder than ever.

Angus stands in front of the wall, lookin' the women over. He's grinnin' like a monkey. My hand curls into a fist. I wanna punch him. So bad. Bastard.

"You have to relax." Jon stands next to me.

I exhale and slowly unclench my jaw, then take a step closer. I try and act like I'm lookin' the women over. It's a blur, though. I can't see nothin'.

"See something you like?" The bald dude is back.

Angus points at a picture. Hadley. She looks like shit. "That the actress? What's her name?"

The asshole smiles. "Hadley Lucas. We just found her a few days ago. She's free tonight, but she's going to be popular."

Angus nods and rubs his chin. He even leans closer to the picture. I gotta swallow down my rage. "Never thought I'd get to screw a celebrity."

The bald asshole slaps Angus on the back. "Well, here's your chance!"

My body shakes, and I have to fight not to punch the bastard. He turns toward me. Smilin' like we're best goddamn friends. I imagine shootin' him. Watchin' his head explode. It don't make me feel no better.

"What about you?"

I pick a girl at random and point to her picture. "She looks good. No, wait." I put a shaky finger on Vivian's picture. "This one. Right here."

The bald dude smiles even bigger. He looks like that goddamn cat from *Alice in Wonderland*. Always hated that movie. "Good choice. She's got a nice pair of tits."

I flinch, and Jon clears his throat. "I helped bring them both in. Had a night with the blonde chick already. She was feisty, but good."

I'm gonna rip his head off.

I swallow and nod. "Sounds like something I'd like."

CHAPTER ELEVEN

VIVIAN

Hadley's body is shaking when she sits down next to me. Her hair is still dripping from her shower. It's already almost dinnertime, and she's barely spoken since she got back to the room. I wish I could think of something to say. Maybe distracting her would be the best thing? It's worth a shot.

"You've never told me about your family," I say.

Hadley stares at me for a few seconds. Her green eyes are blank. She blinks, then clears her throat. "I grew up in Ohio."

I nod like I didn't already know that. She did tell us a little something about her family that first day at the shelter, but I want to get her talking. "Brothers and sisters?"

"An older brother," she says, and her eyes start to focus a little more.

"Were you close?"

Her lips twitch slightly. "Most of the time. I dated a lot of his friends, and he didn't love that. But we got along."

Her body relaxes a fraction, and I smile. "I always thought it would be nice to have a brother. Hell, it would have been nice to have any kind of real family."

Hadley bites down on her lip, and her green eyes narrow on my face. A little color has come back to her cheeks. Yeah, getting her talking was a good idea. Any kind of distraction will help us right now.

"Darla's your mom?"

Shit. Maybe not. My stomach twists the way it always does when I think about Darla, and I nod. I was pretty sure Hadley had overheard that argument, so I shouldn't feel as nauseated as I do. But I can't help it. Darla makes me sick.

I clear my throat. "Yeah. If you can call her that. She gave birth to me, anyway. I haven't seen her since I was ten and she ran off. That's when my dad started beating me..." I swallow, and Hadley nods. Her cheeks get pinker like she's embarrassed or feels bad for me. It's good for her to be focused on my shit rather than her own right now. "Before she ran out, Darla always took the brunt of his anger." I shrug. "Just another day in the trailer park."

"You always talk about yourself like you're such white trash. You don't act like it, though. No offense to Axl, but you can tell just by talking to him where he grew up. Not you."

"That's because I worked hard to distance myself from all that. I didn't want to spend the rest of my life that way." I laugh, and it's one of the most bitter sounds I've ever heard. "I had big plans. I was going to meet a nice guy and get married. Be a soccer mom. All that boring crap I've only ever seen on TV. Ridiculous."

"Why is that ridiculous?"

"Because I was a stripper. I took a few classes at the community college, read a lot of books. Worked hard to make sure I sounded like a nice girl. But at the end of the night, I went to work and took my clothes off for money. I was fooling myself. A nice guy wouldn't marry a girl like me."

Hadley shakes her head, and she almost looks like her old self. Maybe talking about the trivial problems of the past is the best thing right now. Get her mind off the world we're living in.

"That's not true."

"Doesn't matter," I say with a shrug. "Not anymore."

Hadley nods and squeezes my hand. *She's* comforting *me.* Maybe she will be able to come back from this. I hope so. I like

Hadley a lot, and the thought of her letting this destroy her after we've survived so much other bullshit makes me ache.

"You want to hear something that will make you feel better?" I nod, and she actually grins. I almost cry when I see it. "I moved to Hollywood right out of high school. I was *so* determined to make it as an actress. But I was only getting small parts in TV shows and I was barely getting by. I was minutes away from taking a part in one of those late night Cinemax movies. *Minutes.*"

"What stopped you?"

"I got the lead in *Zombieworld*. It was pretty low-budget, but it was popular. It made my career." She laughs, then puts her hand over her mouth. Her eyes are huge and round. Terrified. "It all seems like a nightmare now."

AFTER DINNER, MEGAN IS A LITTLE MORE COHERENT than usual. She asks Hadley all kinds of questions about Hollywood. Questions only a teenager would think to ask. Like if Hadley had ever met Zac Efron or if she could call up any other celebrity any time she wanted to. It's kind of strange, but maybe she's doing the same thing I was. Trying to distract herself from reality.

When the linebackers show up and start pulling women out, Megan shrinks inside herself. Hadley scoots closer to me, and we both sit in tense silence while they make their way through the room. They're headed our way. Linebacker One even glances toward me a few times.

It's Jon. It has to be Jon.

That's all I can think when Linebacker One stops in front of me. He stares down at us with a big grin on his face. "You two are popular."

Hadley squeaks when he jerks her to her feet, but she doesn't fight. I don't either. She's going to Jon. I know it. He promised. But me...the odds that Tat wants another go at me are slim.

My heart pounds so hard it echoes in my ears, totally drowning out the moans of the zombies in the hallway. Linebacker Two stands at the elevator just like before. Hadley sobs. Linebacker One's fingers dig into the bruises on my arm, but I hardly feel it. He shoves me into the elevator right behind Hadley, and we find ourselves squeezed up against the back wall.

KATE L. MARY

I close my eyes when the door shuts and a tear slides down my cheek. Hadley doesn't stop crying and I really wish I could reassure her, but I can't let the linebackers know about Jon. Plus, I'm pretty sure if I open my mouth, I'll burst into tears. All I can think about right now is how it felt to have Tat on top of me. His hot skin against mine. His teeth biting my skin. I start to shake.

What happened with him was nothing compared to what I'm about to face.

The elevator dings, and I open my eyes. We're on the ninth floor. Linebacker One shoves two women out, then grabs Hadley. She yelps, but I can't even look at her as she's dragged away. Something like bitterness squeezes my insides, and for the first time, doubt creep up inside me. Maybe I shouldn't have sacrificed myself for Hadley. Maybe I should have been selfish...

The linebacker comes back, and we continue down. We stop on another floor, then another, and then I'm the last girl. Linebacker One leers at me, and more than once he mumbles something about needing to go out on a run. My stomach clenches until I almost double over in pain, but I don't want him to know how much he's bothering me.

The door slides open on the third floor, and I come face to face with Jon. His eyes meet mine when he steps into the elevator, and my heart plummets. He isn't the man who requested Hadley.

Oh, shit.

Linebacker One jerks me forward and pulls me down the hall. My heart pounds. Please let it be Tat. Please, God. Do this for me. Tat won't be able to get it up. Anyone else, and I'm screwed. Literally.

I let out a panicked laugh, and it comes out sounding slightly hysterical. Am I going crazy? I haven't slept much. I'm starving and probably about to be raped. Throw all that on top of the fact that the entire civilized world seems to have disappeared and been replaced by this madness, I've found and lost my only child in a matter of days, and fallen in love just in time for these assholes to destroy it. Things just keep getting better and better.

Every muscle and nerve in my body screams at me to run, but there's nothing I can do. I couldn't get away from this guy even if there was somewhere to go. And there isn't. I'm totally trapped. There are a few men standing in the hall in front of me. If I took off, they'd stop me for sure. The elevator is at my back, along with

92

Linebacker Two. This place is solid. Like Fort Knox on steroids.

When the linebacker stops in front of a room, my body starts to shake so hard my teeth rattle together. He raps his knuckles against the door, and I wait for what feels like hours. The knob turns, and my heart pounds harder. My stomach lurches when it starts to open, but once again I'm shoved forward before I can register who it is.

The door slams behind me, and I spin around. A strangled sob pops out of my mouth. "Axl!"

Tears fill my eyes, spilling over as I throw myself into his arms. He's sweaty and filthy and smells like death. But I don't care. He's here.

His mouth covers mine, hot and urgent, and he pushes me back against the wall. His hands are everywhere. On my face and in my hair, caressing my arms and my back. Running down over my chest and stomach. It isn't sexual, though. It's like he's reassuring himself I'm here. That I'm still in one piece.

It's the most amazing feeling I've experienced.

"You okay?" he whispers between kisses. His voice is low and rough.

"I'm okay. I'm okay." I'm still crying, and it's all I seem to be able to get out. Even that is shaky.

He pulls back and studies me more closely. His gray, stormy eyes search mine. His hand runs down the side of my face, caressing the bruises left behind by Tat. His expression hardens. "Did they...Jon said..." He swallows, and for the first time since I met him, he looks uncertain. "Did anybody touch you?" His jaw is so tight the words are barely audible. His eyes are hard with unconcealed rage.

I shake my head and hold his face between my hands. "Not really. I mean, he tried but..." A sob shakes my body when the memory comes screaming back. "I'm okay."

His face crumples and he opens his mouth to say something else, but I cut him off with a kiss. I raise myself up on my toes and trace his lips with my tongue. Forcing his jaw to relax. He wraps his arms around me and pulls me closer. My entire body ignites. I can't believe he's here. I was starting to wonder if I'd ever see him again. If we'd ever be able to find a way out of this.

His hands and mouth move down my body, and he pulls my shirt over my head. He runs his tongue down my neck to my cleavage, and his fingers tease my nipple, pulling on the small silver ring that pierces it. When his mouth closes over it, I let out a gasp. I close my eyes and work to block out everything that's happened the past couple days, focusing on nothing but Axl.

We make our way to bed, and Axl pulls his own shirt over his head. Within seconds, we're both naked, and his mouth moves down my body. Teasing and caressing every curve.

"I thought I'd never see you again," I whisper as he kisses his way up my stomach and over my breasts.

His mouth tickles the skin on my neck, sending shivers down my spine. "I never woulda stopped lookin' for you."

I pull him up and kiss him again. "I love you." The words tumble out before I can stop them, but I don't regret it. I should have said it earlier. Never should have left the shelter without letting him know how much I care.

Axl pulls back, and his gray eyes hold mine. He runs his hand down my face and between my breasts, then grasps my hips. When he enters me, I gasp.

"I love you," he says, rocking his body against mine. Slow and steady, like the waves crashing against the shore. "I ain't never gonna let you outta my sight again."

MY CHEEK RESTS AGAINST AXL'S CHEST. HIS SKIN IS STILL wet from our shower. He needed it. Hell, so did I. I trace my fingers up his chest to his shoulder, down his arm. Then I sit up. The knuckles on his right hand are red and cut. Bruised. I lift his hand and press my lips against the cuts.

"What happened?" I whisper against his skin.

His lips twitch, and he pushes a few strands of wet hair behind my ear. "Punched a wall. Doc says it's broke."

"That was dumb." I roll my eyes. "You should have a cast or something."

"Had a brace. It got in the way."

Of course. He's too much of a man to take care of an injury.

I lay my head back down on his chest, then let out a deep breath. "Tell me you guys have a plan."

"We're workin' on it. We can get you and Hadley for a night, but we ain't sure what to do 'bout Megan. She ain't on the list downstairs." His hand sweeps across my head, twisting my wet hair between his fingers. It causes goose bumps to pop up on my arms.

I tilt my head up so I can see his face. Looking into his gray eyes is like standing in the middle of a storm. "She's hurt. She got beat up pretty bad."

He touches my own black eye, and I wince. "Who did this?"

"Is it bad?"

"You ain't seen it?" His eyes cloud over, and he traces my cheekbone with his fingertip.

"No mirrors in the suite. I guess a girl broke one last week and slit her wrists." I swallow, and his jaw tightens. "They took out all the glass after that."

He leans down and kisses my eye, then my cheek. It stings, but almost in a good way. Like he's sucking the poison out after a snake bite. "I'm sorry. I shoulda been there."

"Don't," I whisper. "Let's not focus on that. Let's worry about what we're going to do to get out of this."

He nods and presses his lips to my swollen cheek again. "You got any ideas how we can get Megan out?"

His lips move against my skin, and I sigh. I just want to stay here forever with him and forget about the outside world.

But we have to focus. To figure out what we're going to do to get out of this in one piece. I force myself to sit up even though I don't want to. "I don't know. Right now they're letting her heal, so there's no way to get her out. But maybe she can convince them she's sick so they'll take her to the doctor? I don't know if she can handle it, though. She seems pretty shell-shocked."

"You got any other ideas?"

"I don't know..."

If Hadley or I were going to be there we could get her out, but we won't be. Will she be able to do it? I think about her battered body and the way she shrank into herself when the linebackers walked in. I doubt it. Even though she's been up and talking, she's still pretty messed up. And she's only been able to really talk with Hadley. Who won't be there. We need someone to help us.

Someone who would never in a million years get selected.

Dirty Blonde.

She hasn't had a night away since we got here. Why would she? She reeks. Even if someone picked her from a picture, they'd get a refund the second they saw her. Or smelled her. Word must have gotten around about her. Right?

But can I trust her? That's the real question. She's a total bitch, but that's only because she's a prisoner. We could be her ticket out. Why wouldn't she help us?

It's the only thing I can come up with. It *has* to work.

"I can get someone to help us," I mutter.

Axl nods, then kisses me again. He won't stop touching me. Like he's afraid I'm going to disappear. His fingers trace the bruises on my face over and over again. Even though it hurts, I don't tell him to stop.

"You gonna tell me what happened here?" His jaw is tight again. "I gotta know who to kill."

Something lodges itself in my throat, making it impossible to talk.

I don't want him anywhere near Tat. All I want is for us to get out of here and never look back.

"Nothing," I say. "I got lucky, that's all."

It makes me think of Hadley, and I swallow. Where is she right now? Did the bastard from the other night get her again?

I shudder and close my eyes. "Hadley didn't get so lucky, though."

Axl swears and I open my eyes. His expression is dark. Dangerous. "She'll be okay tonight. Angus has her."

My eyebrows shoot up. "Angus? Seriously?" I bite down my bottom lip. Angus is...unpredictable. But I don't really have him pegged as a rapist. Asshole, yes. But this... "Are you positive she's okay with him?"

Axl nods, but he does it very slowly. "He's on our side."

I trust Axl, but I don't trust Angus for a minute. It's impossible to forget how he acted when we first met. The first time I spotted him was in some hole-in-the-wall diner on Route 66. He looked at me like I was on the menu. And I know he only wanted to stop to give me a ride because of my double D's. Since then, he hasn't missed an opportunity to make sexual comments. Then there was the time he hit me. Yeah, Angus has a dark side. Just how dark, I don't know. Would he hurt Hadley? If he did, he'd never be able to come back to the shelter, which would mean leaving Axl. Angus is an ass, but he loves his brother. I'm sure of it.

WHEN I ROLL AGAINST A WARM BODY, MY HEART ALMOST stops. My back stiffens, and I suck in a deep breath. Fingers trail up my spine. I start to shake.

Then I remember where I am and who I'm with, and I'm slowly able to relax. Axl. I'm with Axl. Safe for the moment.

I crack one eye and look toward the clock. It's three o'clock in the morning. As usual, Axl is awake. I sit up, and my eyes meet his. He smiles, and it makes my insides soften like a stick of butter that's been left on the counter for too long.

"You never sleep," I whisper, running my hand through his dirty blond hair.

He just nods.

"Why?"

He takes a deep breath, and when he blows it out his body feels harder. Like he's turned to stone. Something keeps him from sleeping. Demons or ghosts, I'm not sure, but there's a reason, and I want to know. I want to know everything about him.

"Dreams," he finally says. "Used to be, anyways. When I was younger. Now it's just habit." His Adam's apple bobs when he swallows.

"What are the dreams about?"

He doesn't take his stormy eyes off me. "My mom. The night she died. I was there, in the other room of the trailer we lived in. But I couldn't get to her."

My pulse quickens. I've been waiting for him to open up like this for so long. Been wanting him to trust me. I'm almost afraid to breathe. Afraid he'll stop talking.

"How did it happen?" My voice is softer now, like I'm talking to a frightened animal and if I'm too loud I'll scare it away.

"She was datin' some asshole. Nothin' new, really. They was all assholes. This one, though, he was something different. I knew it right away. 'Course, she couldn't see it. They hadn't been goin' out long, and already she'd showed up with a broken wrist. Seems like violence was the only way she knew how to live.

"When I woke up that night, my room was full of smoke. It was late. Not sure how late, exactly. But I knew I had to get to her. The doorknob was too hot, though. It burned my hand when I tried to open it. I was coughin'. Couldn't see. The only way I was gonna make it was to get out the window, but I didn't want to leave her. She was a bitch but—"

97

"She was your mom."

He nods and purses his lips. "Yup."

"So she died in the fire?"

"Nope," he says. "Bastard set the fire to try and cover up what he'd done. I got out and the fire department showed up. Angus came, too. He lived on the other side of the trailer park and had come runnin' when the sirens woke him. We was both there when they got the fire out. Mom's body was barely burnt, but she was dead. Skull smashed in. She and that asshole had been screamin' at each other earlier that night, but I'd ignored them. Like always. Gettin' in the middle of it usually ended with me gettin' a black eye. Or two. Better to just stay in my room. But seein' her like that... It made me feel bad. Like I shoulda known. Shoulda done something."

I want to wrap my arms around him and pull him against me. To take away his pain. All the shit I went through as a kid, but I never lost a parent. And he lost the only one he'd ever known. Even a shitty mom is still a mom when you're young. I know something about that.

"You couldn't have known, Axl. It wasn't your fault. You were a kid, and she wasn't. She made her choices."

"Still felt like shit 'bout it."

He isn't looking at me now, but I wish he would. I hate the way he puts so much pressure on himself.

I turn his face toward mine, then gently press my lips against his. "You need to forgive yourself. Think of all the people you've helped since this whole thing started. You aren't like her. You're better."

He buries his face in my hair and inhales like he's breathing me in. I hate thinking I have to leave him tomorrow. That I have to go back to that room of suffering when all I want to do is be in his arms, away from this hell we're living in.

"Don't wanna let you go," he says, echoing my thoughts.

"We'll be okay." I do my best to sound reassuring and confident. In reality, though, my insides are like mush.

DIRTY BLONDE'S BLUE EYES SLICE THROUGH ME WHEN I step into the suite. She's watching, just like she said she would. Her lips press together when I lift my head high. Her eyes move down, studying every move I make. No walk of shame for me today. I don't even pretend. I *want* her to notice.

Hadley is already back from her night with Angus. Thankfully, she doesn't look any more broken than she did yesterday. I guess Angus behaved himself. If I find out differently, I'll slit his throat.

She and Megan are huddled together against the wall. Talking. Megan still looks fragile, though. There's no way she'll be able to handle this on her own. We can't leave getting out of here up to her. It's too important.

I catch Dirty Blonde's eye and motion for her to follow me. Her lips press together, but she gets up. She heads toward me while I back into a corner, close to the door. There isn't much privacy in here, so we'll have to be careful.

Dirty Blonde stops in front of me and crosses her arms. Her face is hard. Like a pit bull's. "You're looking awfully happy for someone who just got raped."

I flinch. She just shrugs. This chick is a bitch. Probably was before all this. But I need her. We may not be able to do this without her help.

When I step closer, I have to breathe out of my mouth. Being this close to her is like walking by a dumpster full of sweat and piss. Her breath stinks worse than the zombies on the Strip. No man would want her. Not when there are so many other options.

She may be a bitch, but she isn't stupid.

My mouth is an inch from her ear. "My friends are getting me out of here, and I need your help."

She drops her arms to her side and steps back. Her eyes are huge. "What?"

"You heard me. Now shut up and listen, we don't have much time." I tell her how Hadley and I got here. How I sent Jon to find my friends. How they are ready to break us out of here tonight. Her breathing picks up. Every time she exhales, my stomach twists. I try my best not to breathe in through my nose, but I'm talking as fast as I can and sometimes I don't have a choice. I wish she didn't stink, but I guess if she showered we'd be in trouble.

"So all you want me to do is get that messed-up girl out of here? If I do that, you'll take me with you?"

When I nod, her eyes shimmer. Bitch or not, you can't hate anyone trapped in this situation.

She wipes her nose with the back of her hand and looks

around. Then back at me. "What about everyone else?"

My throat tightens, and I avoid looking at the other women. There are times when you just have to think about yourself. "We can't. There are too many men. We'd never make it out alive."

Her mouth tightens like she's considering telling me to go to hell. Too late, though. I'm already here.

"Can you do it?" I ask when she doesn't say anything.

She nods so hard her greasy hair falls in her face. She doesn't make a move to push it out of her eyes.

I step closer even though I don't want to. The smell is so strong it turns my stomach. "You have to do *whatever* it takes to get her out of this room by nine o'clock. Got it?"

Dirty Blonde's eyes snap toward me. Her lip quivers. She wraps her arms around her chest so tight it looks like she's trying to crush herself. "I will do anything."

That's what I need.

CHAPTER TWELVE
AXL

"What do you mean she ain't available?" My hand throbs from clenchin' it so tight. Maybe I should be wearin' that damn brace. My hand ain't gettin' no better.

"Just what I said." The bald dude shrugs. "The blonde already has a date tonight. You'll have to wait until tomorrow." He grins, and I wanna hit him. If I get a chance, I'm gonna slit this guy's throat wide open. "You must've had a good time with her last night."

Angus elbows me. "Don't sweat it, little brother. I'll let you have the Hollywood chick if you want."

I cough, tryin' to loosen my jaw. "I'll wait."

The bald dude nods and heads back to the front desk, but I can't move. We just handed these bastards a bunch of guns for nothin'. Some asshole already has Vivian tonight, and I gotta find out who.

"Relax," Angus mutters. He looks toward the asshole in the suit. "We'll figure out where she is and get her."

I inhale slowly. That's right. I'll just find out which one of these bastards has her. Then cut his balls off.

Jon motions for us to follow him. We head toward the bar, and when we're a safe distance, he says, "What are we going to do now?"

"Stick to the plan," Angus says. "You two meet the others at the back door and head on up to my room. Hollywood'll be with me. Then we split up. Half go for your sister, half for Blondie."

I wish he'd stop callin' Vivian *Blondie*.

"How we gonna find out where she is?" I mutter. I ain't really talkin' to the others, though. Just thinkin' out loud. We gotta figure out how to find her. And soon. I don't wanna leave her alone with some animal for even a second.

Angus puckers his lips and scratches his head. His hair's gettin' longer. I ain't seen him with anything but a buzz since we was kids.

"Maybe the big fella that brought them girls to our rooms would know. Seems like he's in charge of movin' 'em back and forth."

Sometimes I think Angus is a genius hidden in an asshole's body.

I look at the clock. Almost six. They brought Vivian to me little after seven last night. Don't give us much time. "Let's go find him."

We search all the normal places. Casino, bar, pool. They got a big-ass TV set up in a conference room, and they're constantly showin' movies. Porn mostly. But the big guy ain't 'round.

My insides are in pieces. "What now?" I run my hand through my hair and pace back and forth. "Shit!"

"Shut up," Angus mutters.

I clench my fist and glare at my brother, but he ain't lookin' at me.

"Tom would know," Jon says.

I'm back to wantin' to beat the shit outta that guy. I tighten my fist, and the pain in my knuckles keeps me focused. If I don't find Vivian, this asshole is dead. I don't give a shit 'bout his sister. "Who the hell is Tom?"

"The man in the suit. The one from the lobby."

The bald dude. I nod and take off.

"What're you doin'?" Angus grabs my arm and spins me 'round. "I gotta get upstairs and you gotta meet the others at the back door!"

"Jon can do it," I snap. "I'm goin' for Vivian. I'll meet you in your room."

Angus swears, and his mouth scrunches up. He'd be a moron to try and talk me outta this right now. He don't, though. He just nods and swears under his breath. "Watch yourself, little brother."

Something in his eyes makes me stop. He looks like he's afraid to let me outta his sight. I ain't never seen him look that vulnerable. There's a lot of weird shit goin' on, that's for sure.

I give him a quick nod, then head to the front of the hotel. That's where the bald dude has been every time I've seen the bastard. Actin' all important. He'll be there. He's gotta be.

Just like before, he's standin' at the desk, talkin' to some other prick when I round the corner. Now all I gotta do is get him alone.

The bald bastard looks up when I walk over. Then elbows the other guy. "This is the one."

I stop. They was talkin' 'bout me? My eyes snap to the other dude, but there's nothin' special 'bout him. He's average. Looks like somebody's dad. He's wearin' a Steelers jersey and hat like he's headed to a game. Not sure what they'd want with me.

"This is Dave," Suit Man says. "He's in charge of this whole thing."

The boss.

I clench my jaw, and the pain that shoots through my hand helps me think straight. So this is the guy I'm gonna kill. Not now, though. This ain't the time. I gotta keep my cool or Vivian's in serious trouble.

"Name's Axl," I say, shakin' his hand.

"Hear you brought in some big things. We need more guys like you and your brother around."

"Just wanna pull my weight. The payment ain't bad, neither." My jaw is stiff. Makes it hard to talk. "That blonde was something else. I was hopin' to get another go at her."

Suit man laughs and elbows Dave. "Told you. That girl is popular enough to get even Hector out on the Strip."

"Hector?" The name don't ring a bell.

"Yeah. He probably brought the blonde to your room last night. He's one of the big guys. Looks like he should be in the WWF. This was his night off."

The big guy. I clench my hand even tighter. That's why we couldn't find the bastard.

Dave slaps me on the shoulder, and it takes everything in me not to punch him in the face.

CHAPTER THIRTEEN
VIVIAN

Hadley can barely sit still as we wait for evening to come. Not that I'm doing much better. This is sure to be the slowest day of our lives.

"Tell me something about you," I say when I can't stand the silence any longer.

Hadley shakes her head like she isn't going to talk, but then she blurts out, "My real name is Virginia Lucas."

"What?"

"I changed my name to Hadley when I moved out to California. I went by Ginny when I was younger, but I always hated my name. It seemed like the perfect time to create a new identity."

I let out a low laugh. "I know a little bit about that."

She nods, and I wait for her to say something else. When she doesn't I ask, "Did Angus behave himself?"

She smiles and turns to face me. "A perfect gentleman."

"Angus?" Now it's my turn to smile. "I'm pretty sure that's impossible."

"I'm serious. He was nice. Sympathetic even. I showered and he told me to rest. He sat in the chair and didn't come close to the bed except when he brought me something to drink. He even made me coffee."

"You're lying." I have a real difficult time picturing Angus doing any of that stuff. I didn't think he'd attacked her—she would have told me that—but I was pretty sure he'd made a lot of inappropriate jokes that might have scarred Hadley even more.

"I'm telling the truth. Vivian, he even talked to me about his childhood."

I sit up straighter. "What?"

"He told me about taking Axl camping. Teaching him to fish. Hunt. You should have seen how proud he was of it. He may be a racist ass most of the time, but he did the best he knew how to with Axl."

"Shit." I lean against the wall and let all this new information sink in.

Angus did pretty much raise his brother. He may have taught him some stuff that was ignorant and wrong, but he was a kid too. They're only thirteen years apart. He could have run off, left Axl to get the shit beaten out of him. He could have left him to the system after their mom died. But he stuck around. Let Axl sleep on his couch when his mom was having a bad night. Took him in after she died.

Damn. This changes my whole perspective on Angus.

Not that I don't still think he's an ass.

"I guess I shouldn't be too surprised he was like that with you," I mumble. "He was good with Emily."

"Who's Emily?"

I turn to find Hadley staring at me. I forgot I haven't told her about my daughter yet. It was too hard to think about when we first got to the shelter, and since then things have just been too crazy. I've barely had time to deal with it.

"Emily was my daughter."

Hadley's eyebrows shoot up. "You had a daughter?"

"When I was sixteen. I gave her up for adoption, but when this whole virus thing started, she was all I could think about. That's where I was headed when I met Axl and Angus. My car broke down and I needed to get to California so I could see her. They gave me a lift. I knew getting in the car with them might be a very bad idea, but I was out of options. Turned out to be the best thing I ever did."

"What happened to her? I mean, you found her. I know you did because you just said Angus was good with her."

"She got bit. We didn't know what was going to happen. If she would turn or get better or just die. How could we know?"

"That's why you didn't stick up for James when he was bitten."

I nod and think back to that day. How adamant Hadley was that James, the company employee who was running the shelter, would be okay. She hadn't seen anyone turn so she couldn't know. But I knew. Because of Emily.

"Yeah. She turned and Angus took care of it." My heart splinters in half just thinking about it. The grief is something I'll always carry with me. When I keep busy, I can almost forget it happened. Then all at once it comes back, almost taking my breath away. I didn't know losing something you never really had could hurt so much.

Hadley squeezes my hand, and we lapse back into silence. Megan is on the other side of her. Asleep. She sleeps most of the time. Maybe she can't stand to be awake and face the world. I can understand.

When the door finally opens, my heart leaps and Hadley's hand squeezes mine. There's a third man with them tonight. That's never happened before. I'm not sure whether or not it's important, but it does make me slightly nervous. Do they suspect something? They couldn't. Not unless Dirty Blonde — I forgot to ask her name — told someone. She's sitting on the other side of the room, not looking at me. Did I make a mistake?

My heart thumps with fear and excitement and anxiety as the men walk through the room. Nothing seems off. Linebacker Two and the new man gather women just like always, and Linebacker One heads our way. It's not a surprise, though. We already knew we were getting chosen.

That asshole grins when he stops in front of me. Even though I know Axl is waiting for me, I tense up. It's impossible not to. With all the sobbing going on. All the women cowering in terror. The appearance of the linebackers makes me ache with fear, inside and out.

"Yeah, I know. I'm real popular," I snap.

He grabs my arm and jerks me to my feet. He doesn't say a

word. Just smiles. Why the hell is he so happy tonight? Maybe he just enjoys torturing me. He grabs Hadley too and pulls us toward the door. My eyes meet Dirty Blonde's as I'm dragged by. She nods. No, she didn't tell anyone.

We're herded toward the elevator just like every night, but Linebacker One won't stop smiling. My stomach starts to churn. Something isn't right. He stands close to me in the elevator. He won't let go of my arm. He looks at me the way a person looks at a fillet after not eating for a week. Like he's starving and can't wait to dig in. But that can't be. Axl has me tonight. I'm supposed to be safe.

My heart pounds even faster when the elevator door opens only one floor down. The linebacker pulls me forward. Linebacker Two doesn't step out to hold the door open the way he usually does. Hadley's eyes are huge when the door slides shut. She disappears from view and my heart plummets as tears spring to my eyes. No Axl.

The linebacker drags me forward and I twist and fight, but his hand just grips me tighter. He won't let me go, and my heart pounds so hard it's all I can hear. Desperately, I look up and down the hall. Axl has to be here somewhere. He's looking for me. I know he is. If I can just hold out long enough, he'll come for me. He won't let this man touch me.

Linebacker One stops in front of a door. He grins at me when he slides a key into the lock, and I want to hurl. The door clicks and my stomach jumps, then drops to the floor. The little red light turns green.

"My turn."

"No!" I scream and claw at his face as he pulls me into the room. My nails slash across his cheek, drawing blood, and his fingers loosen just enough for me to get my arm free. I stumble when I run forward, further into the room. Where am I going? What am I doing? I have to fight, to find a weapon! Frantically, I search the room. There's nothing. There are clothes everywhere and a couple shoes. Nothing I can hit him with. Not even a lamp or a book. Nothing more deadly than a tennis shoe.

His hands clasp my shoulders and I scream again, kicking backwards until my heel makes impact. He grunts, and my right shoulder slips from his grasp. I wiggle and squirm, pulling out of his other hand. Then charge toward the window. I still don't know where I'm going. Just away. Away from him and his meaty hands.

He's bent over, holding his crotch. His face is red and scrunched up. "Bitch."

I pant and look around the room. My eyes land on the nightstand, and I rush forward. There has to be something inside. I yank the drawer out, and it clatters to the floor. There's nothing in it but a Bible. My heart pounds even faster.

Linebacker One straightens up. He takes a few steps toward me, then winces. He's still holding his crotch. "You're cutting into my time. Why don't you just make this easy on yourself?"

"Easy! You think there's anything about this that could be easy on me? Fuck you!"

He smiles. "No. Fuck you."

He lurches toward me just as I grab the drawer off the floor. I swing it at his head. It breaks in half when it crashes against his skull. His body slams into the bed. Clearing my way to the door.

I run.

The linebacker growls behind me. The bed creaks, and his feet hit the floor just as my fingers close around the doorknob. I turn it and pull as hard as I can. A jolt goes through my body when it comes to an abrupt stop. I pull again, but it doesn't budge. Why won't it open? Something clatters above my head, and I look up. The safety chain is on! I fumble with the chain, trying to get it free. My fingers shake, but somehow I manage to get it unlatched. He's right behind me. His breathing is all I can hear. I turn the handle and the door comes open, but before I can make a run for it, the linebacker's arms wrap around me.

"No!" I howl.

I scream and kick and fight, trying to get away. He's ready for me this time, though. His arms tighten around my chest, cutting off my air supply. I gasp, and he presses his face against my neck.

"You're gonna wish you hadn't done that."

He tosses me on the bed. I land on my stomach, and my body bounces against the mattress. I crawl forward as I suck in a big mouthful of air. His fingers wrap around my legs and he jerks me back, pinning them down. His hands snake up my thighs, and I swat at them as best as I can in this position, but I'm not making any progress. When his fingers move under my underwear, I scream and squirm and kick. I can't stop him. There's nothing I can do. He yanks my underwear down and shifts positions. His knees dig into my calves, making it impossible to turn over. The sound of his zipper is so loud I'm surprised my eardrums don't burst. I kick harder and try to hit him, but I can't turn. Can't reach him.

"No!" I scream again.

He grunts, and his heavy body drops on top of mine, making it impossible to move. His bare skin against my legs feels hotter than a branding iron. Tears fall from my eyes, and I clamp them shut while I brace myself for what comes next. But he doesn't move. He's so heavy I have a difficult time getting air into my lungs. Then something warm drips onto my face.

"Vivian!"

Axl? My eyes fly open, and I try to turn my head so I can find him, but I can't. Not with the linebacker on top of me. Did I imagine Axl's voice? The linebacker starts to move and I scream, but nothing happens. Someone grunts, and the weight is lifted off me. I suck in a mouthful of air, and the pain in my lungs lessens. Fingers brush against my leg and I jerk away, rolling to my side.

"It's okay," Axl says.

He stands over me, staring down. But he doesn't make a move to touch me again. His gray eyes are moist. They travel down my body, and his jaw tightens. My underwear is still around my knees. I pull them up with shaky hands and search the room for the linebacker. He's laying at the foot of the bed with his pants around his ankles and Axl's knife buried in the back of his skull. I wish he'd suffered just a little bit more.

Tears spring to my eyes, and Axl is at my side in an instant. "I'm sorry," he whispers, pulling me into his arms.

He kisses my temple, but I can't speak. Can't even move. All I can do is stare at the linebacker laying there with his dick hanging out. I must be in shock.

Axl pulls back and turns my face toward his. His eyes search mine, and I blink a few times, trying to get the image of the linebacker out my head. "Was I too late?"

My body starts to tremble as I slowly come back to reality. I shake my head, but my mouth won't form words. The linebacker was so close. If Axl had been a few minutes later, if I hadn't fought so hard...things would have been different.

Axl pulls me against him, and I bury my face in his chest. He's here. He made it. That's all I need to focus on. Not what could have happened. That and getting the hell out of this hotel. I want to put this nightmare behind me. To move on and never think about the linebacker again.

"Where's everyone else?" I ask, pulling away and wiping the tears from my cheeks.

"Angus had to go back to his room and wait for Hadley. Jon's lettin' everybody else in the back. You get somebody to help with Megan?"

My throat burns from unshed tears. I swallow. "Yeah. It should be taken care of."

Axl gets up, pulling me with him. He yanks his knife out of the linebacker's skull and wipes the blade on the bed. I refuse to look at the body again, so I stare at Axl, focusing on his face. On his stormy gray eyes. How they sharpen when he moves. Soften when he looks at me. The way the skin around his scar puckers under his lip when he talks. Any detail that will wipe the last few days out of my mind.

WHEN AXL AND I WALK INTO THE HOTEL ROOM, HADLEY rushes toward us. "You're okay!"

Tears stream down her cheeks and she throws her arms around me. I hug her back. I never used to be a hugger, but right now all I want is for someone to hold me. She probably needs it, too.

Angus stands behind her, along with Jon, Winston, Trey, Nathan, and Darla. I stiffen when I meet my mother's gaze. Why the hell did she bother coming? She never had a problem abandoning me when I was a kid. I can't imagine she was worried about me.

"You doing okay, sweetie?" She reaches out like she's going to touch my face, and I jerk away.

"Don't talk to me," I hiss.

She frowns, but I turn away. We don't have time for a confrontation right now. We have to get to Megan and get out of here before someone discovers the body.

Axl moves so he's standing between us. His hand rests on my lower back. "Let's get upstairs so we can get the girl."

"Megan," Jon says.

Axl glares at Jon out of the corner of his eye. He looks like he's on the verge of punching Jon in the mouth.

"Yeah," Winston says. "We should get a move on."

The men draw their weapons, and I grab Axl's arm. "You have

a gun for me?"

Axl shakes his head. "You girls gotta stay here. It'll draw too much attention if you're walkin' 'round the hotel."

I suck in a deep breath. He's right. Dammit. I don't like the idea of just sitting here doing nothing, but I guess we don't really have a choice.

"I still want a gun," I say.

Axl nods and produces a gun from behind him like it was tucked in the back of his pants.

I flash him a tense smile and take the weapon. "Be careful."

"I'll be right back." His fingers brush my cheek, right across the bruise Tat left.

The men head out, and when the door clicks shut, I flinch.

CHAPTER FOURTEEN
AXL

The hall's empty and so's the elevator. Everybody must either be in their rooms for the night or down in the bar. Hopefully they stay where they are and we don't run into trouble.

We're all too tense to talk, me especially. We got Vivian, so I'm ready to split. I don't give a shit 'bout this girl, much as I hate to admit it. Even to myself. But I made a deal, so I gotta stick by it. Not that Vivian would let me leave without Megan. She's nicer than me.

Angus tilts his knife back and forth, lettin' the elevator lights reflect off the blade. He's the only one that don't look like he's dreadin' what we're 'bout to do. His lips are puckered, and he's playin' with his knife like it's some kinda toy. He's enjoyin' himself too much. It ain't normal. Never thought I'd start to dislike my brother as much as I have the last few days.

It feels off bein' so pissed at him all the time.

The elevator stops, and I grip my knife tighter. Can't fool with all that Angus bullshit right now. Gotta focus so we can get outta this.

The door opens, and I cringe. It reeks of death. They must have zombies up here. What for I got no idea, but I don't like it. The others cough and take deep breaths, shiftin' their feet nervously. Nobody makes a move to step out.

We don't got all day.

My eyes meet Winston's, and he nods. I bite the bullet and step out.

There are three zombies chained up at the end of the hall, probably standin' guard at the emergency exit. They're pullin' on the chains, tryin' to get at the people in the hall. There's a dark-haired girl slumped on the floor. She looks young. Must be Megan. 'Cross from her, a man's leanin' against the wall with his eyes closed. A blonde woman is kneelin' on the floor in front of him, givin' him a blowjob. I blink a few times 'cause I ain't sure if what I'm seein' is actually happenin'. It don't change, but it also don't make no damn sense.

The blonde woman pauses and looks our way, but the man is too preoccupied by his BJ to notice us. The man shoves her face back into his crotch without even openin' his eyes.

"What the hell?" Angus says.

I shake my head. Vivian set this up? Whatever. I don't give a shit, long as we can get outta here.

When I take off toward the man, Jon is right behind me, headin' for his sister. The woman is goin' to town, but she's watchin' me outta the corner of her eye. When I'm two feet away, she stops and gets up. The man's eyes fly open, but it's too late for him. I jam my knife in and out of his throat before he's even had a chance to make a sound. His hands go to his neck and his eyes get huge. Blood seeps between his fingers like a waterfall, then he slumps to the ground, and I turn away.

The blonde woman smiles. She needs to wipe her damn chin. "You must be the people who are going to get me the hell out of here."

"Long as you can keep up," I say, wipin' the blade on my pants.

Jon's kneelin' next to his sister. She don't look good. Most of her bruises are yellow now, but there are a lot of 'em. I don't wanna be a hard-ass, but we got no time to check her out now. We can worry 'bout that once we're back at the shelter.

I jerk my head toward the elevator. "We gotta go."

Jon nods and helps his sister get up. This was too easy. In and out with no problem. It's got me on edge. I press the button, and my leg twitches while I wait for the door to open. I wanna get back to Vivian and get outta this hotel. Outta Vegas. If it's up to me, we'll never set foot in this town again. We can go to Boulder City or someplace else for supplies. Get that water garden thing goin' so we got some fresh food. Maybe Angus and me can even do some huntin' for meat. Whatever we do, we ain't comin' back here.

The door slides open, and two men are standin' there. One is a big bastard, like the guy that brought Vivian to my room, and the other is a small, measly-lookin' dude.

The big guy goes for a weapon, and I rush forward. I jab my knife toward him, tryin' to get him in the gut, but he pushes me aside. My body slams into the elevator wall, and I drop my knife. The big guy's arms go 'round me, squeezin' my chest. All the air rushes outta my lungs. There's yellin' and cussin'. Most of it comin' from Angus. The big guy's grip loosens and I drop to my feet, gaspin' for air. But the second my lungs are full, an arm presses against my throat.

I pull at his arm, and my face gets hot. My lungs are 'bout ready to burst from the need for air. I hear Angus swear, and the man's grip loosens enough for me to get some, but the bastard don't let go. I elbow him in the stomach, and his hold on me tightens again. There's more shufflin' and cussin', and I catch sight of the measly guy strugglin' with Nathan. I try to breathe. Try to pull the big bastard's arm away from my neck, but I can't.

Darkness closes in. I blink, but it don't help. My fingers dig into the asshole's skin, but he just squeezes tighter. My vision starts to go black...

"Axl." I open my eyes, and Winston is starin' down at me.

It takes a second to remember what happened, then I register the gruntin' and swearin' of Angus. I blink. He's 'cross the hall beatin' the shit outta that big asshole. The guy's slumped against the wall and his face is nothin' but a bloody mess. Angus just keeps on poundin' his fists into the guy's nose. My brother's face is red and sweaty, and he's cussin'. Sayin' something 'bout me. I can't wrap my mind 'round what's happenin' exactly.

Nobody moves. They don't try to stop him. Angus has a short fuse and he don't like these guys, so I don't blame 'em. My brain starts to focus and I blink a few times. We gotta go. I struggle to my feet, and the hall spins. Winston steadies me, and I let him. I don't wanna fall on my ass. Angus won't stop beatin' the bastard, and ain't nobody else gonna stop him.

"Angus," I say. My throat aches.

He don't let up. I touch his arm, and he flinches. He spins 'round to face me with his fist in the air like he's ready to beat the shit outta me too. His knuckles are red, and the wall behind the big guy is splattered with blood. The guy ain't movin'. Could be dead.

"Stop, man. You took care of him."

Angus puckers his lips and drops his fist. He just stands there for a few seconds. Then his eyes go to my neck, and they get hard. He jerks the knife outta his belt and jams it into the guy's neck. The asshole sputters and jerks. Blood runs from his neck and sprays outta his mouth.

"Bastard," Angus mutters, pullin' the knife out and stickin' it back in the sheath without even wipin' the blade clean. "Let's get the hell outta this city."

Everybody is already waitin' in the elevator. My neck is sore, and I rub it as the door slides shut. Nobody talks, and I can't even look at Angus. Was that really just 'bout me? Angus has always been a selfish prick. I never thought he really cared all that much 'bout me. Sure, he looked out for me when I was a kid. He let me sleep on the couch in his trailer when our mom was drunk and I didn't wanna go home. He taught me how to hunt and fish. Everything I know. But I guess I never thought he really felt anything for me. Angus don't *feel*.

Guess I was wrong.

CHAPTER FIFTEEN
VIVIAN

Axl won't stop rubbing his neck and every time he does it, I want to scream. My hand tightens on my knife. Axl puts his arm around me as Winston opens the hotel door. He glances up and down the hall. I want out of the Monte Carlo more than I've ever wanted anything in my life. We've had too many close calls, and we're pushing our luck. We need to run, and fast.

"It's clear," Winston whispers. "Stay close and make as little noise as possible."

He doesn't have to tell us twice. We rush from the room like the wave of a tsunami, and hurry down the silent hall. The emergency exit is in front of us, and I keep my eyes focused on the prize. Axl is right by my side. His hand on my back. Hadley and Jon support Megan less than a foot behind us with Trey and Nathan right on their heels. Angus and Darla are next. He's still covered in blood. I don't even care right now that he's holding Darla's hand like they're high school sweethearts out for a romantic stroll. What he did for Axl...I could kiss him for it. Dirty Blonde—Lexi, as it turns out—is in the rear. She keeps to herself. Or maybe no one wants to be close to her. She still stinks.

We reach the emergency exit with no problem and rush down the stairs. My legs get tired after only a couple floors, but I force them to move. Focusing every ounce of energy on each step. Leg up. Leg down. Repeat. It doesn't help. Less than five minutes in, and I'm panting. We've barely eaten the past few days, and sleep hasn't been easy. It's taken a toll on my body. Hadley is puffing away behind me. Lexi has to be struggling even more. She was there longer than us. How long, I don't know. I don't want to think about it, to be honest.

"You alright?" Axl whispers.

I nod and pause for a second, breathing heavily. "Haven't eaten much."

The others have stopped walking as well, giving Hadley, Lexi, and me a chance to catch our breath. I don't want to stop. I want out. But my legs are wobbly, and despite the fact that I don't want the break, I need it.

"We still got ten floors to go," Axl says.

I nod and take a few deep breaths. "I can do it." I'll roll down the goddamn stairs if I have to.

"Let's get out of here," Hadley says.

We start moving again, and this time I ignore the pain in my chest and the heaviness in my limbs. Just a little bit further.

We reach the first floor and pause while Winston slowly opens the door and looks out. My heart pounds and my legs shake. I lean against the wall and close my eyes. All I want to do is get out of here, but I'm so weak.

"Clear," Winston whispers.

Axl grabs my hand, and I force myself to move. Winston is already out the door. When I step into the brightly lit hall, my stomach tenses. My eyes dart back and forth, up and down the hallway. I grip my knife tighter while I wait for angry men to charge us. But there's no one around.

Winston motions us forward. "This way."

Trey is right behind him, followed by Nathan, Angus, and Darla. I grab Hadley's arm and pull her forward while Jon helps Megan. Lexi trails behind, and Axl tries to get her to pick up the pace. His jaw is tense. We walk fast, keeping our footsteps as quiet as possible. From somewhere in the distance, voices echo through the hotel, and I have to stifle a scream. Hadley grips my arm. The voices are faint, though. Probably coming from the casino or bar.

There's a door at the end of the hall with a chain through the handles. And a padlock. Shit! What the hell are we going to do now? I'm ready to panic and make a dash back to the stairwell when Winston pulls a key out of his pocket. Thank God.

When the chain is gone, he pushes the door open. The scent of death floats in like a cloud of noxious gas, and my heart moves to a rhythm that reminds me of a pop song. I'm not sure what's worse. The zombies or the men in this hotel.

Winston's face tenses when he glances out. "It's clear."

The voices behind us grow louder, and we all freeze. I spin around just as two men step out of the casino. Their backs are to us, and they sway a little as they walk. Laughing a lot and way too loud. They're drunk. Too drunk to notice the stench we've let inside. They stumble a few steps in the opposite direction, talking and carrying on as they go.

Hadley tenses beside me. Her breathing picks up and her hands shake. The tremors move up her arms until her entire body vibrates. One of the men is short and pudgy. Balding slightly. I've seen him before.

It's the man who raped Hadley.

"Hadley," I whisper, reaching out to her.

It's too late. She steps forward before I have a chance to stop her and rips the gun out of Jon's waistband. No one has time to react. It all happens too fast. She rushes forward with the gun raised. Her arm is steady when she stops about fifteen feet behind the man. A boom echoes through the hallway, and his head explodes. Blood and bone splatter all over the drunk man beside him.

Hadley drops her arm to her side as men pour out of the casino. I grab the gun out of her hand, then drag her back toward the door. The men pull their own weapons just as Axl fires the first shot. I push Hadley behind me and aim for a familiar face. The chubby guy who groped me in the van. He's unarmed, but I can't forget the feeling of his hands on my breasts. I fire and try not to feel guilty when he falls to the ground, screaming in agony.

The men fire back as I push Hadley toward the door. They're bad shots. Either they're too drunk or they haven't been taught. We may be outnumbered, but thanks to Axl and Angus, we know how to shoot.

The men in front of us go down one by one as Winston yells for us to head outside. Jon is the first one out, carrying his sister with him. I push Hadley out behind them before stumbling into the alley myself. We don't move as we wait for the others. I have no idea where the car is and apparently Jon doesn't, either.

The noise from the gunfire is drawing a lot of attention our way. Zombies flood into the alley. My fingers itch to pull the trigger, but I don't want to draw more. I hold off, waiting until they're closer. Waiting for the others. For Axl, so we can leave and never see this place again.

The rest of our group stumbles out, still firing. Axl is the last one, and I can't relax until I see him step through the door. The men inside continue to fire. The bullets hit the door, the wall behind us, the ground. Zombies scream in response to the noise, and I can't stand still. I look back and forth between the hotel door and the zombies charging us. We have to leave! Axl fires into the building one more time, then reaches for the door. Trey is at his side, covering him. The door swings forward just as Trey's body jerks back. Red sprays across the front of his shirt, and he falls to the ground, gripping his chest.

All the air escapes my lungs. "No! Trey!"

He grunts and pushes himself against the wall. The circle of blood grows larger until his shirt is almost completely stained red. Axl curses and leans down next to Trey, ripping the shirt aside so he can get a better look at the gunshot wound. I release Hadley and drop to my knees at Axl's side, taking the flashlight he hands me. Holding it over Trey with shaky hands. There's blood everywhere, and Trey's face is twisted in agony.

"We gotta move!" Angus yells between shots. I look over my shoulder to see what he's shooting at. The zombies are getting closer.

Winston, Nathan, and Darla join him in taking out the zombies, but no matter how many they take out, more come. We don't have long, but we can't leave Trey. I don't know if Angus and Axl can carry him.

Trey sputters, and blood sprays from his mouth. More gushes from the wound with each pump of his heart, and his breathing has slowed. My vision blurs as tears fill my eyes. It doesn't matter whether or not they'd be able to carry him. His time is almost up. I

120

want to scream or throw something or hit someone in the face. Trey came here to save me, and it killed him.

"Shit," Axl mutters, pressing his hand to Trey's chest. It's not going to help and I can tell Axl knows it, but he doesn't stop. He presses harder like he'll somehow be able to heal everything if he can only hold on long enough.

Trey grabs my hand. He's shaking, and so am I. This whole thing is so damn screwed up. "Tell Parv I love her."

It only makes me cry harder.

I could tell him he'll be okay, but it would be pointless. He'd know it was a lie. I squeeze his hand and nod as I blubber like a three year old. "I'll tell her."

Trey coughs, and more blood sprays from his mouth. He closes his eyes, and his face contorts in pain. I have to look away.

"Axl!" Angus screams from behind us.

Axl looks toward his brother and then down at Trey. He's still breathing, but just barely. Axl starts to get up, but I grab his arm. My chest tightens, and I start to panic. The zombies pour into the alley at our backs, charging right toward us. Trey's defenseless. We can't leave him. My heart constricts, and I sob even harder. It's a hopeless situation. There's nothing we can do for Trey, but leaving him here would be cruel. He doesn't deserve this. None of us do.

"We can't leave him," I say, squeezing Axl's hand. "We can't just leave him to die like this!"

Axl shakes his head, but the door to the casino bursts open before he can answer. A handful of men run out with their guns raised. Axl jumps to his feet, pulling me with him. I don't want to leave Trey, but he doesn't even make a sound when we back away. His chest rises a few times. He opens one eye, but it's brief. It flutters shut, and I want to scream. Axl fires as men pour from the door. I glance toward the casino for just a second, and when I look back, Trey's completely still. A sob breaks out of me, shaking my chest. Is he dead? If he is, I can walk away and not feel guilty for the rest of my life. But how do I know for sure? What if there's just enough life left in him and he turns? I can't live with that.

My hands shake. Axl pushes me back toward Angus and the others, but I steady my gun as best as I can when I raise it. Prayer isn't something I do often, but I do it now. Asking God to help me aim. Begging Him to protect us. To get us out of this.

When I pull the trigger, the bullet hits Trey in the forehead, and

I say a silent thank you as more tears fall from my eyes.

Axl pushes me harder, and I let him. He drapes his body over mine like he's some kind of armor. Or like he's willing to take a bullet for me. I'm backed up against Hadley, and Jon is standing next to her, shielding his sister from the zombies and gunfire.

My face is still moist from tears. I swipe my hand across my cheeks and fire at the dead. I can mourn Trey later, but for now I need to work on saving the rest of us.

"Where's the car?" I yell.

Axl fires at the men and points behind them. Of course we'd be cut off. Nothing can be easy these days.

Zombies rush into the alley to our right and the men from the casino to our left. There are fewer men, and we definitely stand a better chance of getting by them. Although not much of one.

I turn and fire at the men just as Winston and Nathan begin backing toward them, still shooting at the zombies as they go. Angus holds his ground as usual, and Darla clings to his side while she fires her own gun. Winston and Nathan spin around to face the men and shoot, clearing our way to the car. I shoot at the zombies and push Hadley and Jon toward the car since they aren't armed. Hadley rushes forward to meet Winston and Nathan, but Jon stumbles. He's been carrying his sister for a while now. She has to be getting heavy.

"Go!" Axl yells to Winston. "Get the car started."

Winston and Nathan push Hadley and Lexi forward. Axl puts his gun away so he can take Megan out of Jon's arms. Angus has finally stopped firing, and he and Darla take off toward the car. I stay with Axl and Jon. Once Axl has Megan situated, we take off after the others, but more men rush from the casino. Cutting us off yet again.

There are more of them this time, and we're cornered. Zombies pour into the alley at our backs, but they don't come for us. My stomach lurches when I realize why. They're rushing toward the lifeless body of Trey. I'm torn between repulsion and relief. As horrible as it is to even think it, Trey's death may have saved our asses.

We're completely cut off from the others, though. Axl pulls me back, away the car and toward the Strip. Angus is just on the other side of the men, and even in the darkness of the alley I can see the conflict on his face. He doesn't want to leave his brother.

"Get outta here!" Axl yells, and Angus only hesitates for a split second before turning around and heading in the opposite direction.

The men are still firing, but all they're really doing is drawing the zombies toward them. The dead don't seem to even notice us. Between the men firing away at the door and the fresh meat on the ground, we are almost invisible. Axl puts his gun away and pulls out his knife. We can't fire our guns. That would only draw their attention.

"This way," Axl says.

He's carrying Megan when he heads out toward the Strip, keeping as close to the wall as possible. He barely has a free hand, and my entire body is tense behind him as I keep an eye on the dead we pass. Axl won't be able to defend himself if one decides to attack us.

We make it out onto the Strip relatively unnoticed, and I say a silent prayer of thanks. It's getting to be a habit with me.

"What's the plan?" I whisper.

There's still firing in the alley and the zombies are rushing toward the sound, but it won't be long before they notice us. We have to move.

Axl stops and scans the area. "Over there. We gotta cross over to that street and get the hell off the Strip."

I can just make out a street next to the Aladdin casino, but there are a couple hundred zombies blocking our way. Great. Looks like a particularly horrible way to commit suicide.

"Are you nuts?" Jon's voice is high and shaky. He looks even more uncertain than he did that first night in his hotel room.

Axl doesn't even look at him. He puts Megan down next to her brother and takes a couple steps forward, grabbing a zombie headed for the alley. Then stabs his knife through the back of its skull and drags the motionless body over. My stomach churns when he jams his knife into the zombie's stomach, slicing him from sternum to belly button.

When he rips off his shirt and wraps it around his hand, Jon takes a step back. "What are you doing?"

I know exactly what he's doing, and it makes me gag. If I had any food in my stomach at all, I'd be in trouble.

"Camouflage," Axl says, dipping his shirt into the zombie's black ooze.

When Axl starts wiping the goo on Jon's clothes, he tries to push him away. Axl grabs his shoulder with the other hand to keep him still. "Don't move. We don't got a lot of time."

Jon closes his eyes and lets Axl to cover him in the goo. He gags a few times but manages not to puke. I hope I can do the same. Axl does the same to Megan, who barely reacts, before turning to me. The smell is overpowering when he wipes it on my shirt, and even though I try not to, I gag.

"You okay?" he whispers.

I nod and do my best not to think about Trey being dead. Not to worry about Hadley and the others making it out of the alley. We need to focus on *us* right now. We need to get ourselves out of this. Then I can worry about everyone else.

By the time we're all covered in the black goo, screams have replaced the sound of gunfire. Zombies rush toward the alley by the hundreds, trying to jam their way into the small space so they can get to whatever's making that horrifying noise. I can't help feeling a little satisfied at the sounds, thinking about all those girls being held in the suite. Knowing what those men have put them through. If only we could throw the casino doors open and let all these zombies in. That would be justice.

"Stay close and keep your eyes open," Axl says as he steps off the sidewalk and right into the mass of undead clogging the street.

My heart pounds as I follow, keeping as close to him as possible. Megan walks behind me, slightly more alert than before, and Jon stays right on top of her. I grip my knife as I go, scanning the faces of the zombies we pass. It's dark, but the moon is bright. They're even more decayed than just a few days ago—probably a result of the hot desert sun—and the smell is intense. Bile rises in my throat at the putrid scent of death mingled with the smell of excrement and the black ooze. They moan and grunt when we go by, but few look our way. Occasionally, one lurches toward us and I have to bite down on my lip to keep from screaming. But the black goo Axl rubbed on our clothes seems to have fooled them.

At least for now.

CHAPTER SIXTEEN

AXL

I work my way through the zombies on the Strip and head for the street I spotted. Vivian's at my back, holdin' onto my shirt like I'm a life preserver. Every sound outta her mouth makes the muscles in my body tighten. I gotta get her outta here. No matter what.

The stink is awful. There ain't even an ounce of clean air, and every breath hurts as rot fills my lungs. Vivian gags behind me, and even I don't got an iron stomach. When a zombie comes within inches of my face, I heave, and the taste of puke fills my mouth.

I'm sweatin' by the time we get to the other side, but somehow we make it. There ain't a chance to celebrate, 'cause there are just as many zombies on this street as there was out on the Strip. I don't slow. I grab Vivian's hand and keep goin', stayin' as close to the stores linin' the sidewalk as I can.

After about fifteen feet, the zombies thin out. I can't hear the screamin' from the alley no more. Either the bastards have been put outta their misery or we're too far away. Too bad, 'cause that means the zombies here are more interested in us than the ones on the Strip were. And the black gunk on our clothes ain't foolin' 'em.

A few come closer to check us out but lose interest when we keep movin'. It won't last, and I know it. We're pushin' our luck bein' out in the open like this.

A rotten showgirl grabs my shirt as we're passin' by, and my heart goes into double time. The bitch opens her mouth and screams in my face while she tries to pull me closer. Vivian stifles a scream behind me. I move my body so it's blockin' her, then jam my knife into the showgirl's skull. She drops to the ground, and it draws even more of the ugly bastards our way. There ain't as many 'round as there was on the Strip, but they're all suddenly very interested in us.

We gotta move.

"Run!" I yell to the others.

I tighten my grip on Vivian's hand and take off. The zombies are everywhere. My heart pounds in tune with her heavy breathin'. After a few steps, she pulls her hand outta mine and starts hackin' away at the zombies. It makes me sweat. After the last few days, I don't ever wanna let go of her.

We cut our way down the street, takin' out anything that gets in front of us. I forget about Jon and Megan. Even though I feel bad for the girl, I ain't got a lot of respect for Jon. Vivian's my priority. No matter what else happens, I gotta get her outta this alive. That's all that matters.

We make it to the end of the road without losin' anybody. There's a small store in front of us with the door wide open, and I duck inside. Hopefully, there'll be a back way out. We ain't gonna make if we stay on this street.

Vivian runs in behind me, followed by Jon and his sister. Soon as we're all in, I pull the metal gate closed and fasten the padlock. The zombies slam into the metal, and it clangs against the door. But they can't get in. It'll buy us some time.

I pull my flashlight out and move the beam across the room. The store's empty. Looks like it used to be some kind of fortuneteller's place. Assholes and con artists. Whatever. I don't give a shit 'bout all that long as we're safe.

Soon as I know for sure the place is clear, I pull Vivian to me. She's breathin' hard and her heart's poundin'. She stinks like that shit I rubbed all over her, but I couldn't care less. Long as I got her with me.

"What now?" she whispers.

I kiss the top of her head while my insides tighten. I gotta pull through for once. For her. Figure a way outta this. "I'm gonna get you back to the shelter and never let you outta my sight again."

"I know where to go," Jon says.

Every muscle in my body tenses at the sound of his voice. I step away from Vivian and pull out my knife. Shit. I know that asshole ain't totally to blame for this, but I can't help puttin' it all on him.

"*You* gonna get us outta this?" The words ooze outta me like the black gunk in them dead bastards outside. Thick and rotten.

Jon steps closer to me. "Yeah. *I'm* going to get us out of this. Look, you don't like me. I get it. But right now we have to work together if we want to survive this."

My fingers tighten around my knife, and pain shoots through my knuckles. Damn hand. Hasn't bothered me in a while. Must've been the adrenaline. Don't matter how much it hurts, though. The second we're back to the shelter, this asshole is toast.

Jon and me are still starin' at each other when Vivian steps between us. She puts her hand on my shoulder and runs it down my arm. Every part of me relaxes.

"Axl," she whispers. "Calm down." She turns my face toward her. "Ease up on Jon, okay? You're mad, I understand. But I'm alright."

My throat tightens, and that animal starts clawin' at my insides. She's filthy and she smells like the dead, but even in the middle of all that she can make my heart stop beatin' just by lookin' at me. Her fingers run down my jaw, and I wrap my arms around her, ballin' my fists in the shirt she's wearin'.

"If you'd been hurt," I whisper against her ear. My throat threatens to close, and it's all I can get out.

"Shhh." Her lips brush against my cheek, movin' to my mouth. "We are going to be okay."

My insides ache. I haven't been in love since Lilly, and that was nothin' like this. Lilly gave me hope, but Vivian gives me a reason to live.

"What's your plan?" I don't even look at Jon.

He clears his throat. "Helicopter."

My head jerks up. "What?"

"I was a pilot. I worked for a company in Boulder City that gave tours over the Grand Canyon. The owner had a place here in Vegas, too. If we can get there, I can fly you wherever you want to go."

I wanna kiss the son of a bitch.

Vivian pulls away, and I feel cold.

"How far is it from here?" she asks. "How are we going to get there?"

Jon shakes his head, but I don't let him talk. "We go out the back and we get us a car."

"You make it sound so easy." Jon rolls his eyes.

I clench my fist and bite down on my lip. His sarcasm makes me wanna punch him again. My mood swings are worse than Angus's.

I head toward the back to see if there's another door. Need to put some distance between me and Jon.

"No sense arguin' 'bout it," I mutter. "That's what we gotta do."

The back room's small and jammed full of boxes and shit. But there is another way out. 'Bout time something went right.

"Now all we gotta do is rush out into a horde of flesh-eating zombies and find a car that's already gassed up," I mumble as I head into the other room. Piece of cake. Which is something else we'll never have again.

Jon's sittin' on the floor with his sister, tryin' to get her to talk. She don't move. She's barely moved since we got her. She looks like shit, and to be honest, I ain't even sure she wants to be saved.

I wrap my arms 'round Vivian and give her a quick hug, then point to the back room. "No sense waitin'. Let's get outside and find us a car so we can get the hell outta Vegas."

Vivian's hand is in mine when I stop at the back door. I do that thing where I put my fingers to my lips, then duck my head out to look 'round. The alley ain't too bad. Five zombies, that's it. We can take 'em.

I pull Vivian forward, not even checkin' to make sure Jon and his sister are with us. Them dead bastards come runnin' soon as they see me. I take the first out while Vivian gets the second. She wields that knife like a pro. Like she was born for a zombie apocalypse. Crazy as that sounds.

After I jerk my knife outta the last one's head, we take off down the alley. Away from the Strip. Jon's right behind us with his sister while Vivian and me take the lead. When we turn the corner, we get lucky. There are three cars parked on the side of the road less than fifteen feet in front of us. Trouble is gonna be gettin' in.

I put my hand up so the others stop, then scan the road. There are zombies everywhere.

"We're gonna hafta work fast," I whisper. "I'm gonna break the first one's window. If it's gassed up we're good, if not I'll move to the next."

"What if none of them have gas?" Vivian asks, scannin' the road.

"Then we're screwed."

I head out without sayin' anything else, movin' as quietly as possible. The others are right behind me. When I get to the car, I go for the driver side door. Locked. We're bein' quiet, so the zombies don't seem to notice us. Not for long. I take a deep breath, then slam the butt of my gun into the driver's window. It shatters, throwin' glass all over the ground and seat. The moans 'round us get louder, and I jerk the door open, shinin' my flashlight on the dashboard. Less than a quarter of a tank, but there's gas.

"Get in!" I yell.

I don't even wipe the glass off the seat. The zombies are chargin', and I get busy pullin' wires out from under the dash. Vivian slides into the passenger seat. She holds the flashlight so I can see what I'm doin', and I cut the wires. Then strip them. My hands shake. A dead bastard grabs at me through the window. Jon leans over the back seat and jams his knife into the asshole's eye.

The engine roars to life. I sit up and slam it into gear, then stomp down on the gas pedal as another zombie reaches for me through the window. Damn things are everywhere.

"Hold on!"

We fly down the street, and more zombies come runnin'. They grab at me through the missin' window. Without it, I'm gonna be zombie chow if I ain't careful. I press down harder on the accelerator, and we slam into a couple bodies blockin' our way. They fly up, and when they land on the windshield, the thump vibrates through the car. Vivian screams, and it gets my blood boilin' all over again.

Gotta get to that helicopter.

"Where do I go?" I yell over my shoulder to Jon.

I DRIVE RIGHT THROUGH THE CHAIN LINK FENCE. METAL smashes against the windshield with a crash that shakes the whole car. The glass splinters, but it don't shatter. 'Course, now I can't see a damn thing. I stick my head out the window, and the smell of death slams into me. The zombies moan. Just goddamn great.

"You're gonna hafta work fast!" I yell at Jon, then push down harder on the gas. Headin' for the helicopters in the distance.

If Jon answers, I don't hear him. I slam on the breaks, and the tires squeal across the pavement, comin' to a stop 'bout ten feet from the closest helicopter. Zombies are already on their way. Comin' over the fence I just knocked down.

I shove the door open and turn to face the zombies. They're movin' fast.

"Run!" I shout to the others.

Jon rushes his sister to the helicopter as I squeeze the trigger. The head of a one-armed zombie explodes, spraying stinkin' black ooze all over the bastards 'round him. Another shot rings through the air, and I jerk my head to the side to see where it came from. Vivian's firin' on the other side of the car. Dammit.

"Vivian!" I yell as I focus on the dead chargin' us. I pull the trigger and hit another one of the rotten bastards. "Go!"

"I'm staying with you!" I turn to see her shakin' her head.

I swear and fire two more times, takin' out a couple before runnin' to Vivian's side. She's firin' into the chargin' monsters like a pro. God, she's hot.

"Get to the helicopter," I yell, shovin' her behind me and turnin' to fire again.

"I won't go without you!"

There's no time to argue. The helicopter comes to life behind us, and the roar of the propeller drowns out the screams of the dead, now less than four feet from us. I grab Vivian's arm, and we take off toward the chopper. They're right behind us. I can't hear 'em, but their stink is so strong I know they're there.

The wind whips Vivian's hair in her face and stings my eyes. We reach the chopper, and I shove her toward safety. I spin to face the masses and squeeze off three quick shots, backin' up as I go. My legs hit the helicopter, and Vivan pulls me in. They're still comin', though. It's like a wave of death and rot and stink and screams. The helicopter moves, and I grab the side so's I don't fall out, still shootin' the zombies that just won't stop runnin'. Vivan fires over my head. So close to me it makes my ears ring.

We're up. Three feet off the ground. A zombie snatches my foot, and I jerk back, almost fallin' over. Vivian shoots him in the head, and he goes down. Five feet. A tall bastard grabs the helicopter, and I pull the trigger. My gun clicks. He screams, and his feet come off the ground as the helicopter moves higher. He won't let go. I grab my knife and kneel down, holdin' onto the door as I drive the blade into the top of his skull. His hands let go, and he falls onto the heads of the zombies below him.

My heart's poundin' when I sit back up and wipe my blade clean. We're in the air. Too high for anymore of 'em to get us. Safe.

I stand up and slide the door shut, then turn to face Vivian. The helicopter sways in the wind. She's a mess. Her hair's tangled. She's covered in black gunk. Her face is covered in bruises.

But she's here. Alive.

My throat tightens, and I grab her, pullin' her against me. Her whole body shakes, but it's too loud in here to talk. My mouth finds hers, and she pulls me closer.

We made it. We fuckin' made it.

CHAPTER SEVENTEEN
VIVIAN

We got out alive. I almost can't believe it.

The helicopter soars into the air, and I squeeze Axl tighter. Just to reassure myself he's here. This whole thing has been a nightmare, and all I want right now is to put it behind me. His lips find mine, and he coaxes my mouth open with his tongue. It's sweet and gentle. Like he's savoring the taste of me, and even though we both stink and neither one of us can catch our breath, I follow his lead. This moment is too precious, too triumphant to be ignored.

When Axl pulls away, he moves his mouth to my ear. "Gonna ride up front!" He has to yell over the roar of the helicopter. "Gotta tell him where to go!"

He gives me one quick squeeze, then climbs up next to Jon and puts a headset on. I can't take my eyes off him. Not even when I sit next to Megan. Like if I look away all this will disappear.

The helicopter sways, and Megan bumps into me. I reach out to steady her, but she doesn't react. Doesn't blink. She stares off into nothing. She looks worse than the zombies, and in this light, her bruises are darker. I can't imagine the amount of damage there is on the inside.

She isn't going to be okay.

The men are talking in the front. Axl is giving Jon instructions on how to get to the shelter. Maybe telling him he's an ass. I know he wants to beat the shit out of Jon, and while I won't let that happen, I'm not going to stop Axl from telling Jon how he really feels. I know how awful this whole thing has been for him. How useless he's felt. Axl has a right to call Jon every name in the book if he wants.

I slump in my seat and buckle my belt. Now that we're out of danger, exhaustion hits, and my limbs suddenly feel heavy. Like I'm too weak to even lift a finger.

The helicopter is loud but soothing. My eyelids grow heavy, and I lay my head back. Allow my eyes to shut. My body to relax. To accept one very important fact: we are going to be okay. We have our supplies from Sam's and enough fuel for a while. The medical equipment we got on our fateful trip to the hospital. Everything we need to make a stand in the shelter. We shouldn't have to go out again for a long time. And now that we know what we're up against, we'll be smarter. We'll avoid Vegas. We can be safe. Axl can be safe. That's all I really wanted, anyway.

A sudden gust of cold air rushes through the helicopter, and the aircraft sways. My eyes fly open, and my heartbeat goes into triple time when I see Megan standing at the open door. Her hair whips around her as wind rushes in. She holds onto the side of the helicopter and stares down over the city.

No!

I scramble to undo my belt, but my body is exhausted. My fingers too slow. I can't get the button to obey.

Megan turns her head slowly and looks over her shoulder. Toward her brother. Jon's eyes get huge and he shakes his head. Everything seems to move in slow motion.

I jerk at my belt even harder, but it still won't budge.

"Megan!" I scream, desperately pulling against the belt holding me in.

Megan steps forward slowly, dramatically. Like she's walking out onto a stage. Her hands drop to her sides, and her body falls from sight.

Jon screams. The helicopter sways, and wind whips through

the aircraft. Jon tries to get out of his seat like he can stop what just happened if only he can get back here, but he's still buckled. Axl grabs his shoulders and yells at him over the noise as the helicopter jerks us back and forth.

My belt finally comes undone, and I'm thrown from my seat. I land right by the door. I pull myself forward and look out over the desert. I can't see Megan, but I can tell where she fell. A mass of bodies has converged on a small area, crawling over one another. Trying to get at the damaged girl who threw herself to her death. Every muscle in my body turns to Jell-O.

The helicopter evens out, and I roll over, away from the sickening sight below. Jon has stopped trying to climb back, but he's sobbing. My own eyes fill with tears, and I squeeze them shut. It was all for nothing. Everything we've been through. Hadley being violated, Trey dying, all of us risking our lives. It was all to save a girl who was beyond saving. She died back in that casino. What's worse, I knew it before I saw her standing at the door.

AXL AND JON SHOUT BACK AND FORTH TO EACH OTHER IN the front of the helicopter. I can't hear a word. The rotor's too loud, and my heart pounds so hard it thumps through my head like a drum. The helicopter veers to the right, and I grip my seat so hard I can feel the stitching against my palm. We swoop down, circling the shelter yet again while the men yell. I just want out. Only there's no way we'll be able to land inside the fence. The small landing pad is already in use, and the cars take up the rest of the space. That means landing in the desert and making a run for it. Not my favorite plan of the night.

I lean closer to the window and practically press my face against the glass. All the cars are there, which means the others have already arrived. Hopefully, they all made it safely.

Axl pulls his headset off and leans back. He motions for me to get closer, and when I do, he presses his lips against my ear. He still has to yell over the noise of the aircraft to be heard, though. "We're gonna have to land outside the fence! Get ready to run!"

Even though I already knew it, my heart still races. There are zombies around the fence by the dozens. How the hell are we going to make it in alive?

"We're gonna hafta climb the fence!" he yells again.

Great. The good news just keeps coming. I'm not wearing shoes. Or pants.

I don't complain, and I don't ask questions. I just nod and pull back, and when my eyes meet Axl's, he looks like he wants to say more. But it's too loud and there's no time. The helicopter moves lower, and Jon gives us a thumbs up. We need to be ready.

Jon circles to the back of the shelter and swoops down. My stomach drops as he takes us in, and the closer we get to the ground, the harder my heart thumps. *This is our best chance. Most of the zombies are at the front. We'll be okay.* I repeat it in my head over and over again like a mantra.

Saying it to myself a thousand times doesn't make me feel any better.

Axl rips his headset off and climbs back. My hands shake so bad I can't get the seatbelt off. He does it for me and pulls me to my feet. When he throws the door open, the sticky desert air rushes in. It's cool but still moist from the heat of the day. The rancid smell of death is so strong that my stomach contracts. We're three feet off the ground.

"Get ready to run!" Axl yells.

I nod and focus on the ground coming up to meet us. Axl will be with me the whole time. I'm fast. I've made it out of stickier situations. The monsters are still pretty far away. It isn't as bad as I'm making it out to be. We'll make it. Piece of cake.

I let out a bitter laugh. I sound like my own personal cheerleader.

When we're a foot off the ground, Axl jumps. His boots hit the desert floor and he stumbles a little before motioning for me to follow. I leap from the helicopter without a second thought. The wind from the rotors swirls around me and whips my hair into my face, making it impossible to see. When I slam into the sand, it catches me by surprise. The impact vibrates up my legs. Small, sharp stones pierce the bottoms of my feet, and I fall forward. My hands fly out in front of me, and my knees hit the sandy ground. Specks of rock and earth dig into my skin. I can hardly breathe.

Axl doesn't give me time to recover. He grabs my arm and hauls me to my feet, then pulls me toward the fence. We keep low as we run under the rotors. His fingers dig into the bruise left by the linebackers, but he doesn't ease up. He's going too fast for me. My feet trip all over one another, but his grip on my arm keeps me from falling.

When we reach the fence, he pushes me forward. "Climb!"

I look back and forth between Axl and the fence. Between the zombies and my reason for life. "What about you?"

The helicopter's engine dies, and the moans of the dead break through the night sky. They're louder than the roar of a hurricane. More menacing than a tornado. I can't leave Axl.

"I'll cover you," he yells. He spins to face the zombies. They round the corner. Fifteen feet away at the most.

I grab his arm and pull him to the fence. "Come with me!"

He shakes me off and looks down at my bare feet and legs. "You ain't protected. Go!"

There's no way to convince him, plus he's right. I'm much too exposed. I turn to the fence and climb. The metal digs into my hands and feet. The moans grow louder, and my legs shake, threatening to give out. I keep my head up so I won't look back. Axl will be more focused if I'm safe. He can take care of himself. He *will* be okay. My heart races even faster.

The fence is high. Maybe ten feet. My arms ache as they slowly pull my body up. I'm not even halfway there and already I'm shaky.

A shot rings out behind me, and I scream.

Keep moving. Don't look down.

The wind blows, showering me with bits of sand. My eyes sting and tear up. I blink, but it doesn't help. A few tears slide down my cheeks. I hang onto the fence with one hand and use my free one to rub my eyes. They burn, but there's no time to worry about it. I squint as more tears fall and pull myself up a little more. Halfway there.

Axl grunts and Jon curses. Something slams against the fence, and the whole thing shakes. I grip the metal tighter. Fingers claw at my foot, and I scream. Kicking at them. They wrap around my ankle. I kick harder, and the fence sways. I can't get away!

My fingers curl around the metal links, and I glance down. What was once a man—his face now half-rotten—grips my ankle. His foul teeth chomp, and he moans like he's in pain. Jon is on the ground, struggling with a zombie. Another one has Axl pinned against the fence. His knife is on the ground.

"Axl!"

I kick harder, trying to get free. The zombie pulls my foot

toward his mouth. I'm too high, though. He can't bite me. But he could still scratch me. Then I'm screwed.

He jerks my foot harder, and I scream when the metal slips from my grasp. I slide down a few inches before I manage to stop myself. My fingers grip the fence tighter. The muscles in my arms strain as I struggle to get away. His fingers wrap around my ankle tighter and he pulls, but I hook my fingers around the metal. The fence digs into my skin, and I squeeze my eyes shut, screaming from the exertion.

A gunshot rings through the air, and my body jerks. The hand slips off my ankle, and I plant my feet on the fence, gasping for air. My eyes fly open to find Winston, Angus, and Nathan running toward the fence. There are even more people behind them.

Axl is still on the ground.

My legs shake, but I can't make myself move. "Angus! Help him!"

The zombie is right on top of Axl. He holds the creature at arm's length, and they struggle on the ground. He's still unarmed. They slam against the fence, and the whole thing shakes. I'm panting and trembling. I can't force myself to move. Not when Axl is still in danger.

Angus lifts his gun, then lowers it. He swears before charging toward his brother.

"Shoot it!" I scream.

"Can't get a good shot."

"Dammit, Vivian," Axl grunts. "Climb!"

My arms quiver from holding on. I don't want to leave him, but I *have* to move. Angus *will* get him. He'd never let Axl die.

I slowly pull myself up the fence. The metal feels like razors slicing my flesh, and my feet scream at me to stop. My arms wobble harder with each inch. I reach the top and throw one leg over. My inner thigh slides across the top of the fence, and a sharp pain makes me scream. A trail of blood slides down my leg.

I'm straddling the fence when it shakes. I grip it to keep steady, ignoring the metal piercing my skin. My heart pounds so hard it threatens to burst from my chest. Is a zombie climbing up after me? I jerk my head around and my racing heart evens out. No. It's Axl and Jon. Thank God!

"Go! Go!" Axl yells

I swing my other leg over and the fence slices my calf. My arms are weak and I can barely hold on as I lower myself. My feet find a good position, but my legs wobble. They're as flimsy as pipe cleaners. The fence slips from my grasp and I lose my footing. My body slides down the chain link and I hit the ground with so much force it vibrates through every bone in my body.

I don't move. My legs are too shaky to support me and I can't breathe. I gasp for air while blood runs down my legs and it drips onto the sand. Zombies scream and claw at the fence. Nothing feels real.

Axl drops to the ground next to me and grabs my face between his hands. "Vivian, are you okay?"

His hands brush down my legs, over the cuts, and I wince even though I don't really feel it. He grabs my foot and looks it over.

"I'm okay," I manage to get out. "He didn't get me." My mind snaps to attention, and I grab his arm. "Are you alright?"

He pulls me against him. Having his arms around me feels like home. "I'm okay. We're all okay."

Tears fill my eyes, and I rest my head on his shoulder. We're okay. We made it back in one piece.

My gaze lands on Jon and I shudder. No, not all of us.

EVERYONE SEEMS TO BE GATHERED IN THE COMMON AREA when we finally make it inside. Hadley is on the couch, still dirty, and Parvarti is with her. Crying. My already damaged heart cracks a little more. With everything else going on, I'd forgotten about Trey.

Lexi stands off to the side, leaning against the wall. She should get a shower. She isn't any cleaner than the last time I saw her. Her eyes meet mine and she smiles, but it's shaky. How long was she at that hotel before we got there? How much did she have to endure before she got too dirty and smelly for the men to want her? I don't think I want to know.

"Do you need me to look at those cuts?"

Joshua's voice slices through my thoughts. I tear my eyes away from Lexi and look down at my legs. They're filthy. Streaked in blood and dirt. I'd forgotten all about the cuts, but I have no clue how. They throb, but they're just little cuts. Do they really need a doctor? I have no idea.

"I don't know," I mumble.

Axl's arm goes around my waist, and I lean my head on his shoulder. My legs wobble.

"We should get 'em clean."

I nod, but I don't want to go to the clinic. All I want to do is take a shower and crawl into bed with Axl. And never leave the shelter again. The outside world is too crazy. Everyone has gone insane.

"I'm going to shower," I say. "I'll let you know if I need you to look at them. But tomorrow. Not tonight. I'm just too tired."

Axl's arm tightens around my waist when he leads me toward the elevator.

My fingertips brush Hadley's shoulder when I go by, and she nods. "I'll be there soon."

AXL AND I STRIP, THEN TOSS OUR CLOTHES IN A PILE ON the floor while the bathroom fills with steam. They're going to be trash, anyway. They're covered in zombie guts.

I step into the shower and sigh when hot water runs over me. Down my face and hair, over my shoulders and breasts. Stinging the cuts on my legs. Axl is right here, his hands following the water's path. His fingertips brush against the cuts. He kisses them. The one on my right calf, another right behind my left knee. The one on my inner thigh. I run my fingers through his hair as his lips moves back up my body, burning my skin.

"Don't ever leave me again," he says, running his lips up my neck.

"Never," I whisper.

Our lips meet. His tongue sweeps over my mouth, and I open to him. His hands move down my spine and over my ass. He lifts me up and I wrap my legs his waist, pressing my back against the wall. The tile feels cold against my skin. I gasp when he slides inside me. My hands tangle in his hair as he starts to move. His mouth slides down, kissing a hot trail over my neck.

"Axl," I say between gasps. "I love you. I've never loved anyone else."

He thrusts harder. My legs tighten around his waist. His mouth covers mine, and his kiss is more than confirmation that he feels the same way.

"I love you," he says against my lips.

140

MY STOMACH GROWLS. THE BED IS SOFT AND WARM AND I don't want to get up, but I'm starving.

Axl is asleep with his arm draped over my waist. That's a first. I don't want to wake him, so I gingerly roll towards the edge of the bed. His hand slides across my body as I move, and when it flops onto the mattress, I hold my breath and wait for him to wake up. He doesn't stir.

I slide out of bed and pull some clothes out from the dresser. Underwear and another dress that doesn't cover much. It seems to be the only thing in this condo. After my time at the casino, I'm not very anxious to wear revealing clothes. Give me a turtleneck and jeans.

I step into the hall and gently ease the door shut behind me. I've only taken two steps when voices freeze me in my tracks. It's almost two o'clock in the morning. Why is Hadley up? And who's she talking to? Lexi? I pause and listen. No. Jon. I didn't expect that.

"Megan wouldn't have wanted you to give up." Hadley's voice is shaky like she's crying or trying not to cry. I'm sure she took Megan's death hard. She really bonded with that girl.

"She gave up."

"Jon, you just can't understand. What she went through—" Hadley takes a few deep breaths. "She couldn't face all this zombie bullshit and deal with the trauma, too. She was too young, and it was just too much for her."

My stomach twists. I'm sick thinking about what that bastard did to Hadley. At least she got her revenge. I just wish he'd suffered a little more. Or saw it coming, maybe.

Jon lets out a sigh as big as the Grand Canyon. "Did she talk to you much? Did she tell you what happened?" His voice is tense, strained.

He can't really want to know the details. Can he? It would just be more torture. One more thing to keep him up at night. One more thing he could punish himself for.

"We talked, but not about that. About the past. About you and your parents. She was so grateful you risked so much to get her out."

"Then why did she do it?" His voice cracks, and there's rustling like Hadley's moving closer to him.

141

"Not everyone can deal with it." Hadley's voice quivers. It makes me want to throw up. I hope she can pull through. That she doesn't let this destroy her the way Megan did.

"I'm sorry," Jon whispers. "I know what happened to you. It was because of me."

"No. It was those men, not you." She exhales, and for a second, I don't think she's going to say anything else. Then she says, "I don't want to talk about that. I just want you to promise you won't give up. For Megan."

"What's the point? What are we fighting for? Even if we are safe here, there's nothing for us. No future. We'll never be anything more than what we are here. We'll never be able to move on. No families, no kids. No relationships. All we'll ever be is stuck underground, fighting for our lives."

"You don't know that! This thing could end as suddenly as it started. We don't know what's going to happen," Hadley says. "And who says we can't have something more? We start things over from here. Create something new."

Jon lets out a bitter laugh. "Like what? Start dating. Maybe I'll take you upstairs and we can watch a movie in the theater."

"We can just start with something simple," Hadley whispers.

There's movement, but I can't tell what's going on. Someone jumps to their feet. Then Jon says, "Stop. What are you doing?"

There are more footsteps, and I have the urge to look around the corner so I can figure out what's going on. Jon sounds so panicked. So confused.

"Kiss me," Hadley says. "I need this... The last man who touched me..." She doesn't talk for a second, and when she does, it's strained. "Help me forget."

Oh my God. I shouldn't be listening to this. It's too private, but it's too late to go back to the bedroom now. I don't want them to hear me. To know I heard. I hold my breath and press myself against the wall.

"I need to feel something else. To get rid of the feeling of him on me —" Her voice cracks.

"But if it hadn't been for me —"

"Stop. This is what I need. Do this for me."

She sounds desperate, and only a few seconds later, they're kissing again. The sound is unmistakable this time. Footsteps move my way. They can't find me here.

I duck into the bathroom and press myself against the wall. They're still kissing when they go by. Hadley's shirt is off, and she's working on Jon's jeans. They look frantic. I hold my breath and stay where I am. When the bedroom door clicks shut, I finally relax.

I have no idea what to make of that.

My stomach growls again. Food. That's why I got up.

THE ELEVATOR STOPS ON THE FIRST LEVEL — THE COMMON area. My stomach isn't growling anymore thanks to a can of corn and jar of Vienna sausages, but I couldn't get my mind to shut off enough to go back to sleep. I need a drink. Especially after hearing that whole thing with Hadley and Jon.

When the door slides open, the room is quiet but the lights are still on. Doesn't anyone sleep around here?

I step out and freeze. Angus sits on the couch. Alone. Reading. I never took Angus for a reader. Other than *Penthouse*, that is. I really wouldn't have been surprised to find out he *couldn't* read.

He doesn't look up, but he has to know I'm here. What could this redneck asshole be reading? Curiosity moves my feet forward, and I squint, trying to see the title.

"You gonna just stand there gawkin'?" he says without looking up, and I nearly jump out of my skin.

I put my hand over my pounding heart and shake my head. Damn him. "Just trying to figure out what you're doing."

I walk across the room so I'm standing right in front of him. My eyes narrow on the book. A western.

He still doesn't look up, but he purses his lips, and his eyebrows pull together the way they do when he's annoyed. "Readin'. What the hell does it look like I'm doin'?"

"Just surprised, that's all."

When he finally looks up, his eyes are dark. "Thought I couldn't read or something? I may be trailer trash, but I ain't stupid."

He sniffs and grabs the Coke can off the table in front of him so he can spit into it. I guess he found time to stop for dip on the way back from Vegas. Goody.

I resist the urge to roll my eyes, then head over to the bar to fix myself a drink. I'm not going to let Angus scare me away. He goes back to reading, and on an impulse, I pour him one too. He won't turn it down. I put the glass on the table in front of him and throw myself into the chair. Cool liquid jumps out of my glass and lands on my hand, and I lick it off before taking a drink.

Angus picks up his drink. He doesn't thank me. He takes a sip, and his gray eyes study me over the rim of the glass. He has something on his mind.

When he lowers the glass, he says, "Didn't know she was your mama when I started screwin' her."

Every muscle in my body pulls tight, and I grip my glass so hard I'm surprised it doesn't shatter. "She told you."

He takes another drink and purses his lips again. "Biggest problem with her is that she don't ever keep her trap shut. If she weren't so good in the sack I wouldn't put up with it."

I cross my arms over my chest, almost spilling my drink. I'm not sure why. Maybe I'm trying to protect myself from the truth. Or from others knowing the truth. Axl knowing is one thing, but I don't want anyone else associating me with that woman.

"Don't sweat it," I manage to get out.

"I ain't sayin' it woulda mattered, I'm just sayin.'"

Is he just trying to get a reaction out of me? Why bring it up if he doesn't care? I study him and blink. What the hell? His expression is soft—for Angus—and his eyes aren't as dark.

"I know what it's like to come from shit. That's all." He purses his lips and goes back to his book. "You know how it is. Axl's spilled the beans 'bout all that."

He's being sympathetic. It brings to mind what Hadley told me, about how he acted when they were alone. Maybe Angus does have softer side. I almost laugh. Angus is full of surprises.

I down the rest of my drink. "Don't worry about it. She's nothing to me anyway. I should have left her ass in Vegas."

Angus snorts. "You wouldn't have. That ain't you. You're the one always runnin' off to save people. Draggin' Axl with you. He's like a goddam puppy these days."

He snorts again and goes back to his book like he doesn't expect me to respond to that. As if I could let it go. Axl isn't a puppy. If anything, he's finally learned how to be his own man. After all those years of doing what Angus says, Axl has a mind of his own now. That's what Angus hates.

And me. I'm pretty sure he hates me.

"Why'd you pick me up?" I say. "When my car was broken

down on the side of the road, why did you bother?"

Angus sniffs. "Thought you might be grateful. I saw you at that diner. A rack like that's hard to miss." He glances up and flashes me a monkey grin. "'Course, you only had eyes for my brother from day one, didn't ya?"

"Not from day one, no. Axl was…different. I could see it right away."

"A pussy, you mean." I stiffen, but he waves me off. "He's always been too soft, my baby brother. Woulda gotten the shit beat outta him on a daily basis if I hadn't been there to toughen him up. Not that it matters. You came along and wiped all that away. Made him weak."

I get to my feet, torn between the urge to punch Angus in the face and stomp out of the room. "Axl isn't weak. He's a good man, and it takes a big person to overcome all the bullshit they've been raised with."

"Whatever you say, Blondie."

Angus goes back to his book, and my face gets hot.

Typical Angus. Just when I'm starting to soften toward him, he has to show his true colors. I turn on my heel and head back to the condo. Before I say or do something I'll regret.

CHAPTER EIGHTEEN
AXL

I jerk awake and jump outta bed. Somebody's poundin' on the condo door. Vivian's eyes pop open, and she sits up. I don't wait for her. I take off, tearin' through the condo to see what's goin' on. Could be anything. Zombies. Asshole rapists come from Vegas. Maybe all the food got up and walked away. With the way things have been goin', nothin' would surprise me.

When I rip the door open, Nathan takes a step back. His eyes get big, and they move down. Shit. Forgot I was naked.

"What's goin' on?" I snap.

He turns his face away and rubs the back of his neck. "Sorry, but we need your help with Angus."

Shit. What's that asshole done now?

I head back to the bedroom, yellin' over my shoulder, "Let me grab my pants."

Vivian is already dressed. "What's happening?"

"Angus," I say, pullin' my jeans on. "Dumb bastard can't go a day without causin' trouble." I don't even bother grabbin' a shirt or shoes before headin' out.

Vivian's right behind me, wearin' a dress that shows off every curve. No bra. I hate it. Hate that others can see her. Hate what she went through and that I wasn't there to help. Hate that it could happen again.

Gotta get her some different clothes.

Nathan's standin' in the livin' room when we run out. Hadley's there with that asshole Jon. Not exactly sure where he came from, but he's zippin' his pants. Weird shit goin' on 'round here. Nathan looks 'bout as uncomfortable as a kid who walked in on his parents doin' it.

"What's he done now?" I ask as we run up the stairs. "I hope this ain't got nothin' to do with Winston. I'll beat the shit outta Angus."

"Not Winston," Nathan says. "That rich guy. The one who brought you guys here."

"Mitchell?" Vivian asks.

"Yeah. Angus is giving him a pretty good beating. Doesn't look like he plans on stopping anytime soon, either."

"Bastard deserves it," I mutter, but I move faster. Angus'll kill him.

We hear the yellin' before we get there. A couple people—Winston, maybe the doc—tellin' Angus to stop. Mitchell beggin' for mercy. Angus cussin' up a storm. Never heard him sound so angry. And that's sayin' a lot.

When we run in, Angus has got Mitchell backed into a corner. The bastard's face is covered in blood. His nose is broken for sure. Angus stands over him, his face red and hard. Like a bulldog gettin' ready to attack. His fists are bloody.

"You pussies wanna let this asshole off the hook after he locked us out? Hell no! I ain't lettin' this guy get away with it. His ass is mine, and when I'm done with him, he's zombie chow."

He grabs Mitchell by the collar and pulls him back up, then slams his fist into the asshole's face two more times before lettin' him drop. Angus spins 'round to face everybody with a big grin on his face. It gets even bigger when he sees me.

"Come on over, little brother! Let off some steam." He kicks Mitchell, who grunts. The bastard's head rolls back and forth like it's barely attached to his neck. "I can share."

"Damn," I mutter, takin' a step closer. "That's enough, Angus."

Angus frowns and moves my way. "You wanna let this guy

off, too?"

"You know I don't. But look at him! He got what he deserved. What you gonna do? Kill him? You ain't a killer."

Angus spits on the floor. "We're all killers now, little brother. How many men you kill last night when we was leavin' that casino? How many would you've killed to get Blondie back? You woulda killed 'em all. I know you." He points at me and spits again. "This mother's dangerous. We all know it. He'll stab every last one of us in the back if he gets a chance."

"What can he do?" Vivian asks. "Angus, look at him! He can barely move. He's not going to do anything now but cower in his room. He'll be too scared."

Angus puckers his lips and glares at Vivian, and I step in front of her. "Let the doc fix him up. He ain't gonna cause no more problems. Vivian's right."

Angus gets right in my face. "You're wrong."

We stare at each other for a few seconds, and nobody moves. Angus puckers his lips so tight they look like a dot on his face. He shakes his head. He swears, then spins 'round and storms outta the room.

"Shit," I mutter, lookin' over at Mitchell. His eyes are closed and his face is a bloody mess. If I didn't know who he was, I wouldn't recognize him.

"Joshua!" Vivian yells, rushin' to Mitchell.

I don't move, and I don't like seein' her helpin' him. Why does she care so much anyhow? The bastard woulda watched us get eaten alive if Hadley hadn't stepped in.

"I'm gonna go talk to Angus," I mutter, turnin' away. I ain't interested in helpin' the bastard out. He's lucky I didn't let Angus throw him to the zombies.

Darla answers the door when I knock. Angus is right behind her, wipin' the blood off his fists.

"How'd you turn into such a pussy?" he growls, tossin' the towel on the counter. "It ain't my doin'. I did everything I could to do right by you. No way you learned that mercy bullshit from me."

I shut the door and throw myself on the couch. "It ain't 'bout just me, Angus. This is about the group."

He puckers his lips, and Darla goes to him. She puts her hands on his shoulders. Kisses his neck. Makes me sick.

"So you woulda let me kill the bastard if it'd been up to you?"

149

I shrug and stare at my bare feet. "Don't know, but it don't matter. It ain't up to me. Them people don't wanna see you beat a man to death. Not even a man like that. There's enough violence in this world. We all been through too much as it is."

"He's right," Darla says, and my head snaps up. I don't want her takin' my side. "This is a safe place. Nothing else out there for us."

I get to my feet, resistin' the urge to spit. She leaves a bad taste in my mouth. "Listen to her, bro. We got nowhere else to go."

"Like you'd leave," Angus spits at me.

I wanna cuss when I pucker my lips. Just like Angus. "Why would I?"

"If it weren't for Vivian, you would."

I can't help lookin' at Darla, but she don't look no different. Same blank expression on her face as always. Like she ain't got nothin' in her head.

"I love her. I ain't gonna apologize for it, and I ain't gonna let you talk me out of it this time either. Not like with Lilly."

Angus puckers his lips, and Darla just stares at me. Does she care 'bout Vivian at all? It don't seem like it.

This time, I do spit. Then I turn and head for the door. Bein' 'round the two of them ain't good for me.

Vivian is waitin' for me in the hall. Leanin' against the wall wearing nothin' but that skimpy dress. Even though it makes me uncomfortable, a jolt goes through my body. Somehow, it affects my heart and my crotch at the same time.

"Is he pissed?" she asks.

"He thinks I'm pickin' you over him."

"What do I have to do with it?"

I shrug and look at the floor. Angus has been spittin' out here. There are little brown circles on the gray carpet.

"Probably just reminds him of Lilly."

"The girl you got the tattoo for?"

I look up, and I can't help smilin'. "You jealous?"

She smiles too, but it ain't happy. "She's probably dead."

My smile melts away. 'Course she is. I hadn't thought 'bout that. I cared 'bout Lilly, even after we broke up, and I hate thinkin' she's gone.

"We dated when I was seventeen," I say. "Senior year. She lived in the trailer park too, but she worked hard in school. Studied,

150

did extra work. She was applyin' to college and tryin' to talk me into it. My grades weren't bad. Just average. I never thought 'bout goin' to college though, not 'til Lilly. But she made me think it could happen."

Vivian puts her hands on my shoulders like she's tryin' to comfort me. Not sure I need it, but I don't stop her. Anytime she wants to touch me she can. "Angus didn't like that?"

"He said she was settin' me up for failure. That I should just accept who I was."

"He was wrong. Maybe he was jealous, or maybe it was his own insecurities. I don't know. Whatever it was, he was wrong."

"He was probably just repeatin' what our mom always said to him." I swipe my hand through my hair. "Don't matter now."

"It does because he's still trying to keep you down, Axl. Don't listen to him."

I shrug again and pull her toward the elevator. It ain't something I like talkin' 'bout.

CHAPTER NINETEEN
VIVIAN

Hadley is in the kitchen when we get back to the condo, and Lexi sits at the small dining room table. I almost don't recognize her. She's clean, and she has her blonde hair slicked back into a ponytail. She's wearing more of the condo's cast-off clothes. She doesn't smell. All clean and dressed like this, Lexi is actually really attractive. It makes my stomach roll, because I know she was probably popular when she first got to the Monte Carlo.

She gives me a hesitant smile when I walk in. Like she doesn't know what to say or how to act in this situation. I can't blame her, really. I don't have the first idea what to talk to her about.

"Coffee?" Hadley asks, not even looking up.

"Please." I grab a couple muffins and toss one to Axl. Then lean against the counter and unwrap it while I look around. Where did Jon disappear to?

Lexi clears her throat, and I jump. The muffin slips from my fingers, but I manage to catch it before it falls.

"Sorry," she says. "I just wanted to thank you for saving me."

Axl disappears into the back bedroom. Probably to get a shirt. He's been uncomfortable around Hadley since I told him she thought he was hot. Of course, now there's Jon... I'm not sure what that all means.

"I'm just glad it worked out." I can't look directly at her, so I focus on my muffin. Lexi may have gotten out, but we left a lot of other women behind. "I wish we could have done more."

My statement is followed by total silence. What is there to say? We did what we had to. Doesn't mean we have to feel good about it. Those other women... Well, hopefully some kind of miracle comes along so they can get out, too.

Axl comes back—with a shirt on—and leans against the counter next to me. His fingers rub circles on my lower back, sending tingles through my body. Lexi looks away. Her hands shake. Hadley squirms. The atmosphere is tense. I don't know have a clue what to do about it. It's going to take them some time to get over what happened.

If they can.

The door opens, and Lexi lets out a little yelp. Hadley's mug slips from her hand. It drops to the floor and shatters, spraying coffee everywhere. The hot liquid hits my calves, and I jump back, slamming my teeth into my lower lip to keep from cussing. Dammit.

"Oh my God! Vivian, I'm so sorry!" Hadley grabs a towel and starts dabbing at my legs, they're covered in little red dots. Every time she brushes the towel against one, it stings.

"It's okay," I say, trying to brush the towel away. Her hands are shaking. I grab them in mine. "Hadley, it's okay."

She bites her lip and finally drops the towel. Her green eyes swim with pain and misery. I should have done more to protect her. There had to have been some way. Something I could have said or done. Something...

I know it's not true, but it doesn't stop me from blaming myself.

"What's going on?" Jon asks from the living room.

"I spilled my coffee." Hadley stares at the puddle of coffee on the floor.

Axl kneels down so he can get a closer look at the burns on my legs. "You gotta go see the doc now." His fingertips brush a red spot the size of a golf ball right next to the cut on my calf. I wince, and he shakes his head. "You're goin'."

I'm pretty sure Axl is overreacting, but before I can say anything Hadley gets up, and I notice she has burns on her legs as well. She didn't even react when the coffee splashed on her.

"Hadley, you're burnt."

She stares down at her legs and blinks. Once. Twice. Three times. She just keeps staring.

"Come on," Axl says. "You're both goin' to the clinic."

I don't put up a fight. There's no way the little red spots on my leg need medical attention, but I want Hadley to go. I'm not sure if Joshua can even do anything for her. It's not like he has a magic pill she can take that will make her forget what she's been through, but it will make me feel better. A little.

JOSHUA IS STILL CLEANING MITCHELL'S INJURIES WHEN we walk in. With the blood washed off his face, the full extent of Angus's fury is visible for the first time. It isn't pretty. Both Mitchell's eyes are swollen, and his once perfect nose is purple and crooked. His lower lip is split on the right side and his upper lip on the left. He has a big gash on his right cheek and another just below his eye. His shirt is off, and on top of everything else, purple spots have already started to form on his abdomen.

Mitchell glares when we walk in, and Joshua barely looks up from cleaning the cuts. "What's going on?"

"I spilled my coffee." Hadley looks dazed.

Joshua's head snaps up, and his eyes narrow on Hadley. He presses his lips together, then looks at me. I can see the question in his eyes, and I know he's asking me if she's okay. I shake my head.

"You okay?" Joshua asks softly. I've never hear his voice sound so gentle. Not like he's a rough guy or anything, but this is a side of him I've never seen. I guess some doctors do have bedside manner.

"They got some burns on their legs," Axl says. He glares at Mitchell, who glares right back.

Joshua nods slowly for a few seconds, giving Hadley a closer look. He sighs and goes back to cleaning Mitchell's cuts. "I'll take a look at it in a minute."

The door opens behind us, and I turn to find Winston standing there. Staring straight at Mitchell. "I was looking for you, Axl."

He doesn't take his eyes off the battered man on the table for even a second. Axl and I look back and forth between Mitchell and Winston. Something's up. Winston motions for Axl to follow him, then turns and walks out of the clinic. Now what?

Axl nods and squeezes my hand. "Be right back."

"That's all I can do for now," Joshua says, stepping away from Mitchell.

Mitchell doesn't even look at him. His face is swollen and purple, but he looks more pissed off than hurt. Like it's Angus's fault. Sure, he went too far, but Mitchell asked for it. You can't be a selfish prick and expect no one to retaliate. Especially these days. Especially when you're living with Angus.

Joshua turns, and his eyes go to Hadley. She's staring at the wall, barely moving. Her shoulders are so tight they look like they're made of cement. "Hadley, I don't know what happened out there but—" He breaks off and looks at Mitchell. "Why don't you come back to the office so we can talk in private?"

Hadley nods, but she doesn't really seem to be focusing. Joshua leads her to the back. Leaving me alone with Mitchell. My favorite person.

I don't look his way. Just because I have to be in the same room with him doesn't mean I have to acknowledge he exists. My foot taps against the floor rapidly, making a slapping noise that echoes through the almost-empty clinic. Mitchell shifts, and the vinyl bed he's sitting on crunches under him. My skin crawls. I cross my arms over my chest and tap harder. Faster.

"So what's this I hear about Vegas?" Mitchell says, making me jump. "The Monte Carlo, right? I heard they've got some guys there who have cleaned the place out."

My foot stops moving, and my head snaps up. I narrow my eyes on his face, but I can't respond. Who the hell does he think he is? After everything he just went through with Angus, he's dumb enough to bring this up? To me! He doesn't know the hell I went through out there. And it could have been so much worse.

Either he's dumb or glutton for punishment, because he doesn't let up. "You just have to walk in and they'll give you a room?"

My jaw tightens, and I stand up straighter. Mitchell stares at me, but I can't figure out what he's thinking. His face is too battered and his eyes too swollen to really get a good read on him. Is he interested in going there? He'd fit in, although I can't see him running around on the Strip. Risking his life isn't really his style. Not even for sex.

"Pretty much," I snap, clenching my jaw.

"They don't make you go out to get supplies if you don't want to?"

I glare at him unblinkingly. Is he serious?

"Doesn't sound like a bad set-up," he says when I don't respond.

My body jerks. I bolt forward and slap Mitchell across the face so hard my hand stings. He falls backward, right off the bed, and lands on his head. His legs hit a tiny metal table with gauze and a few small instruments on it. It clatters to the floor, echoing through the room.

"What the hell?" Joshua runs out of the back room and stands looking back and forth between me and Mitchell just as the clinic doors fly open. Axl and Winston come running in.

"What happened?" Winston asks.

Axl purses his lips and stares at me for a few seconds before turning to Mitchell, who scrambles to his feet. His lip has started to bleed again. The blood drips down his chin and falls onto the floor.

"You people are fucking crazy!" he yells. "You're worse than the zombies!"

I haven't moved a muscle since I hit him. Every inch of my body is tight, and I can't even blink. Mitchell deserves everything he got. Now I wish we'd let Angus beat him to death. Or better, we should have thrown his ass over the fence and let the zombies rip him apart.

"IT DOESN'T MEAN HE'S GOING TO DO ANYTHING," Winston says for the tenth time.

"Don't mean he won't," Axl snaps.

He won't stop pacing the living area. Or swearing. Sophia and Moira had to shut the door to the theater because Axl's language was getting out of control. His fists are clenched, and he has his lips pursed. He looks just like Angus. For once, though, the similarity between the brothers isn't what I'm focused on. At the moment, my only concern is Mitchell, what he might do, and if it will put us at risk.

"So what do you suggest?" Winston asks. He's as calm as

usual, taking Axl's temper in stride. They're a good balance.

"Throw the bastard out!" Angus yells from across the room.

"Shut up!" Axl snaps. He runs his hand through his hair and shakes his head, swearing again. Then he goes back to pacing.

"Axl?" Winston says calmly.

"I'm thinkin'!" He stops and purses his lips. Again. "We talked 'bout the weapons." Winston nods. "What else can we do?"

"You mean other than throw him out," Nathan says.

Axl purses his lips even more. He looks like he took a bite out of something bitter. "Do we got another option?"

"We're not doing *that*," Winston says firmly. He turns and looks at me. "You were the only one there. What did you think was going on in Mitchell's head?"

I know exactly what was going on in his head. "He sounded like he would love to be there. But I don't know." I exhale and chew on the inside of my cheek. "This is Mitchell we're talking about. Do you really think he'd have the balls to do anything about it? You think he'd be willing to risk his ass to get there?"

"No." Winston's voice is firm. "I don't."

"Nobody's asked the obvious question," Nathan says. "Do we care?"

No one moves. No one breathes. The silence stretches across the room, and I stare at my hands. At the little crescent moons still on my palms. Barely visible now. Where I dug my nails into my skin when Emily was sick. When she died. Mitchell was such an asshole. He wanted to leave her behind to begin with, and he was so adamant she would turn. Then after it happened he was so smug, acting like we had all been fools. But we didn't know. Anything could have happened.

"If he wants to leave, he can go," I say.

Axl stops moving and presses his lips together so firmly they look fused. After a few seconds, he forces them apart and says, "We got two problems with that." Winston nods like he's giving Axl permission to go. "First, the cars."

He's right. Shit. It would mean Mitchell taking one of our cars. We need them. All we have left is the Nissan, Trey's Cadillac, and the sedan Nathan had when we found them. We lost the Explorer.

Nathan lets out a big gust of air through his mouth. "We can't lose a car."

"What's the second problem?" Winston's watching Axl like he

knows what he's going to say. Like he's thinking the same thing but wants confirmation.

"Asshole knows where the shelter is."

I'm pretty sure everyone in the room sighs after that. I can't think of a worse scenario. Mitchell running off to the casino, telling them where we are. It wouldn't turn out good for us, that's for sure.

"That's it, then," Nathan says.

"Unless we wanna throw him to the damn zombies, we're stuck with him." Axl grinds his teeth together, and his hands ball into fists. For a second, I think he's going to hit something. He doesn't. Thankfully.

"And you pansies still ain't willin' to do that?" Angus snaps, walking over to stand in front of the group. That vein is back on his forehead, and his lips are more pursed than ever.

I don't want to come to Mitchell's defense, but as much as I hate him, I just can't lose sight of who I used to be. Things haven't changed that much. Have they? Mitchell's still a human being. On the outside, at least.

"Not until he gives us good reason," I say. "We can't throw him out just because no one likes him."

Angus swears and stomps out of the room like a kid who didn't get his way. I'm torn, though. Maybe Angus is right. There's something about Mitchell that bothers me.

CHAPTER TWENTY
AXL

Vivian's asleep, so I slide outta bed and grab my pants. My mind won't shut off, and I can't just lay here. I got too much to do.

When I step into the hall, Jon is comin' outta Hadley's room. He freezes when he sees me like he's been caught doin' something wrong.

"Relax," I mutter. "I ain't your mama."

He follows me to the livin' room. I wanna tell him to leave me the hell alone—I still don't like the bastard—but I gotta cool it. I don't wanna be a hothead like Angus. That shit's gettin' old.

"You don't sleep?" he asks.

I slouch into one of them oversized chairs and shrug. "Too busy thinkin'."

"There's a lot to think about these days." He sits on the couch and leans forward. "This about that rich guy?" I nod. "He's bad news. He cornered me earlier, started asking me all kinds of questions about the Monte Carlo. Hinting around about me flying him out of here."

I sit up straighter. "What'd you say?"

Jon shrugs and runs his hand across his eyes. He's got bags under 'em. "I told him he could hitchhike. If I go back there, it will be to blow the whole damn place to pieces."

"Ain't a bad idea," I mutter.

I lean back and stare at the ceiling. There I go again, puckerin' my lips. Mitchell's worryin' me, though. Winston and me took care of the weapons—we wanted to be sure Mitchell couldn't get his hands on 'em—but the cars are another thing. Angus has the keys to the Nissan and the Cadillac, but Nathan's got the keys to the other car. He won't give them up. Don't want Angus to have all the power. Not that I blame him. But I don't think he gets what a little weasel Mitchell can be. I don't trust him.

"We gotta amp up security," I mutter.

"What?"

I jump to my feet. "We can't afford to have him steal one of them cars. If something happens and we gotta get outta here, we'll be screwed. We got over twenty people now."

"We're going to be screwed either way, then," Jon says. I narrow my eyes at him, and he sits back. "I mean, we have two eight-passenger vehicles and one five-passenger car? That's not going to cut it with twenty-five people."

"We got the Sam's truck."

Jon slowly nods. "Yeah. It would be nice if it were stocked and ready to go. Just in case."

He's got a point, but I ain't gonna tell him. "In case of what?" I ask. I think they call that playin' devil's advocate. Don't know exactly what it means, but I heard it before.

"Anything could happen. Haven't we learned that? Someone else who bought a condo could suddenly show up, and maybe they don't want to play nice. The air filtration system could break. We could be attacked. Mitchell could decide he doesn't want to live anymore, and he could throw the doors open and let everything on the surface in. We should have some kind of emergency plan in place."

"Shit."

I go back to pacin', runnin' my hand through my hair and not even carin' that my lips are puckered again. Jon's right. Why the hell didn't I think of this before? What would we do if we had to get outta here real fast? Nobody would have a clue what to do. We'd be dead.

"We gotta get some people together." I head for the door, cursin' myself for my own stupidity.

Jon jumps up. "Now? It's two o'clock in the morning!"

"Don't give a damn. We shoulda done this right away. We were so happy to be safe that nobody even stopped to think how trapped we are down here."

He runs after me. "Who are you going to get?"

I stop. Shit. Here's the tough part: do I get Angus? He's resourceful, but he ain't exactly thrilled to be with these people. Still, if I don't get him, it could make things a hell of a lot more difficult. For all of us. He hates not bein' in the loop. Especially now that he's on this crazy power trip.

"We'll start with Winston."

"DAMMIT." WINSTON LOOKS OVER HIS SHOULDER toward the bedrooms. "We should have thought of this already," he says, quieter this time.

"No shit," I mutter.

"So what are you thinking? Get a group together to discuss it?"

I look at Jon. I wish he weren't here. Winston I can trust, but I don't know Jon. Talkin' 'bout my problems with Angus 'round him don't seem right.

"We do that, and I'm gonna hafta bring Angus in."

Winston nods, but he don't blink, like he knew I was gonna say it. "And you don't want to." It ain't a question. He knows that's why I came here in the middle of the night.

"I think it would make things tough."

"How about we talk it out first? Then bring him in so he thinks he's involved."

"But we already got all the plans made," I say. Winston's a genius. "That sounds 'bout right."

"So what were you thinking?"

I swipe my hand through my hair and look over at Jon. He ain't said a word. "Jon suggested we load some supplies in the Sam's truck. Have it ready in case we gotta get out fast."

"Sounds reasonable, but it's not going to be easy. There are more zombies up there than ever."

"I could fly the helicopter out, draw them away."

I pucker my lips. Dammit. Wish I could stop doin' that. "That's a thought."

"Then what?" Winston says. "Do we want to leave a fully-stocked truck out there where someone could just take it and leave?"

"We gotta hide the key," I say. "Angus'll have to give it up if we do this."

Winston rubs the back of his neck. He looks at me like he ain't sure I can handle it. "Will he?"

"He will," I say. "I'll make him."

Winston gets up and stretches. He looks as tired as Jon. As tired as I feel. "That means we're going to have to drag all that stuff back up the stairs."

I exhale and lean back, starin' at the ceiling. "Damn."

"WE GOTTA DO IT NOW," I SAY FIRMLY.

Angus don't look thrilled, but we managed to make him think he was in on the plannin'. "Yeah, before that prick gets wind of it," he grunts. He's drinkin'. He's been drinkin' a lot lately. Reminds me of our mom. Ain't a pleasant thought.

"This is going to suck," Nathan says.

"It'll go faster if we get every person we can." Winston scratches at his beard and looks around the room. "And we're going to need someone watching Mitchell's room to make sure he doesn't come out. We need to get this done, and fast."

"I'll watch the bastard," Brad says.

Of course he'd offer. That asshole never wants to put himself in danger. He's the prick who left us in Boulder City when we got the fuel truck. He was pissed enough that we made him go, but soon as we had that truck, he refused to go further. Refused to put himself in harm's way. Asshole.

"Fine," I mutter, headin' toward the stairs. "Let's get Al up and that other teenager—"

"Jhett," Nathan calls after me.

"Whatever. They can help."

Angus is right on my heels. "You gonna wake Blondie up?"

"No," I snap.

"Don't gotta bite my head off," he growls. "I ain't the asshole that's makin' us do this."

I smash my lips together to keep from sayin' something I'll

regret. Like he would be the asshole doin' this if it weren't for me. He'd be right there with them bastards at the Monte Carlo. I hate to admit it, but truth is, I can see it happenin'. I can see Angus takin' out all that rage on them women. Makes me wanna hurl.

Angus grabs my arm and turns me to face him. "That what this is 'bout?" he growls.

I shake his arm off. "Don't know what you mean."

"This attitude you got toward me. It's about the Monte Carlo, ain't it?"

I look over my shoulder. We don't got time for this shit. Not now. I wanna get movin'. Havin' a blowout with Angus right now is a waste of time.

"We don't got time—."

"No," Angus says, steppin' closer. That little vein is all popped out on his forehead, and his face is as red as a tomato. "We're gonna talk 'bout this." He puckers his lips and spits, then wipes his mouth real slow, like he's tryin' to decide what to say. "That what you think 'bout me? That I'd be there with them pervs if it weren't for you?"

My jaw tightens, and I take a step back. "You looked pretty excited to see them pictures when we was there."

Angus spits again. "Pictures is one thing. I ain't a rapist."

I clench my jaw tighter. Wish I could believe him. "If you say so."

Angus puckers his lips so much that they're like a tiny circle on his face. He looks like he's gonna hit me. There's something else in his eyes, too. Hurt? No. Angus don't get hurt.

"We got work to do," he says, spittin' at my feet again.

SWEAT DRIPS DOWN MY BACK AND MY HAND IS KILLIN' me, but I keep movin'. The desert air ain't hot, but we've been carryin' boxes up the stairs and out to the truck for over an hour, so I'm sweatin' anyways.

"We only have about ten more minutes!" Winston calls, jerkin' his head toward the helicopter.

Jon's flyin' in circles close to the ground 'bout a hundred yards out. Most of the zombies are followin' him 'round, goin' crazy tryin' to get him. But there ain't much fuel, so we gotta hurry.

"Incoming!" Nathan yells.

I drop the box of canned soup I'm holdin' and spin 'round. One of the bastards must've gotten bored with the helicopter or noticed we was out here. He's comin' 'round the front of the truck. Practically runnin'. I jog toward him with my knife raised and swing it at his skull. He swipes at me, but he's too slow. My blade sinks into the side of his head before he can get me, and he goes down.

"I think we'd better get the truck locked up!" Al yells, pointin' behind me.

The helicopter swoops 'round, movin' back toward the fence. He must be gettin' low.

I grab the box off the ground and grunt when pain shoots through my hand. I ignore it and run for the truck, shovin' it toward the back. "Let's get outta here!"

My hand throbs, much as I don't wanna admit it. Dammit. I wish I hadn't punched that damn wall.

"You okay?" Joshua asks as we run toward the fence.

"Nope, but there ain't nothin' I can do 'bout it."

"You can take it easy."

"Ain't no such thing no more."

Angus is the last one through, and he's got the keys in his hands. He throws the padlock back on the gate after Winston shuts it. Winston's eyes follow the keys when Angus stuffs them back in his pocket. I gotta get Angus to give me the key, and it ain't gonna be easy after our talk.

Jon lands the helicopter and everybody heads toward the shelter, but I grab Angus and pull him back. "We gotta talk."

"'Bout what? How this is a dumbass idea and we should just kick the bastard out." He spits again, and it comes awfully close to landin' on my shoe. Guess he ain't over being pissed.

"This whole thing ain't just 'bout Mitchell. This is 'bout bein' prepared. Anything can happen."

Angus puckers his lips and grunts.

"I need the key to the truck, Angus."

The vein on his forehead pulses. "Why's that?"

"We gotta put it where we can get it fast. In case we gotta make a run for it."

Angus spits again, and this time it does land on my shoe. I curse and take a step back. He don't look sorry. In fact, he looks kinda happy 'bout it.

"Where's that exactly? In Winston's pocket?"

"No, you idiot. We gotta hide it somewhere. Up here, probably. Someplace we can grab it as we run out."

He puckers his lips again, but he nods. "What're you gonna do, hide it under a rock?"

I scan the area, but there ain't much 'round. "We're gonna hafta bury it. Close to the fence would be best."

"Can't just bury a key, it'd get lost," Angus says, diggin' in his pocket. He pulls out his can of dip and dumps it out, swearin' when he does it. "Don't got much left, you better be grateful."

He sticks the key inside. When the lid's back on, he practically throws it at me. It hits my chest and almost falls to the ground, but I manage to catch it. I just stand there, starin' at it. I ain't never seen Angus do something so selfless. Most people wouldn't think much of it, but I know my brother. That's a big sacrifice for him.

"Thanks," I mumble, then head toward the fence. "Next to the gate would be best."

He follows me, and the zombies start goin' nuts. I get down and dig in the sand, right next to the fence post. It'll be an easy place to find.

"Watch yourself," Angus says, jabbin' his knife through the fence when a zombie reaches for me.

When the bastard falls, a big chunk of rotten flesh is ripped of his hand by the metal links. It falls right next to the hole I'm diggin', and I stop long enough to toss it away. It smells bad enough out here.

When I'm done, I get up and brush the sand off my jeans. "Let's get back inside. It smells like shit out here."

Angus just nods.

We almost bump into Brad when we get to the bottom of the stairs. He's standin' next to the control room, starin' at the monitor over Al's shoulder.

"Thought you was watchin' Mitchell," I say.

"You guys were done." He keeps starin' at the screen, like he's watchin' a movie.

"He give you any trouble?"

Brad shrugs but don't look away. "Never saw him. It's the middle of the night. Why would he be up anyway?"

I nod, but he still don't look at me. What's he starin' at so hard? There ain't nothin' on the screen but zombies. And the truck. Was he watchin' us hide that key?

"It's gettin' late," I say.

Brad finally looks at me. He nods and heads back toward the common area. "See you folks in the morning."

I pucker my lips. "Don't trust that guy."

"Never met a Brad that wasn't an asshole. Remember the one you used to play ball with, back in the day? How I beat the shit outta him?"

"I remember." 'Course I remember. Angus got arrested. "I think it'd be best if we moved that key."

Angus spits on the floor. "I'm on it."

CHAPTER TWENTY-ONE
VIVIAN

Arthur's sitting in the common area by himself when I walk in. It's early—not even seven—and Axl is still asleep. I didn't want to bug him, and the condo was too quiet.

Arthur looks up and smiles. He's always so happy. It's a nice thing to have around. "Good morning, Vivian."

"Morning," I say, taking a seat next to him. "What are you doing up so early?"

"I've always been an early riser." He's still smiling, but his face is pale. There are bags under his eyes, and he's thinner than he was when I first met him. It's like he's slowly shrinking away.

"Have you been feeling bad?"

"Oh, nothing more than usual. Tired mostly. It's not going to be long for me, Vivian. I knew it before this all started. The cancer should have taken me last year."

He doesn't seem sad, just resigned. But it hurts me, deep in my bones. There's been too much death lately to think about someone else going. Especially Arthur. There aren't many people who are able to make living underground cheery. We've been a pretty depressed group. Of course, that's to be expected after everything we've been through. But somehow Arthur doesn't seem to let it get to him.

"I'm sorry." My voice is thick, and I think I'm really saying it to myself. Pretty pathetic.

"You know, in some ways I wish I'd gone before all this started." He frowns and tilts his head. "Does that sound ungrateful?"

It's the first selfish thing I've ever heard him say, and it's not like I can blame him for feeling that way. If it weren't for Axl, I'm sure I'd have the same thought.

"No." I have to pause so I can swallow the lump clogging my throat. "I think it's normal. I'm sure we've all had moments like that. I know there have been times when I've thought it would've been better if the virus had taken me."

He pats my leg, and that same easy smile is back. "You're going to be fine. You and Axl are tough, you'll make it through this. And you'll bring people with you. We wouldn't have made it this far if it hadn't been for him, you know."

My throat tightens, and I have to blink away the tears. "That's what I've been telling him."

"He's a good man." Arthur exhales and leans back, closing his eyes. Maybe he's in more pain than he's letting on. "I'm ready for this all to be done."

I guess that's my answer.

I can't think of a thing to say, so we lapse into silence. It's nice, though. Relaxing. Arthur is good company to have.

A few minutes later, the elevator opens and Parvarti comes out, followed by Jessica. I haven't really seen Parv since Trey was killed. She looks awful. Her face is swollen and her hair's a mess, but she and Jessica are talking. Jessica knows something about loss. She had a fiancé before the virus hit. Maybe she and Parvarti can get through this together.

Footsteps pound up the stairs, and Angus comes stomping into the room, followed by Axl. He still looks groggy. My heart sputters, and I jump to my feet. Can't we go twelve hours without a major crisis?

"You seen Mitchell?" Angus growls.

"No," I say, shaking my head and turning to Arthur, who is now fully alert. "You were here first."

"I haven't seen anyone this morning, and I've been up for an hour or so."

Axl swears and runs his hand through his hair. "Brad ain't in his condo, either."

I can't see the connection. "So?"

Axl purses his lips and looks like he's trying to decide what to tell me. Is he keeping something from me? "We loaded some supplies last night. Set up an emergency plan for gettin' out. Brad watched Mitchell's door while we loaded the truck."

"We gave them the perfect chance to plan their getaway," Angus growls.

He heads toward the control room, and Axl follows. I run after him with my heart pounding. They set up an emergency plan and didn't involve me? And why would Brad run out with Mitchell? He's a coward, but he's safe here. He wouldn't be interested in what's going on at the Monte Carlo. Would he?

Angus shoves the door to the control room open, and Al almost falls out of his chair. "What the hell?"

"You been watchin' them screens?" Axl asks.

Al nods and glances over his shoulder before looking at the brothers. His cheeks get red and he looks down at his hands. "Yeah. I mean, mostly."

"Shit." Axl steps forward. "Al?"

Al looks up, and he cheeks get even redder. He grins like he's about to reveal his greatest achievement. "Lila was here for a few hours and we—" He looks back down and squirms in his chair. "You know."

Al and Lila? Seriously? When did that happen?

"God dammit," Angus yells, pushing Al's chair out of the way. It rolls to the other side of the room and hits the wall. Al almost falls out of it.

"The Sam's truck is still here!" he yells.

Axl studies the four monitors. He won't stop shaking his head. "So are the cars."

"They didn't take a damn helicopter and they didn't walk."

My stomach drops. The fuel truck. "Did Brad still have the key to the fuel truck?"

Angus and Axl both spin around at the same time. They have identical expressions on their faces.

"Dammit!" Angus kicks a trashcan across the room. It slams

against the wall and spills the contents all over the floor. Including a couple used condoms.

Axl swears under his breath and turns to Al. "Can you see the fuel truck from down here?"

Al is shaking in his Nikes when he pulls himself out of the chair and steps around Angus. He acts like he's afraid if he gets too close, Angus will hit him. "I can move the camera."

None of this makes sense. How would Mitchell and Brad have walked out of the shelter and driven off without anyone seeing it? "But wouldn't the alarms have gone off if they'd gone out there?"

Al shakes his head, but doesn't look away from the monitor as the camera slowly pans across the surface. "We had to turn the motion sensors off after the zombies showed up. They would have been going off like crazy."

That makes sense. "And there's no alarm on the door?"

"Not unless you break it down. Mitchell had the code."

He stops moving the camera and stands up. Nobody moves. There's a blanket spread across the top of the fence, flapping in the breeze. The fuel truck is gone.

"They climbed the fence," I whisper.

Angus swears again and glares at Al, but Axl steps between them. "Lay off, Angus. It ain't his fault. We shoulda taken the key."

"Damn kid," Angus mutters.

"Like you never skipped out on work so you could get laid," Axl says. "There's nothin' we can do 'bout it now. They got the truck. We're just gonna have to get the other one."

My stomach has dropped so low it's on the floor. Under my feet. "Before *they* do. Brad knows where it is."

Angus's lips pucker even more. "I gotta get a drink."

He storms out, and Al sinks into the chair. He puts his head in his hands and stares at the floor. Poor kid.

Axl slaps him on the back. "Don't worry 'bout it. We'll make it work."

Al nods, but he doesn't look up. I think he's afraid he disappointed Axl.

I grab Axl's hand and pull him out of the room. My face is hot, and I'm mad at Axl for the first time in a while. He made plans and didn't include me? It doesn't make sense.

"Why didn't you wake me up?" I say when we're in the hall.

"No need. We took care of it."

I cross my arms over my chest. "Seriously? That's all you have to say? I want to be involved in all this! You can't leave me in the dark because of what happened in Vegas."

Axl's stormy eyes flash. "What happened? You mean you gettin' kidnapped and almost raped? You mean me barely makin' it in time—" His voice catches in his throat, and he looks away. "I ain't gonna lose you. Not if I can help it."

My heart aches. I pull him close and wrap my arms around him. "Death is always going to be a possibility for us now. We're just going to have to deal with it."

"No," he says firmly, wrapping his fists in my dress and pulling me closer. "Not if I can do something 'bout it. You're gonna stay here and you're gonna be safe."

He's talking about going to get that other fuel truck and leaving me behind. Which will never happen. I can't let it. He doesn't realize that letting him out of my sight will hurt me as much as it would hurt him if I ran off while he stays behind. I can't let him go off and leave me here alone to wonder if he's okay.

His mouth covers mine, and the argument dies on my lips. Another time.

I JERK AWAKE WITH MY HEART POUNDING IN MY EARS. My body is drenched in sweat, and I'm gasping. The pounding gets louder. More shrill. Why won't it stop?

It's not my heart.

When I jump out of bed my legs get wrapped in the sheets, and I end up falling on my face. The room vibrates from the alarm and throbs through my skull. Drowning out my own racing heart. It can only be one thing.

"Axl!" I shout, trying to be heard over the wailing. He doesn't answer.

I kick my legs, trying to untangle them from the sheet, and pull myself up. The bed's empty. Where the hell is he? Before I can do anything else, the door flies open and light pours into the room. Axl rushes toward me, grabbing my dress off the floor and flinging it my way.

"What is it?" I yell.

"Don't know."

I pull the dress over my head and grab some underwear while

he runs for the closet. My hands shake. I almost fall over when I pull the underwear on. Axl digs through the closet until he finds his pack. He pulls out a couple guns and some knives. He must have stashed them here. He's always prepared. Thank God for that.

Axl thrusts a knife into my waiting hand and pulls me out the door. Every light in the condo is on, and Hadley and Jon stand in the middle of the living room looking as terrified as I feel. The wailing hasn't let up. It even seems like it might be getting louder.

"What's happening?" Hadley screams.

Axl throws a gun to Jon. "We're gonna check it out—"

The wailing stops, and none of us moves. The silence is even more threatening than the noise.

Axl and Jon lock eyes, and dread shoots through me like an icy bullet.

Axl turns toward me. "You two stay here."

I nod even though I want to argue. I can't leave Hadley alone.

Jon opens the front door, and the scent of death drifts in. Axl swears, and Jon coughs. My stomach lurches. Hadley whimpers. My legs turn into something solid and root themselves to the ground. Like they're buried in a grave of my own fear. I should comfort Hadley, but my legs won't work. The men step out into the hall, and just before the door shuts, someone screams. Every hair on my body stands up.

"They're here," Hadley whispers.

"How did they get in?"

She doesn't answer. Not that I expected her too. Neither one of us moves. I stay frozen in place, staring at the closed door with my knife clutched in my trembling hand. Waiting for Axl to come back. Praying he does.

Minutes pass, and my body starts to shake.

When the door finally swings open, Hadley screams, and my heart jumps to my throat. Axl rushes in, but Jon isn't with him. Where is he? Dead? Helping others? There's no time to ask.

"Come on!" Axl motions for us to move.

My feet finally break free, and I fly toward the door, grabbing Hadley's hand as I go by. Axl grips my arm and jerks me forward. Toward the stairs. There's screaming behind us. Moans fill the air, echoing off the walls. The atmosphere is thick with rot and blood, and the combined smells make me gag. The sound of a gunshot rings out, and I jump.

174

"What's going on?" I scream. I don't even recognize my own voice.

Axl pulls me faster, and Hadley yelps behind me. "Zombies! They're everywhere. Somebody let 'em in!"

We turn the corner and a body lurches at us, clawing at the air right in front of Axl's face. He ducks and pushes me back against the wall as he brings his knife forward. The blade sinks into the monster's neck. Black goo sprays everywhere, coating the wall and Axl's arm. But the thing doesn't go down.

Axl swears and jerks the blade out. He stabs it upward this time, and it hits the zombie just below his cheek, then sinks into its useless brain. The monster falls and rolls down the stairs, knocking Hadley down a few steps. I grab her hand and haul her back up just as Axl pulls me forward.

The clinic is on the next floor, but all the lights are off. The hallway and stairwell are dark, and I can't see a thing. Not even the shape of Axl in front of me. Footsteps pound on the stairs ahead and behind us, but it's impossible to tell how close they are. Or whether they're human. My arm shakes, and Axl squeezes my hand tighter, pulling me with him as he climbs.

Hadley screams behind me, and her hands slips out of mine. I jump and lose my grip on Axl's hand as I spin around to find Hadley. It's too dark though, I can't see a thing.

"Hadley?" I whisper, trying to keep my voice down. The pounding in my ears nearly drowns out the sound of my own voice.

Axl clutches at me in the darkness. "Vivian!"

I ignore him and search for Hadley. She couldn't have gone far! "Hadley?" I say louder this time.

"I'm here," she calls. Her voice shakes and echoes through the darkness. "I'm comin—"

The words are cut off by a strangled cry. I step down, trying to get to her. My feet slip and I tumble down a few steps, bumping into something in the darkness. A hand grabs my ankle. I scream and kick at it, bringing up my knife.

"It's me!" Hadley says. "I fell."

A sob breaks its way out of my chest, and tears fill my eyes. Oh my God. I thought she was gone. I thought a zombie had me. I thought it was the end for all of us.

Footsteps pound right next to my head. "Vivian." Axl grabs my forearm and pulls me to my feet.

I reach for Hadley and somehow find her in the darkness. Her hand clasps mine just as more footsteps pound on the stairs behind us. Whoever it is pants like they're out of breath. It can't be a zombies.

"Axl?" Winston calls out. He isn't alone. Several other people are behind him, breathing just as heavily as he is.

"We gotta get outta here," Axl says, pulling me forward.

"Jon and Angus are rounding everybody up," Winston says.

Footsteps thump against the stairs behind us, but it's impossible to tell how many people there are. Hopefully everyone.

"What are we going to do?" someone sobs—Parvarti? Her voice is distorted, and it's hard to tell who it is with all the noise.

"We gotta get to the truck," Axl calls back.

He pulls me closer and puts his face right against mine just as we reach the common area. The light blinds me, and I blink as his lips move against my ear. "Angus buried the key to the truck in one of his old dip cans. On the surface. In the sand. Take three steps to the right when you walk outta the shelter, then dig!"

I'm shaking. Why is he telling me this?

"You're coming—"

Three zombies charge us, and Axl pushes me back. He runs forward, ripping his gun out as he goes and squeezing off two quick shots. Two of them fall, and when Axl reaches the third he drives the blade of his knife into its eye socket.

More run through the door. The smell is overwhelming. Like a tidal wave, almost knocking me down with its force. The zombies scream as they come toward us. There are so many! I count as my heart beats faster and faster. One, four, six. Ten. They keep coming, pouring through the doorway. Screaming as they run our way.

Axl swears and fires his gun. He spins back around. "Down! To the clinic!"

Winston moves toward the stairs, but more rush out of the open doorway. We're cornered. There are so many. They close in on us, and we have to retreat. Only there's nowhere to go. Axl and Winston fire at the advancing zombies, and my eyes scan the group. They're the only ones with guns. Moira and Sophia are here with the kids. There's Anne and Jake. Jessica and Parvarti and Arthur. None of them have weapons. All Hadley and I have are knives.

Axl and Winston fire as the dead advance. The bodies fall to the ground, but there are more behind them. They're never-ending. The moans and screams are louder than the alarm was. More terrifying. The room is rotten. The putrid air soaks into my pores, making my already queasy stomach roll. My hands shake, and I squeeze my knife, but there's nothing I can do. Axl would never let me get close enough to use it.

Winston's gun clicks, and my stomach drops to my knees. He and Axl look at each other, and I can see it written on their faces. This is the end. When Axl turns back to look at me, his face is distorted thanks to the tears shimmering in my eyes.

"No!" Arthur yells, pushing his way out of the group, past Winston and Axl. Charging toward the mass of bodies.

Everyone around me screams, and I take a step forward, but Axl grabs my arm and pulls me back. The monsters moan and wail as they converge on Arthur. He pushes past them, howling in pain when they bite and scratch at his skin. Blood pours from the wounds, but he keeps moving, dragging himself through the throng to the other side of the room. Leading them away from us.

The zombies go wild from the fresh blood, completely forgetting about us. I can barely see through my tears. Axl's arm wraps around me and he pulls me into the dark stairwell. My feet drag, and I can't stop shaking my head. Like I'll somehow be able to erase what just happened.

I should have stopped him. I should have done something.

Footsteps and heavy breathing echo behind us as we descend into the darkness once again. Axl doesn't let go of my hand for even a second. His fingers dig into my mine, and Arthur's screams echo in my ears. Is he still screaming, or am I imagining it? I have no clue, but I do know the tears won't stop coming. All I want is for the screaming to stop.

The stairwell's clear. When we make it to the medical level, Axl jerks me to the right, heading toward the clinic. He slams his shoulder against the door, and it opens with a bang. The lights are on in the back, and they illuminate the hallway just enough for me to see the zombies charging up the stairs behind us.

"Axl!" I push away from him and swing around just in time. My knife stabs into the head of the nearest one just before his fingers wrap around Axl's arm.

The zombie falls, and a chorus of screams, some human and

some not, ring through the stairwell. Axl tries to shove me into the room, but I won't let him. I stand my ground, bringing my knife forward while three more rush toward us. The other women and children run for the clinic as Winston, Axl, and I hack away at the incoming bodies. We take them out, but no matter what we do more keep coming, charging up the stairs behind the others.

I'm already panting when one breaks through the crowd and slams into me, knocking me against the wall. Axl swears and grabs the zombie's head, trying to jerk him back. A chunk of its scalp rips away, and black ooze pours out. Over the zombie's face as he chomps his rotten teeth at me.

Axl grabs its shoulders and jerks the monster back, then stabs him through the skull as soon as it's off me. He pulls me to my feet with shaky hands and shoves me toward the door.

"Go!"

More feet pound on the stairs before I can move, and Axl spins around. He steps forward with his gun raised just as Angus rounds the corner. His face is red and covered in black goo and sweat. He's followed by Al and Lila, Joshua, Nathan, and Jon. They're all panting and splattered with black zombie blood.

Angus pauses, looks toward the stairs, then turns back to his brother. "We gettin' outta here?"

Axl shakes his head. "Common area's blocked."

The others are frozen on the stairwell behind Angus.

"How the hell we gonna get out?" Angus growls.

Axl shakes his head, but he's cut off when more zombies pour down the stairs. He shoves me back yet again, and this time I don't try to resist.

I rush toward the clinic door and yell over my shoulder, "Inside!"

Lila is right behind me, followed by Joshua. Al heads our way just as a zombie rounds the corner, grabbing him and pulling him down. Angus and Axl fire at the zombie while Lila screams behind me. Winston's out of bullets and Jon must be too, because they both charge into the room. The head of the zombie holding Al explodes and he crawls forward, climbing to his feet. Angus and Axl back in, firing. Al scrambles in after them. He grabs the door and pulls it shut as he runs. A bullet smashes into a zombie's head, blowing part of his jaw away, but it doesn't quite hit the mark. The zombie leans forward and sinks what's left of his teeth into Al's hand. Al screams and falls into the room just as Winston slams the door shut. Al sits on the floor, staring at his hand.

Nobody moves. Zombies bang against the door, straining to get in, but it's completely silent in the clinic. My heart pounds, and I gasp for air. My lungs tighten until they threaten to collapse, and I can't take my eyes off Al. He doesn't move a muscle. I don't even think he's breathing. Blood runs down his hand and drips onto the floor. He just sits there, staring at the bite.

Then suddenly, Al's head snaps up, and he thrusts his arm toward Joshua. "Cut it off!"

Joshua inhales and blinks, and within seconds he's charging toward Al, scanning the room as he goes. His eyes land on Angus and he screams, "Your belt! Angus! Give me your belt."

Everything in my head is jumbled and confused and nothing makes sense. I can't focus. Belt? I can't figure out what's going on. My eyes follow Angus as he rips off his belt. It all seems to be moving in slow motion. He tosses the belt to Joshua, who loops it around Al's arm. Right above the elbow. Joshua's hands shake when he pulls it tight.

Al's eyes are huge as he watches Joshua tighten the belt, and everything suddenly snaps into focus. I take a step back and shake my head. Is this real? We can't really be thinking about doing this!

Joshua squeezes Al's shoulder. "We should do it high, just to be sure."

Al's lip trembles, but he nods. My body starts to shake. How is he handling this better than I am? It isn't my arm, but my stomach rolls so much I'm sure I'm going to be sick.

Joshua swipes his hair out of his face, and his eyes search the room. They stop on Axl's knife, but before Joshua even has a chance to ask him for it, Axl is handing it over.

Lila backs away, shaking her head. Her hand grips her throat, and her bottom lip trembles. "You can't be serious! He'll die!"

She looks like I feel, but her words seep into my brain, and it starts to feel a little less muddled. I pull myself together. This is the world we live in now. This is the stuff that happens. If we don't do this, Al is dead for sure. This way, he just might stand a chance.

Joshua doesn't even look up. "He's dead if we don't do it."

"At least give him something to knock him out! Something for the pain!" Her face is pale, and she's shaking.

Jessica rushes to the terrified girl's side and tries to comfort her, but Lila pushes her away and sinks to the floor. Sobbing. Shaking. She closes her eyes and balls her hands into fists, and her face gets so red I expect her to scream.

Joshua ignores her. "I need alcohol, something to sterilize the blade."

I remember seeing a bottle on the table when Joshua was cleaning Mitchell's cuts. "I'll get it," I say, running to the other side of the room.

It's right where Joshua left it, and I barely pause as I scoop it up off the table and rush back. I kneel down next to Joshua and take the lid off. I can't stop looking at Al. He's shaking, and I squeeze his good hand, trying to give him some comfort. There's not much else I can do.

"Can we give him morphine?" I whisper.

Joshua pours rubbing alcohol over the blade. "I locked up all the meds and the key is in my room," he says through clenched teeth. "We're running out of time. We have to do this *now* if we want to stop the infection from spreading."

"You don't even know if it will work!" Lila screams.

Al grabs Joshua's arm. "Do it." His voice is amazingly calm.

"Kid's got balls of steel," Angus mutters.

No one else says a thing.

Joshua nods, and Al lays back. He squeezes his eyes shut and clenches his fists. His good hand is wrapped around mine, and he squeezes my fingers so hard the bones crunch together. I bite down on my lip and let him do it as Joshua positions the knife over his arm. I don't want to watch, but I can't look away.

Joshua exhales slowly through his nose. "I'm going to need someone to hold him down."

Lila whimpers. Moira and Jessica rush the children to the back of the room, and Nathan follows his wife. Angus lays across Al's legs while Axl and Winston take his arms and torso. I stay where I am, clutching his hand.

"I'm sorry," Joshua whispers.

My eyes squeeze shut, and I hold my breath. Al inhales sharply and every muscle in his body tenses, followed by a jerk. Then he lets out a scream. His body shakes. When his hand crushes mine, I can't keep my eyes shut any longer. I open them to find tears streaming down his face. He thrashes, and his screams grow louder. My heart pounds harder with each sound he makes. The agonizing cries echo through the room, drowning out every other sound.

"Hold him tighter!" Joshua says.

Axl lays his body across the teen's chest. His face is covered in sweat. Beads of perspiration drip onto Al's shirt as the poor kid writhes under Axl. Screaming louder. Axl's jaw tightens, and he closes his eyes.

"Halfway there," Joshua says through clenched teeth.

Blood pools under Al's arm, creeping across the floor as Joshua cuts. My stomach lurches, and I have to look away when I catch sight of bone. My stomach won't stop rolling, and my face heats up. I close my eyes and inhale slowly, trying to fight against the nausea. I can't be sick right now.

Al's screaming stops abruptly, and his body goes limp. His remaining hand releases mine and drops to the floor. My fingers tingle as the blood starts flowing again.

"He's dead!" Lila screams. "Oh my God! He's dead!"

My throat tightens, and my heart pounds even harder than before. Al's face is covered in sweat and dirt, and every muscle is relaxed. Is he dead, though? I can't tell.

Lila keeps screaming.

"Shut up," Angus growls at her.

Joshua continues to cut and the men ease off, but don't let go. "He passed out," Joshua says, almost to himself. "Vivian, check his pulse."

I hold my breath and press two shaky fingers to his neck. His veins thump against my fingertips, and I have the overwhelming urge to shout for joy. "He's alive!" I gasp. "He's alive."

Al's arm thumps to the ground, and the sound is louder than any gunshot. More devastating than any explosion. Angus, Axl and Winston sit back, but I can't move. Neither does Joshua.

"I'm going to need something to cauterize the wound," Joshua says. "Does anyone have a lighter? Anything?" No one answers, and he swears. He swipes his hand through his hair. "We're going to need to get to one if we don't want him to bleed out."

Joshua cleans the stump, then starts to wrap it in gauze. Lila rushes to Al's side. Tears stream down her cheeks, and she brushes the hair off Al's sweaty forehead. I didn't even know she cared.

"What do we do now?" I ask.

Joshua shakes his head. He looks ten years older than he did this morning. "That's not up to me."

"We can't just sit here," Hadley says. She hasn't spoken since we got to the clinic. I've never seen her look so pale or shaken.

The room is silent. Too silent. When did the dead stop banging on the door?

"They're gone," I whisper.

Every head turns toward the door. I hold my breath, waiting for the banging to start as the zombies throw themselves against it. Nothing happens.

"Where'd they go?" Winston asks.

Axl purses his lips and swears. "My guess? I'd say whoever let them in killed them off. Right now they're probably out there raidin' our supplies."

"But who let them in?" Hadley asks. "How did they get here?"

"You know exactly how they got here," Winston says calmly. "Mitchell."

"Are you sure?" Joshua asks, sitting back. His arms are red up to his elbows, and his shirt and pants are saturated in Al's blood. He doesn't even try to clean it off. "Did you see anyone out there? I only saw the zombies."

Axl shakes his head. "No, but Mitchell had the code. We all know he did it."

Angus jumps to his feet and kicks the side of a desk. "Shit! I told you we shoulda let the damn zombies have him! Now look what's happened."

My heart drops as reality falls on my head. "They're going to take all our food and weapons." We worked hard to get that stuff. Lost people. Almost lost ourselves.

"Not the weapons," Axl says, heading to the back of the room.

I jump to my feet and stumble after him. "What do you mean?"

"We hid the weapons after Angus beat the shit outta Mitchell. Didn't want him to slit anybody's throat in the middle of the night."

"Where'd you hide them?"

Axl pulls a key out of his pocket and stops in front of the stainless steel refrigerator. The one that's supposed to be full of blood and medicine. When he rips the doors open, I see that it's full of weapons.

I exhale and slump against the counter. At least something's going right.

Angus grabs my elbow and pulls me back. I jerk away, but he doesn't look offended. His gray eyes are more serious than usual, and my heart jumps. Something is wrong.

"What is it?"

His mouth turns down, and he looks away like he can't stand to meet my eyes. "Couldn't find your mama."

I blink and suck in a deep breath. How do I feel about that little bit of news? I don't have a damn clue.

CHAPTER TWENTY-TWO

AXL

We get busy unloadin' the weapons. That teenage girl is on the floor next to Al, cryin' like crazy. It's gettin' on my nerves. I didn't even know they had something goin' on 'til yesterday.

Some of the women head over to see what we're doin'. Hadley — who ain't lookin' so good right now — and Anne.

Moira's with them. She's wringin' her hands, and her face is red from cryin' when she leans against her husband.

"We need to find the rest of our people," Nathan says. "Lexi, Darla, Jhett, and Arthur."

"Arthur's dead," Vivian's voice shakes. "He saved us." She turns away, then goes back to pullin' weapons outta the fridge.

Moira shakes her head and steps back. "But the others?"

"Jhett was up in the control room when this all started," Winston says calmly.

Moira's face gets even redder. She's a mess, and she ain't even lost somebody she loves. Nathan says something in her ear 'bout watchin' the kids, but she don't move. When he picks up a gun, she 'bout loses it. I ain't got time for their drama, so I turn back to the weapons. Let Nathan deal with his own wife.

"What's the plan?" Vivian asks, loadin' her gun.

I tense and shake my head. "You and Anne are gonna stay here and stand guard while Angus, Winston, Nathan, Jon, and me take a look 'round. See what we can see."

Vivian frowns, and I get ready for a fight. No way am I lettin' her go out there. It's too dangerous and I wouldn't be able to concentrate.

Winston steps in. "Axl's right. We need you two here."

Angus shoves a second gun in his waistband. "Let's get movin'.

We don't wanna let them bastards get any more of our shit than they already got."

We head to the door, and Vivian grabs my arm. "Be careful."

"I don't plan on lettin' any of them bastards kill me," I say, kissin' her forehead. "Not today, not ever."

The doc is sittin' on the floor next to Al still. The kid's face is white and sweaty, and the bandage on his arm is soaked with blood already. Not sure if he's gonna make it, but the kid's got balls. I'll give him that.

"How's he doin'?"

The doc shakes his head. He's lookin' bad, too. Older than he did when we first picked him up. "I need something to cauterize the wound and the key to the cabinet so I can get him some morphine. An iron would work. I have one in my condo."

I glance back toward the small metal cabinet. Can't shoot it open, not without ruinin' the meds inside. We maybe could pry it open. It looks pretty sturdy though, so I doubt it.

Shit. Why the hell can't anything be easy? "Your condo's on nine?" The doc nods, and I slap him on the back. "I'll get it. Where are they?"

The doc jumps to his feet. "First bedroom on the right. The key is sitting on the top of my dresser. The iron is on the shelf above the washer."

"I'll get them," I say, turnin' toward the door.

The doc grabs my arm before I can take a step. "Axl. Hurry."

Like we need more pressure.

I head toward the door where the others are waitin'. Angus looks more tense than usual. Probably 'cause Darla's missin'. He seems more concerned than Vivian. Ain't sure if she cares or not. It's weird Angus does, though.

"Let's head out," I say, pullin' out my gun and givin' Winston a nod.

He pushes the door open, and we all tense, but the hall's clear of anythin' movin'.

"Just bodies," Angus says, steppin' out. "We go down first."

"Why down?" Jon asks.

Angus puckers his lips. "'Cause I said."

"Shut up, Angus," I say, pushin' past him and headin' toward the stairs. "We start at the bottom and clear it out. Plus, we gotta get the key for the doc. Al needs them meds."

There are bodies everywhere, and the floor is slick with black gunk. I gotta be careful not to slip when I step over 'em. The lights flicker, and the hall reeks. Death and blood. Should be used to the smell by now, but I ain't. It makes my eyes water and the back of my throat spasm like I'm gonna lose my lunch.

"Lotta fuckin' zombies," Angus mutters behind me.

"You think they just opened the door and let them in or what?" Jon asks.

I wish they'd shut the hell up. My gun's raised, and my whole body is like steel. My finger's over the trigger, and every sound makes it twitch.

We reach level six, and I stop, holdin' my breath. There's talkin' in the distance. And laughter. A door closes one level below us, and I move, runnin' down the stairs with my gun ready, jumpin' over bodies. I pass a bloody mess — not a zombie — and my eyes land on a mass of blonde hair. That chick from Vegas or Vivian's mom. Hope whoever it was, she went fast.

My finger's over the trigger when we round the corner to level seven, but the hall's empty. There's only one condo on this floor. Anne and Jake, I think. Must've been where the bastards went.

"You wanna go in?" Angus whispers, comin' up beside me.

I pucker my lips — dammit — and nod toward the door. "Pull it open."

We all stand to the side with guns raised while Angus grabs the knob. He glances my way and I nod, tensin' even more when he turns it. He rips it open, and I step forward. There are two guys in view, one to the right and the other to the left. I squeeze off one quick shot, gettin' the one to the right in the shoulder before turnin' to the second. He's got his gun out, but before I can fire, Winston takes care of him. The bullet gets him in the neck. The bastard goes down without a sound, but the first guy's screamin' and cussin' on the floor.

"Watch my back!" I yell, runnin' toward him.

His gun is layin' next to him, and there's a pool of blood on the floor. He's grabbin' at the gunshot wound, screamin' his head off like a baby. When he sees me he looks 'round, then gropes the floor as he searches for the gun. I get to it first and kick it aside. It flies across the room and hits the fridge with a metallic bang that I can barely hear over this guy's cussin'.

"Shut the hell up," I yell, kicking him in the ribs. I press my gun to his forehead. "Anyone else in the apartment?"

His face is red and covered in sweat. He shakes his head.

"What 'bout everyplace else? How many of you are there?"

This time he just sneers at me. "Fuck you!"

Angus grabs the guy's shoulder and digs his thumb into the gunshot wound. "I think you outta show a little more respect when a man's got a gun to your head."

The guy screams and shakes, and more sweat breaks out across his forehead. He swallows when Angus lets go. He's pantin' like a dog in heat.

"We brought a whole truckload." His voice shakes, and his eyes dart over toward Angus, who is leanin' against the counter. "Twenty guys, maybe. I didn't count."

"You come from Vegas? The Monte Carlo?"

He nods, and a drop of sweat runs down the side of his face. "Some guys showed up yesterday with a truck of diesel."

We were right. Mitchell. Shoulda let Angus kill him.

"They told the boss all about this place." The man pauses and swallows. "They said you were the people that caused all the problems a few days ago. You stole some girls and killed some guys. The boss has been cleaning it up for days."

My hand clenches into a fist, and I slam it into his nose. The guy howls in pain, and blood sprays from his nose. "We didn't steal nobody! They was our people!"

Winston grabs my arm and pulls me back before I hit him again. I want to. And more. "We don't have time for this. We have to get back to Al."

I take a deep breath and nod. "Yeah." He's right. I gotta control myself.

"Whatcha wanna do with this bastard?" Angus asks. He kicks him in the ribs again.

"Whatever." I flex my broken hand. It's throbbin' all over again. "I gotta get to level nine."

Angus shakes his head, and something flashes in his eyes. "You ain't goin' by yourself." Is he worried 'bout me? No. That'd be dumb.

Winston nods toward Nathan and Jon. "Go with Axl. We'll be right behind you."

Angus glares at Winston and spits. It lands on the guy at our feet. "You gonna try and stop me from killin' him?"

"Nope." Winston's eyes cloud over.

I leave them to it, motionin' toward the others as I head to the door.

We go down, steppin' over more bodies. The air is so thick with death it takes a few minutes to smell the smoke, but by the time we hit nine, I can't ignore it. It's nothin' like a campfire. It's toxic. Chemicals.

"Something's burning," Jon says behind me.

"Yup."

Nathan shakes his head and sniffs the air. He coughs. "Why would they do that?"

"Make sure we couldn't use the place. They didn't want none of us to live."

"Shit," Jon mutters.

"Yup," I say again.

I stop when we get to nine and spit on the floor, tryin' to get the taste outta my mouth. The air's contaminated with more than just death down here. My throat feels raw from breathin' it in, and my lungs burn. My eyes sting, too.

There are two condos on nine.

"Which is his?" Jon asks.

I shake my head and motion toward the one to the right. "Try this one first."

Jon pushes the door open while Nathan and I stand back with our guns raised. Nothin' moves, and the condo's dark. Quiet, just like the hall. We go in and search the livin' room and kitchen. It's clear. Don't keep my heart from poundin'.

I jerk my head toward the hall. "First room on the right."

189

When I push the door open, I spot the key right away. A little silver thing on a black string. I grab it and shove it in my pocket. Now for the iron.

There ain't a sound but our breathin' when we head back out. Jon rounds the corner first, and before I can even take a step into the livin' room, he goes down, screamin' when a zombie slams into him. Nathan swears behind me and I raise my gun, but I can't get a good shot. Jon's strugglin', and the bastard is chompin' at anything he can get close to. His camo is covered in black gunk, and his scalp is rotted to the bone.

I whip my knife out and jerk the bastard up by the collar, shovin' him away from Jon. When the zombie comes back at me, I jab my knife into the side of his head. Black shit explodes outta the wound and leaks from the zombie's eye sockets, drippin' onto the carpet.

Jon trembles and stares at his hands.

My jaw tightens. "You got bit."

Nathan tenses and raises his gun, but Jon shakes his head. He flips his hands around a few times, starin' at them with wide eyes. "No. I don't know how, but I didn't. He was right on top of me!"

I shove my knife back in its sheath and grab Jon, haulin' him to his feet. "Good. Let's get the iron and get outta here before another one jumps us."

Angus and Winston are just comin' down the stairs when we step out into the hall.

"You get what you need?" Winston asks. I don't miss the blood splatters on his clothes and neck. It's even worse on Angus.

Not that I care.

I hold the iron up. "We gotta get upstairs and get everybody out. There's a fire somewhere."

Something behind us grunts. I drop the iron and spin 'round. There are a few bodies piled up on the stairs. They're movin'. One of them bastards must still be alive—or whatever they are. Don't matter though, 'cause we're leavin'.

"Leave it," I say, scoopin' the iron up off the floor. "We gotta get outta here."

"Help!" comes a muffled voice from behind me.

I spin back 'round to see the bodies twitchin' even more and a hand stickin' out from underneath.

"Son of a bitch!" Angus shoves his gun in his waistband and

190

runs down the stairs. He throws a few bodies aside, and a tangle of blonde hair pops out. She lifts her head, and I cringe. Darla. Not sure if that's a good thing or a bad thing.

Angus helps her to her feet. She's covered in the black gunk, and right away she starts talkin' a mile a minute. "So glad you boys found me! I got separated and there were zombies everywhere. I was hiding and then these men came through, killing all of them. They said something about the Monte Carlo and I didn't want them to find me, so I rolled these bodies on top of me when they weren't looking. I knew they'd never look under a pile of zombies."

Angus kisses her right on the mouth. I wanna spit. Instead I pucker my lips. Shit.

"You ain't bit, are you?" I ask. Darla shakes her head, and I turn away. "Good. Then let's get the hell outta here."

Seven levels up, trippin' over zombies the whole way. But everything is quiet, and the higher we go, the less toxic the air is. It's still rotten with death, but there ain't no smoke or chemicals like down below. Fire must be on one of the bottom levels.

"What do you think they're burning?" Jon asks, puffin' away behind me.

"Probably the whole bottom level," Winston says. "It's where everything we need to keep this place running is. Generators, air filtration system."

"They must've turned all the alarms off," I mutter. "Otherwise the fire alarm would be goin'."

"That's just great," Angus growls.

"When I was hiding, some men ran by," Darla says. "They was talking about loading up our supplies and getting outta here. Said they wanted to take that truck."

"We gotta get to the truck," I mutter, movin' faster.

Vivian rips the clinic door open before I even have a chance to turn the knob. Her gun is raised and her face tense, but she relaxes when she sees us. She takes a step back and pulls the door open wider.

"What did you find?"

I give the iron and key to the doc, and my mind goes to work. Makin' a list of everything we gotta do to get outta here. "Lotta dead zombies, two bastards from the Monte Carlo and a whole buncha smoke." Her brown eyes get big, and I take her hand. "They must've started a fire. We gotta get out."

Al's awake. His face is whiter than before and covered in sweat. His whole body shakes. That rich bitch is holdin' his hand. Maybe she ain't such a bitch after all. She's cryin', and she looks pretty tore up 'bout the whole thing.

"How you doin'?" I ask, kneelin' down beside Al.

Vivian leans down too, and she wipes the sweat off his face. Even gives the girl a tissue so she can wipe her nose. She don't, though.

Al nods, and his jaw gets even tighter. "O-okay. G-good t-thing I'm right h-handed." He tries to smile, but it looks more like he wants to cry.

I put my hand on his shoulder and nod. Angus was right. The kid's got balls of steel. "We're gonna get you outta here. We're gonna get everybody outta here."

Al swallows, then looks toward the stump. "It w-worked. I kn-knew it."

We still gotta wait to see for sure, but I nod anyways. No sense kickin' the kid when he's already down.

"What made you think to try it?" Vivian asks.

It's a good question. I never woulda thought of it, that's for damn sure.

The kid swallows, and when he looks up, he's grinnin' a little. Looks proud of himself, too. "Z-zombie fan. Remember?"

He takes a deep breath and closes his eyes. Looks suddenly like he's gonna puke or pass out or scream.

Vivian squeezes the hand he's still got. "I guess we all should have watched more zombie shows."

Al opens his eyes and tries to smile. It don't work.

The doc comes back with a shot, and the kid's face relaxes a bit. Soon as the meds are in his system, Al closes his eyes and lays back.

"Now what?" the girl asks. She sniffs and wipes a bunch of snot off her face with her sleeve, not the tissue Vivian just gave her. I bet she ain't stopped cryin' since the kid got bit. Damn. It's funny how fast people can form bonds in the middle of all this shit.

The doc swallows, and his eyes move across the room. "The iron. We have to stop the bleeding and get him stable so we can move."

"Axl," Winston calls.

Winston and Angus are whisperin' like schoolgirls, not like two men who don't like each other. Angus puckers his lips and looks over toward Al. Right away I know they ain't callin' me over to tell me good news.

"What?" I snap. I know what they're gonna say, and it pisses me off. Not 'cause it ain't true, but 'cause they're right. Why can't anything be easy anymore? The poor kid had to lose his damn arm, but even that might not be enough.

"You know this might not work," Winston whispers. "He could still turn."

My jaw tightens, and I look over at Al. His face is totally relaxed now. Even as the doc brings the iron over and the girl starts cryin' again. Vivian and Hadley are there tryin' to comfort her, but she's freakin' out. I turn away. I can't watch no more.

"We had to try," I mutter.

"Of course we did," Winston says. "But we need to be on the lookout for any sign he's going to turn. That's not going to be easy with the morphine in his system."

"Shit." I run my hand through my hair. It's sweaty and stuck to my forehead. "You sayin' we don't give him nothin' for the pain?"

Winston frowns and looks like he's gonna be sick. He ain't the only one. "Yes."

"Shit," I mutter again, turnin' away. They're right, but I don't like it. "We'll deal with all that after we get outta here. For now, we gotta load up and make sure the way out is clear."

"Okay." Winston nods and looks 'round. "I want the five of us to head up first and make sure the coast is clear. Then we can come back for everyone else. How does that sound?"

"Sounds 'bout right," I say, pullin' my gun back out. "Jon! Nathan!"

Jon jumps up from where's he's sittin' with Hadley and runs over. Nathan has a tough time gettin' away from that wife of his.

I stop by the doc and Vivian on my way to the door. "We're gonna have to get outta here pretty fast. Anythin' you wanna take better be ready." They nod and I point over my shoulder, just to make sure they understand. "All them medical supplies we risked our lives to get. We need 'em."

The doc gets to his feet. "Got it."

"We'll take care of it," Vivian says. She grabs my hand. "Axl."

"Yeah."

"Watch your back."

"Let's get a move on," Angus says, rippin' the door open.

193

The closer we get to the common area, the louder the voices are. Angus is in the lead, and I take up the back. I'd rather be up front, but Angus insisted. The men up there are laughin'. Bottles clink against each other. They must be raidin' the bar. Guess they think we're all dead. Either that or they're dumb as shit.

The second one is probably more like it.

Angus stops just outside the door and holds his hand in the air. Three fingers in the air. Then two. Then one. When he puts the last one down, we charge into the room. Two shots are fired before I even step through the door. The men are behind the bar just like I thought, and we must've caught them by surprise. Two or three of 'em take cover, but the three that were out front are dead within seconds.

"How many?" I yell, duckin' behind a chair.

"Three!" Angus shouts from behind the couch.

Winston crouches next to me. Jon and Nathan must be with Angus 'cause I don't see 'em. The men behind the bar are swearin', yellin' about guns. Sounds like they either aren't armed or they're empty. Either way, it's good for us.

"We gotta go now," I hiss.

Angus shakes his head. He must not be able to hear the men. His hearin' has always been a little fuzzy. We can't afford to wait, so I elbow Winston and jerk my head toward the bar. Winston nods and we take off, keepin' low as we run forward.

Angus swears, and there are footsteps behind us. More shoutin' comes from the bar and when I reach it I jump on top, aimin' down and squeezin' off two shots before I've even have a chance to take it all in.

My bullets take two of them out. The third guy's squeezed his way up under the bar. He pushed some bottles onto the floor so he could get on a shelf. Dumb shit. He's wedged himself in, and now there's nowhere for him to go.

I throw my legs over and drop down right in front of him. His eyes get huge. He's young, sixteen maybe. My jaw tenses, but I can't afford to show mercy. Not after the mess Mitchell caused. I press my gun to his forehead and he opens his mouth—maybe to beg for his life—but I pull the trigger before he has a chance to say a word.

"You moron!" Angus growls. "What were you thinkin'?"

I rip my eyes away from the lifeless kid and get up. "I was

thinkin' we caught 'em by surprise and we should take advantage of it. I was right."

Angus's face scrunches up and he spits. "Whatever. Don't do that again." He turns and heads toward the control room. "Let's make sure the rest of this place is clear."

"All the food we had stored here is gone." Nathan shakes his head. "They must have cleared it out while we were downstairs."

"We've seen eight guys now," Winston says. "That guy swore there were at least twenty."

"Asshole coulda lied," I say.

Winston glances toward Angus and shakes his head. "Doubtful."

Angus nods, and I get the uncomfortable feelin' my brother mighta tortured that guy. I don't care 'bout the man so much, but I hate thinkin' Angus is capable of that. Not after all the other horrible shit I been thinkin' 'bout him lately.

"He was tellin' the truth," Angus says, headin' toward the door. "Let's check out the control."

Jon is draggin' his feet, and he's barely said a word this entire time.

"You got something goin' on in that head a yours?" I ask. My gun's up and I keep my eyes forward, but I can hear him sigh.

"You guys may be able to take all this killing in stride, but I can't."

I pucker my lips. Dammit. "Even after what happened to your sister?"

"Leave her out of this!"

Time for some tough fuckin' love. "Can't. She's part of it. We all are. This is the messed up world we live in now. Get used to it."

Jon don't say nothin'.

When we get to the hall that leads to the control room, the floor is covered in blood and black shit from the zombies. There are bodies layin' 'round, but something else, too. My body tenses when I notice the fur. Dogs.

"That's how they got the zombies down here," Angus grumbles, kickin' at a carcass with the toe of his shoe. "Opened the doors and sent the dogs down. Zombies followed 'em."

"Bastards," Jon mutters. Least he cares 'bout something.

"Let's keep movin'," I mutter. The dogs are the least of my

worries. They're just animals. I don't appreciate animal cruelty or nothin', but we got people to take care of. Women and kids. People who need us to focus. Can't let a few dead dogs distract us.

The door to the control room is wide open. When I turn the corner, I swear and lower my gun. Jhett's on the floor. Or what's left of him. His body is ripped to shreds, but even with all the bite marks, I can see his throat's been slit. A big gapin' cut right across the front of his neck.

"Now you feel bad?" I spit at Jon. "He was just a kid!"

Jon shakes his head and looks away.

"Pansy," Angus mutters, pushin' his way into the room.

Red lights are blinkin' all over the control panel, but the cameras are out. Green words flicker across the computer screen. I lean forward so I can read them.

"Fire on bottom level," I mutter, scrollin' down. "Air filtration system damaged."

"What else?" Nathan asks.

I stand up and turn away from the screen. No reason to keep readin'. "We're screwed if we don't get out. That enough for ya?"

"Okay," Winston says. "What now? We're pretty certain there are people on the surface still. Do we go up and try to take care of them or bring everyone upstairs first?"

"Let's get everybody up here," I say. "At least to the shelter on the surface. Then we can decide what to do. We gotta get to that truck before they leave with it, and the air down there ain't good. Can't leave everybody underground to suffocate."

CHAPTER TWENTY-THREE
VIVIAN

My stomach is in knots and I can't sit still. I open the door every two seconds. There's nothing but death in the hall, though. No noise. No Axl. Nothing.

"They'll be back," Anne says, dropping another bag next to me on the floor.

That should be all of it. At least the medical supplies are pretty much ready to go when they get back. If they get back.

I nod and try not to pace, but I can't stop. Lila is still crying and Al's face is covered in sweat. The morphine didn't keep him from screaming when Joshua cauterized the wound, and it didn't keep me from almost throwing up.

Then there's Darla. She's like a bad penny. And she won't stop staring at me. She has something on her mind, but every time she tries to catch my eye, I look away. I've got too many other things going on to focus on that drama. That's the drama of the past. Not liking your mom. What a joke. I'd love to go back in time when I had those problems. Not here. Not now. Now we've got real problems. Big problems. Running from mad men who want to abuse us and trying not to get eaten by zombies. We're trapped underground in a place that was supposed to be safe, and if those men get ahold of us we'll be going right back to Vegas.

"I'll kill myself before I let that happen," I mutter.

Anne arches an eyebrow. "What?"

"Nothing."

The door opens behind me and I squeal, spinning around with my gun raised. It's Winston. I press my lips together when Jon and Nathan follow him in, then Angus. When Axl walks through the door, I almost burst into tears. I'm wound so tight even the smallest thing is going to make me snap.

I'm in his arms before the door is shut. Shaking. God, why can't I stop shaking?

He doesn't let me go, but he pulls me toward the middle of the room. "Everybody get your shit together. We gotta get to that Sam's truck and get out."

Moira is clinging to Nathan like she's never going to let him go, and Lila is still crying. Hadley looks dazed, but Jon's there to help her. We're a sad group compared to just a week and a half ago when we were enjoying the pool. We only got a few hours of rest before hell fell down on our heads once again.

"What's the plan?" I ask Axl. Still holding him. I'm as bad as Moira. I can't seem to keep my hands off him.

"It ain't gonna be easy," Axl says, lowering his voice. "We know they're on the surface, but we don't know how many. But we gotta go. The fire's on the bottom level and the air in here's gonna get real bad real fast. You gotta be in charge of gettin' them women and children outta here." His stormy eyes search mine, and I swallow. "You're strong. You can do it."

My throat is tight. "What are you saying?"

"I'm sayin' we're gonna try and hold 'em off. Me and Angus, Winston, Nathan, and Jon. But you gotta get the others to safety. Get to the truck, get them in, and drive."

I shake my head. I can't stop. He can't be serious. Not after everything we've been through. "I don't want to leave you."

"We'll be right behind you in the Nissan." The corner of his mouth twitches. "I worked hard to steal that thing, I ain't gonna leave it." His hand rests on my cheek, and I lean into it. "And I ain't gonna leave you, neither."

My bottom lip quivers and my eyes sting, but I fight against it. He's right. We have to work together to get out of this. I can't just worry about me and Axl. This is about all of us.

"Where do I go?"

"Drive east. Toward them mountains. We'll meet there."

"Okay," I whisper. It's the most difficult thing I've ever had to say.

Axl pulls my face toward his, crushing his lips against mine. I wrap my arms around him. The kiss hurts deep inside me. Like my soul knows this might be its last chance to touch these lips, to hold this body.

"Axl!"

Angus's voice brings me back to reality. Everyone stands by the door, waiting for us. I take a deep breath and do my best to control my rapidly beating heart. This is the time to focus on the task at hand. To be ready. I can't be distracted.

Winston walks to the front of the group. His hand moves to the doorknob, but he pauses and looks us all over. "Everyone stay close. If something happens, fall back."

My body stiffens when he opens the door. I expect something to jump out at us, man or monster, but the hall is empty.

Winston moves forward with Jon and Angus right behind him. The rest of us file out in one silent wave of tension. I end up somewhere in the middle, carrying a bag of guns. It weighs me down. Makes my already heavy legs feel like they weigh a hundred pounds each.

Hadley and Sophia carry bags of medical supplies, Angus another bag of weapons. Nathan is practically carrying Moira and Liz. Joshua and Axl support Al at the back of the group, and I can't stop looking over my shoulder to make sure they're okay. Hopefully nothing comes up behind us.

We move up the stairs in a huddled mass, clinging to each other as we trip over the bodies. The air is polluted. Full of noxious fumes from the fire and the foul stench of death. The smoke stings my eyes and my throat, and around me people start to cough. Every breath I take feels thick, and my lungs are painfully tight. One of the kids—Liz, I think—starts to cry.

Voices float out of the common area when we get close, and the air fills with something more lethal than rot or chemicals. Rage, terror, misery. Suffocating anxiety. The group slows, and I push my way forward, up next to Winston, Angus, and Jon. The voices get louder with each step we take. They have to be able to hear us coming. There are too many of us to be quiet.

"What's the plan?" I whisper.

Angus's jaw tightens, and he frowns down at me like he doesn't think I should be put in danger. Is he going to try to protect me now too? That would be a first. I didn't think Angus had a chivalrous bone in his body.

"Sounds like three or four," Winston says.

"We gotta just go." Angus pauses when more people cough behind us. "We don't get out soon, we're goners."

Winston glances at me. "You ready?" I nod and drop my bag to the ground. "Then let's do it."

The three of us run out, and I fire at the first thing I see. My bullet hits a man in the chest, and he falls to the ground as another dives behind the couch. Angus and Winston fire, but only one more goes down. A fourth ducks behind the bar, firing in return. Angus grunts and hits the ground, and I fall to my knees next to him. His sleeve is bright red, and he's cursing up a storm.

"Bastard!" he yells. He rolls to his side and shoots at the man. The bullet hits the man in the head, and he drops to the floor.

I'm trying to pull the sleeve of Angus's shirt aside so I can see how bad it is. He won't sit still, though. I put my arms on his chest and force him against the ground. "Let me look at it!"

His face is tense, but he stays down this time. "It's just a graze."

I pull his sleeve up and sigh in relief. He's right. The bullet left a two inch streak across his left bicep, right under the Confederate flag tattoo.

"It looks okay."

He grunts and drags himself to his feet. "Told ya."

Winston and Jon haul the fourth man to his feet and push him forward. He falls right in front of Angus, who grins and slams the heel of his boot against the man's nose. Blood sprays everywhere.

The man screams, and Angus leans closer. He grabs the guy by his collar and pulls him up, so their faces are only inches apart. "Got your attention?" The man nods, and Angus smiles even bigger. "Good. Now, you're gonna tell us how many men are on the surface. You do that, and I won't gut you."

The man's lips tremble. They move rapidly, but no sound comes out for a full ten seconds. "T-ten," he says. "Maybe more."

Angus nods and smiles like he truly appreciates the man's honesty. The guy starts to relax.

"Thanks." Quick as lightening, Angus slams his knife into the man's throat and lets him go. His body drops to the floor.

"You're enjoying this too much," I say, getting to my feet. But none of us even blinked when he did it. Like we're used to death and killing now. I guess we are.

Angus uses his jeans to wipe the blood from his knife. "Naw. I just like finally having an outlet for all this rage."

I let out a laugh just as someone slams into me. My body bangs against the wall. My gun drops to the floor as all the air leaves my lungs in a puff. I'm gasping when the person spins me around, putting my body in front of his. Using me as a human shield.

I'm facing Angus, Winston, and Jon when Axl walks into the room. His gun is drawn and every muscle in his face clenches. He takes a step closer. The man holding me tightens his grip and presses a knife against my throat.

My eyes flit down, and my heart almost stops. His arms are covered in tattoos. Demons and snakes and naked women. It's Tat.

"Nobody move or I'll cut her open," Tat says. "And enjoy it. Isn't that right, baby?" He leans forward, and his tongue slides up the side of my face like a slippery snake. I flinch and jerk my head to the side, but the blade pricks the skin on my neck.

"Buddy," Axl says. "I'm gonna blow your fuckin' brains out."

Tat laughs, and the sharp point of the knife digs a little deeper into my throat. Threatening to break the skin. I hold my breath as my legs tremble. "So you must be the boyfriend who broke her out. Too bad you didn't get there earlier. I had a real good time with her before you showed up." He presses his mouth against my ear. "Just wait 'til we get back to Vegas. The boss isn't going to care this time. He's going to let me do whatever I want with you."

Axl's mouth jerks, and he drops his gun. It clatters to the floor, and Tat relaxes. He leans his face forward again like he's going to say something else. Faster than a bullet, Axl rips the knife out of his belt and flings it toward us.

I squeeze my eyes shut as Tat's whole body jerks back. A yelp of terror pops out of my mouth. Tat's arms fall away. There's a thump. I crack one eye and look down. Tat's lifeless eyes stare back at me. Axl's hunting knife is buried in his forehead.

Axl is by my side before I even get a chance to fill my lungs. He pulls me against him, squeezing me so tight I can't breathe again. This time, I don't care.

"I'm okay," I say. "I'm okay."

He steps away, but he doesn't relax. He takes a deep breath like he's trying to steady himself, then rips the knife out of Tat's skull. "We gotta go."

WE MAKE IT TO THE SURFACE SHELTER WITHOUT SEEING anyone else, but after the confrontation in the common area, everyone is silent and tense. Stepping into the shelter only makes things worse.

The door is open a couple inches, and male voices travel in. Several of them. Angus peers through the opening, and I hold my breath. A minute goes by. Two. Angus steps back. He frowns.

"Looks like six. They're busy loadin' a truck and holdin' the zombies off."

"What about the Sam's truck?" Axl asks.

"Doors are shut. Either they ain't tried to open it yet or they ain't gonna."

"What do you think?" Winston asks.

Angus purses his lips and scratches his chin. "We got a shot. They're awfully busy and the zombies are on their side of the fence."

"So the five of us go out first and distract them." Winston looks at me. "Vivian gets the keys and gets to the truck. Then what?"

"First, we gotta cut a hole in that fence closer to the truck. Something big enough for everybody to squeeze through." Axl looks at his brother. "We still got them bolt cutters in the car?"

Angus spits on the floor. "Sure do."

"Good," Axl says. "Vivian, you get that key and get to the truck. Soon as it's started, Anne's gonna get everybody movin'."

Anne bites her lip and pulls Jake closer. The kid's eyes are huge. "I can do it."

Axl tilts my face toward his. "Remember where the key is?"

I want to grab his hand and never let it go, but this isn't the time. "Three steps to the right and dig."

"Okay. Let's do it then," Winston says. He turns to Jon and Nathan. "You two ready?"

Jon nods, and Nathan pries himself out of Moira's iron grip. She won't stop crying, and it's starting to get old. He kisses her and practically shoves her toward Liz. She's still blubbering. I have the sudden urge to slap her, but I don't think it would help. With the way she's acting, it would probably make things a million times worse.

Axl drops my hand. My heart sinks to the ground when Angus eases the door open. I hold my breath, waiting for gunfire. But nothing happens. After a few seconds, Angus nods and ducks out, followed by Axl, Jon, Nathan, and Winston. As soon as they're gone, Anne and I run to the door and peer through the opening.

The men from Vegas are loading a truck in the distance. Occasionally, one has to break away from the group to kill a stray zombie. Axl and the others have disappeared. I'm not even sure which way they went.

"Can you see them?" Anne hisses.

I shake my head and grip the door, waiting for a signal. Angus steps out of the shadows and falls in line with a group of men carrying supplies. He has something in his hands, but can't I tell what it is. Maybe a box or something. Where the hell did he get it? My shoulders tense and I wrap my fingers around the door knob, squeezing it tightly. They're going to notice he isn't with their group. They have to!

He walks up to the truck and nothing happens. The man in front of him loads his box and turns away. Angus kneels and lays his on the ground. He's tying his shoe! What the hell is he doing tying his shoe at a time like this?

"What does he have?" Anne asks.

"I don't know, I can't tell!" My heart pounds so hard it's all I can hear.

We both move closer. Angus fumbles with something, then there's a little spark. It catches and a small flame goes up. He looks around, then kicks the box under the truck before getting to his feet and walking away.

"Is it a bomb?" I say, almost to myself.

Anne shakes her head and turns to the rest of the group. "Hold on! There's going to be an explosion," she hisses.

When the truck explodes, I can feel the rush of heat on my face. A fireball bursts through the air and the men go crazy. The two closest to the truck catch fire. They scream and run as flames lick at their clothes.

I'm frozen until Anne shoves me toward the door. "Go!"

I rip the door open and stumble to the right. One step, two, three. Falling to my knees, I dig like crazy. I scoop the sand aside as fast as I can as it collects under my nails. I don't feel anything. The sand runs through my fingers and I dig faster. Where is it? I force my fingers deeper, but come up empty. Maybe Angus took bigger steps than I did. I move my hands forward a few inches and plow through the sand. My hand brushes against something solid. Plastic. Wrapping my fingers around it, I pull it from the sand and jump to my feet.

The fire is still raging when I take off toward the fence with the can clutched in my hand. The key clangs around inside. The sound is louder than the gunfire or the screams. I run past the Nissan, and the fence comes into view. The hole the guys cut is straight ahead.

A man runs out in front of me, and I raise my gun, pulling the trigger before he even notices me. He falls, and I leap over him, pushing my way through the fence. The newly-cut metal slices my bare arms, but I keep moving.

I finally rip the can open when I get to the back of the truck. My hands shake as I unlock the door, and twice I almost drop it. Somehow, I manage to get the lock undone and slide the door open.

Spinning around, I scan the area, looking for Anne and the others while keeping an eye out for any danger. Zombies or otherwise. The truck is still burning on the other side of the fence, and gunshots ring through the dark night. There are no zombies in sight, though. They must all be gravitating toward the burning truck.

Joshua comes running through the darkness, supporting Al. I rush forward and hold the fence aside so he can get through. Darla is right behind him, pulling two of the kids with her. More and more people rush toward me. One by one, they squeeze through the fence.

Anne comes through last, sweating and breathing heavily. "That's everyone."

"Let's get the door shut and get out of here."

We run to the back of the truck just as Parvarti pulls herself up.

I have to jump up so I can grab the strap and pull the door down. "Everyone hold on. We're getting someplace safe."

When the door is shut, Anne and I run to the front of the truck. I pull myself up, but just before I duck into the driver's seat, I pause and look back toward the fighting. Where is Axl right now? I want to see him, just one time before I drive away. Just in case.

But I can't see anything other than the fire and a few faceless men running around. And I can't wait. Everyone is counting on me.

I have to think of their safety first.

I climb in and slam the door. "Hold on," I say as the engine roars to life.

CHAPTER TWENTY-FOUR

AXL

Soon as the truck explodes, I move. I run out from behind the Nissan and head toward the fire, keepin' low to the ground. Two men are on fire, runnin' 'round in circles while the flames trail behind them. There are more men chasin' 'em — probably tryin' to get them to roll on the ground — and a few more lookin' for us.

I raise my gun as I move and fire two quick shots. One man goes down, but I miss the second one and he turns toward me, firin' in my direction. He's a lousy shot. It misses me by a mile. But now the other men know I'm here, and more turn my way. They fire and I duck, throwin' myself behind the sedan.

Angus comes outta nowhere, sinkin' down next to me. "You see that truck?" he says, leanin' down so he can look under the car.

I ignore him and inch forward, lookin' 'round the back of the sedan. Three, maybe four guys. And then there are the zombies. The fire is attractin' 'em like crazy.

"How long we gonna wait?" Angus asks. He's layin' on his stomach, slowly inchin' under the car.

"Just 'til that truck drives away," I say, copyin' him. The sand scratches my arms, and sweat drips in my eyes. "Where're the others?"

Angus grunts and fires two quick shots. What the hell is he firin' at? I can't see a damn thing.

"Over by the other car," he says, firin' again. This time two zombies fall down.

"Stop wastin' bullets," I mutter.

A man runs out in front of me, and I fire. He falls to the ground but don't die. He's screamin' and twistin' 'round on the ground. I swear and shoot again. He stops movin' this time.

Axl pulls the trigger again. "I'm just firin' so they stay where they are. They won't come lookin' for us if they think they're gonna get shot."

Damn. Sometimes Angus surprises even me. You wouldn't think he had a lick of sense by talkin' to him, but he's smart.

The roar of the truck's engine cuts through the air, and I jump, hittin' my head on the bottom of the car. Damn.

Angus laughs and fires two more times. "Guess Blondie's good. We gonna haul ass now?"

"Let's get the hell outta here," I say, inchin' back.

The fire's still roarin', but I can't see a single livin' person. Just zombies. Dozens of 'em. They're stumblin' in from the desert like they're headed to a buffet.

"We got incomin'," I say when Angus is standin' next to me. "We better get movin'."

We head toward the other cars, and I search for our people while we move. There's firin' somewhere, so they gotta be in the area. Angus keeps shootin' as we head to the truck, and I let him. I gotta find the others so we can get the hell outta here.

I finally spot them crouched down next to the Cadillac. Winston waves at me and I turn to get Angus just as he swears and runs off, firin' and cussin' like a madman.

"Angus!" I yell, but he don't listen.

He keeps runnin', shootin' as he goes. A few men are visible on the other side of the fence, kneelin' in front of a vehicle that ain't burnin'. Angus is runnin' toward them, and they're shootin' at him. He's out in the open. Totally exposed! What the hell is that dumbass doin'?

Then I see Mitchell cowerin' behind a car. That's gotta be who

Angus is goin' for. No way I'm gonna be able to get him to come back now. Not with that asshole standin' there.

I run after Angus, yellin' over my shoulder to the others, "Cover us!"

They start firin' at the men, who duck behind the car. Mitchell looks up. He must see Angus comin' for him, because he takes off runnin'. Right into the desert. Not sure where that idiot thinks he's goin', though. There are zombies everywhere. Mitchell's armed, but he ain't even tryin' to shoot. He's just runnin'.

Angus runs past the truck where the other men are hidin' and barely pauses, firin' twice before takin' off after Mitchell again. I'm pantin' and sweatin', but I keep goin'. When I reach the car, the two men that was hidin' there are dead.

Angus tackles Mitchell, and they roll to the ground right in front of a zombie. They don't even seem to notice. Mitchell squirms, tryin' to break away, but Angus rolls him over and starts beatin' the shit outta him. The dead bastard is right on top of them, leanin' down with his mouth open. Ready to take a big ol' bite outta Angus. I fire, and his head pops like a balloon, rainin' black ooze all over Angus and Mitchell.

One down, but there are more comin'. I don't wanna waste bullets, so I put my gun away and pull out my knife, standin' over Angus while he pounds Mitchell over and over again with his fists. Mitchell ain't even conscious anymore.

"Angus," I yell as I slam my blade into a zombie's eye. "Just kill him so we can go! There're zombies everywhere!"

Angus gets up and wipes the sweat off his forehead, pullin' out his gun. "Shoulda done this the first time," he says, pushin' his gun against Mitchell's forehead.

I hold my breath while I wait for him to pull the trigger, but he don't. After a few seconds he puckers his lips and shoves his gun back in his waistband.

"Angus!" I yell. "We gotta go!"

"Bullet's too good for this bastard," Angus mutters.

He grabs Mitchell by his collar and hauls him up. The bastard's face is covered in blood. His eyes are swollen, his lip split. All the cuts from a few days ago are open, and there are new cuts on top of those. He barely looks human.

I take a step closer. "Forget him!"

Angus slaps Mitchell a few times. "Wake up, you prick."

Mitchell groans, and his right eye opens a crack. Angus's mouth curls up into a sadistic smile. He drags the bastard closer to the advancin' dead. Mitchell's conscious, but just barely, and his arms flap at his sides. My feet are rooted to the ground as I watch.

"This is what you deserve," Angus says when he stops.

Mitchell's eyes open wide—or as wide as they can—and he shakes his head. The zombies are close when Angus hurls Mitchell across the desert. The bastard screams when he hits the ground at their feet. He rolls onto his side and tries to crawl away, but a zombie grabs him by the foot before he can get two inches. Angus don't move, and neither do I. It's like the rest of the world has disappeared, and all I can do is stand there and watch a dead man take that first big bite outta Mitchell's leg.

Angus stands there grinnin' while the zombies converge on Mitchell. The prick is screamin' and thrashin', tryin' to get away. They've got him surrounded now, rippin' him to shreds.

He was a bastard, but I still can't stand to watch. I finally get my legs to move and jog over to where Angus is standin'. I grab his arm and pull him toward the gate. The Nissan is comin' our way.

"We gotta go!"

Mitchell's still screamin' when I spin 'round. A man steps outta nowhere and swings a bat at Angus's head. It hits him right in the temple, and Angus grunts. He drops to the ground, and I duck when the man swings again. I recognize him right away. The boss.

He swings a third time, and I charge, just like I did back in my high school football days, tacklin' him. We tumble to the ground and he loses his bat, but I lose my knife too. Don't matter. I start punchin' him, and all I can think 'bout is Vivian and all them other girls at the Monte Carlo. How sick this dude is. How I wanna gut him. My fist slams into his nose, and he screams when the bone snaps. Blood pours out. I swing again, hittin' him with my already broken fist. Pain shoots through my hand and up my arm and I scream, but I swing again anyways.

The Nissan pulls up next to me and the doors fly open, but I don't stop. I'm aware of Winston haulin' Angus to his feet, but I still don't let up. Then Winston's standin' over me, pullin' on my arms. I fight against him, tryin' to punch the bastard more. All I can see is red.

"Axl! We have to go!"

Gunshots bring me back, and I blink. Zombies are closin' in on us. Nathan and Jon are firin' at them. My hands and knuckles are red, and the man underneath me is sputterin' and spittin' up blood.

"Let's go!" Winston calls again.

I nod and stumble to my feet, grabbin' my knife off the ground. The man's eyes follow me. I ain't leavin' him alive. No way in hell. I kneel down and put my blade to his neck, then press in just enough to puncture the skin. His eyes get huge, and he sputters even more, tryin' to talk through the blood. Don't matter what he has to say, though. Not to me.

"Should leave you for the zombies," I say. He shakes and his lips move. "But I wanna watch you bleed out."

I slide my blade across his neck, and it opens wide. Blood pours out like a fountain. The man grabs at it, tryin' to hold himself together. His eyes are wide and his lips keep movin', but no sounds come out. It only takes a few seconds. Then his hands drop, and I wipe my blade on his shirt and get up.

Winston is waitin' by the car, firin' at the zombies headed our way.

"Let's go!" I yell, joggin' up to meet him.

He nods. Jon and Nathan are already climbin' back in. Angus is passed out on the seat, and there's blood runnin' down the side of his head.

"Shit," I mutter, starin' at my brother. Hope he don't got a concussion or nothin'.

There's a gunshot.

Flames shoot through my shoulder, and a million stars burst behind my eyes before everything goes black.

CHAPTER TWENTY-FIVE

VIVIAN

By the time I pull up to the base of the mountain, my hands ache from gripping the steering wheel. I've never driven a truck this big, so the drive was bumpy and difficult. Anne's been gripping the *oh shit* bar most of the ride. The truck stops with a jerk, and we lurch forward. My chest bangs against the steering wheel, and I bite down on my lip. That's what I get for not wearing a seatbelt.

"You see anyone behind us?" Anne asks, looking in the side view mirror.

I squeeze the steering wheel tighter even though my palms already hurt. If I don't, my whole body will start to shake. "No one."

"Then we're not being followed."

She's right. I have to look on the bright side here. Not the side that says Axl isn't driving toward us and he may very well be dead. That won't help anyone, least of all me.

"Let's make sure the coast is clear, then check on everyone," I say, pushing the door open and hopping out.

My bare feet hit the sand, and I yelp when a sharp rock digs into the bottom of my foot. The air is cold, and the wind howls, blowing sand into my face and whipping my hair around. But it's fresh air. No hint of death or smoke from the fire that's still burning in the distance. It's clear.

At least for now.

Anne is already sliding the door open when I get to the back of the truck. Someone inside screams, and one of the kids starts to cry.

"It's just us! We're safe now," she calls out.

Hopefully she's right. So far, it's clear. But nothing else has gone our way. Why should this be any different?

My stomach tenses as I turn my back to the truck. Watching the flickering light of the fire in the distance. The sky above it is blacker than everywhere else thanks to the giant pillar of smoke. I can't stand being so far away. Not knowing what's going on.

"What now?" Hadley asks, coming up to stand next to me.

She shivers and crosses her arms over her chest. The gesture must be catching like a yawn, because as soon as she does it, my body copies hers. Goose bumps pop up on every inch of my flesh. I'm wearing nothing but one of those ridiculously skimpy dresses and a thong.

"We just have to wait," I say, and my teeth chatter.

I'm shivering within seconds. People start moving around inside the truck. Even though I don't want to turn away from the shelter, I do. They have flashlights and lanterns on, and for the first time, I get a really good look at everyone. Pajamas and bare feet. Hadley isn't wearing pants, just a long T-shirt. No one is dressed, and there's nothing we can do about it. Our extra clothes are gone. Lost along with all our personal belongings. We have the supplies in the truck. Food and weapons, hunting and fishing gear, camping stuff. The men didn't think to pack clothes, though. We're in trouble.

My eyes meet Joshua's when he hops down. His skin is painted red.

"How's Al?"

Joshua runs his hand through his hair—it's stained with Al's blood—and sighs. "In pain. I can't give him anything or we won't know if he's going to turn."

Hadley winces, but I nod. "I know." I still don't like it, but they're right.

"What do you think is taking them so long?" Anne asks.

I press my lips together and resist the urge to snap at her. "I don't know," I say through clenched teeth.

Hadley shivers, and I put my arm around her shoulders. She's been almost nonexistent through this whole thing. I miss the strong Hadley.

"How are you?" I whisper.

She swallows. When she shivers, I don't think it's from the cold. "I'll be okay."

Her lips are pursed, and it makes me think of Axl. God, please let him be okay. Let us all get out of this alive. Haven't we been through enough?

"You want to know something?" she says. "I'm mad that I shot him in the back of the head."

It takes me a second to realize she's talking about the man who raped her. My mind is all Axl right now.

"Why?"

She lets out a bitter laugh. "I wish I'd been able to cut his throat and watch him struggle for air."

"Don't worry. He's in hell now." I squeeze her shoulder tighter.

"Is he? I was kind of thinking this was hell. Maybe we're the ones who died from the virus, and this is the hell that's been chosen for us."

My stomach sinks, and I can't think of a single thing to say. There are moments when I can't imagine hell being worse than this.

Hadley sighs and turns away. She heads back toward the truck, but she doesn't climb in. She just leans against it like she can't stand on her own.

Darla jumps down, and everything inside me tightens even more, twisting around until all my organs and muscles are one giant knot. She made it. Of course she did. Now that I have some perspective on the whole thing, I guess I'm grateful. It's not like we've had time to deal with the past.

"You gonna tell me to take a hike?" she asks.

I shake my head, and she almost smiles. One corner of her mouth pulls up. I'm not really sure what the look means.

"I was real glad we got you out," she says. "I know you don't think much of me, but I'm still your mama. I never forgot about you. There were even times when I regretted leaving. Not him."

She spits and her mouth twists into a grimace. "But I did wonder about you."

Give me a break. "How sweet."

"You know if he survived all this?"

My lips press together, and for a full twenty seconds, I can't make them move. Then I say, "No idea. I left the day I turned eighteen and haven't seen him since."

She smiles for real now. "You ran out on your daddy?"

"Guess I learned something from you."

Darla's hair blows across her face, and she brushes it away. My whole body shivers. The air feels colder all the sudden. Maybe it's just the company.

"Gotta say, ever since this zombie thing started I've been hoping he survived the virus. It'd be nice to think he got ripped apart by one of these guys. Don't you think?"

She grins and I want to disagree with her, but I can't. Of course, if I was being honest, I'd tell her there were moments when I'd wished that about her. I won't be honest, though. Not now. Not when I have other things to focus on.

We lapse into silence, and I shuffle my feet. She doesn't leave. I wish she would. She's a distraction, but not a good one. Her presence just makes all this more painful.

"Are those lights?" Anne calls out.

My heart leaps, and I step forward, like the six inches of space I just covered will get Axl to me sooner. Like if I can just run fast enough, I'll find him and we'll be together and I'll be able to prove Hadley wrong. This *isn't* hell. It can't be. Not as long as I have Axl with me.

Joshua pulls his gun out and checks to make sure it's loaded. "You're right. We better be ready just in case."

My heart pounds as the two little balls of light get closer and closer. They bounce over the uneven ground, moving slower than a snail. Jessica and Parvarti come out with weapons. Darla is still by my side, and even she has a gun. Someone pulls the door shut, leaving Moira and Lila inside with the kids and Al. Nobody moves while the lights approach, getting so close I can't look at them anymore without putting a hand over my eyes.

We should move. If it's the men from Vegas, we'll be easy to pick off. Standing here in the open like this. Part of me doesn't care, though. If it isn't Axl, I don't want to walk away from this. Not just

216

to go back to Vegas. I know Hadley doesn't either.

The car slows and stops four feet in front of me. It's the Nissan. I can tell even before the lights turn off. Even though I know I shouldn't, I run forward, stumbling over the sand and rocks. My gun is up, but my hand shakes so hard I would never be able to hit a thing. All I want is Axl to be here with me. To be okay.

The passenger door opens, and Jon jumps out. Winston is in the driver's seat. Nathan and Angus climb out of the back. A trail of blood runs down the side of Angus's head and he's cursing, yelling for Joshua. He's *actually* calling him Joshua. He's never done that before. It's always been doc.

No one else gets out, and the ball of tension inside me explodes. Hadley was right. This is hell.

"No!" I scream, throwing myself at Angus. "Where is he? Where's Axl?"

My voice shakes, and tears fall from my eyes. I'm not even sure anyone can understand me. I'm a blubbering idiot, but I can't do anything other than ask for Axl. He's all I want.

Angus grabs my arms, but he doesn't push me away. He just holds onto me. Is he hugging me?

Joshua runs up, and then Hadley is next to me, pulling me back. Jon and Winston drag Axl out of the Nissan. He isn't wearing a shirt, and there's blood everywhere. On his shoulder. His chest. Running down his arm in little droplets that look like black ink against the desert sand.

"What happened?" My voice shakes as much as my body, and Hadley is still holding me, but no one answers.

"Up in the truck!" Joshua yells. "Get as many lights and lanterns as you can. And the medical equipment. Get everything!"

He stares at his hands. Then looks at Axl. "Shit, shit."

"What?" I scream.

"I have Al's blood all over me. This isn't going to be sterile."

My fingers dig into Hadley's arm, and I just stare at Joshua. What's he talking about? My mind won't focus, and I can't figure out what he means. Then it hits me like a punch in the gut. Surgery. That's what he's talking about. Axl's been shot. Joshua needs to get the bullet out. Infection. We're in the desert. Sitting on a pile of dirt. Joshua has to do surgery with dirty hands, dirty instruments. Axl could die.

Everything feels fuzzy. Joshua is in the truck now, and Axl's lying on the floor. Angus and Jon are still turning lights on. Thank God we have so many. Axl's body jerks. Is he conscious?

"I want to be with him," I whisper, pulling away from Hadley.

She doesn't try to stop me. Not that she could have.

I pull myself into the truck where Axl is lying on his stomach. The gunshot wound is on his left shoulder blade. Joshua's digging in it. Axl groans, and my insides quiver. I step forward, but someone pulls me back.

"Give him some space, Blondie," Angus whispers.

He keeps his arm around me and steps back until he's leaning against the wall. He *is* hugging me. I look up. His lips purse and his eyebrows pull down. His gray eyes shimmer. There are actually tears in Angus's eyes.

"He's gonna pull through," he says. I don't think he's talking to me. "He's a strong son of a bitch. Been through worse than this."

Axl grunts, and my entire body jerks. Angus hold onto me tighter, and all I can do is stare at Axl's body lying on the floor, his fists clenched. I can just make out the side of his face. There are little beads of sweat on his forehead.

"Didn't Joshua give him anything for the pain?"

Angus shakes his head. "Axl told him not to. Said to save it."

Axl jerks again, and without thinking, I bury my face in Angus's chest. He rubs my back. Where did this guy come from? Oh, yeah. Axl is hurt. He's the only person Angus really cares about. This might be the only thing that could actually bring out the human in Angus.

After what feels like days, Angus relaxes his hold on me, and I look up. Joshua sits back and pours rubbing alcohol over Axl's shoulder.

"I know you wanna do it, so just go," Angus whispers, dropping his arms.

He's letting me go for Axl's benefit, not mine, but I don't care. I stumble the short distance across the truck, practically falling next to Axl. Joshua covers the wound with gauze. Axl's jaw is so tight. His eyes are closed, but he opens them when I touch his face.

"I thought you were dead," I whisper.

He grabs my hand and presses it to his lips. "Told you I wasn't gonna let them bastards kill me." His voice sounds rough.

"Why didn't you take some morphine? We have it."

He grunts, and his jaw tightens even more. "Gotta save it.

Something worse could happen."

"Worse than getting shot?" My throat tightens as soon as the words are out.

Yes. Something worse than getting shot could happen. Look at Al.

Axl just squeezes my hand.

"That's all I can do," Joshua says.

Angus stands at Axl's feet like he's afraid to get any closer. "How bad is it?"

Joshua runs his hand through his hair. His hands are even redder now. "We'll just have to wait and see. Hopefully he doesn't get an infection, but we won't really know the full extent of the injury until it's healed. He may have some permanent damage, but it's hard to say."

Axl moves like he's trying to sit up, but I put my hand on his back. "What are you doing?"

"We gotta figure out what we're gonna do," he says, letting go of my hand and pushing himself up with his good arm. His face tenses and he swears, but he manages to get up. He takes a few deep breaths before saying, "Can't stay here."

A gust of wind blows through the truck, and I shiver. He wraps his good arm around me. His skin is damp with sweat and blood. He's going to be cold soon, too.

"We gonna head out now?" Angus asks. He still hasn't moved from his position at Axl's feet.

"Gotta get someplace warm," Axl says.

I scoot closer, trying to get warm and ensure Axl doesn't get cold. "We don't have any clothes and most of us aren't dressed."

Anne and Hadley climb into the truck and come over to join us. We're all gathered around. All the adults except Al and Lila.

"Where do we go?" Hadley asks. Jon puts his arm around her and she doesn't move away or tell him to stop. That must mean something, but I don't know what's going on with those two.

"We could go with your original plan," Winston says. "Find a farm. Figure out a way to fortify it."

Jessica sighs and leans against her dad. "You mean go back to California?"

Winston shakes his head. "Not necessarily. There are other places. We need to figure out what would be safest."

"There's nothing safe no more," Darla mutters.

"Anybody got suggestions?" Axl arm tightens around my shoulder when he talks, and he winces.

"Up in Wyoming or Montana, there would be ranches and things," Joshua says. "Those areas were less populated, so in theory there would be fewer zombies."

Moira speaks up for the first time. She's clinging to her husband. "Then we'd have to worry about winter."

Winston scratches his chin and stares at the ground. "Could be rough with no electricity."

"We could go south," I say. "It would be warmer."

"But more populated," Joshua replies.

Angus hasn't said a word.

Axl looks up at his brother. "What're you thinkin', bro?"

There are little beads of sweat on Axl's forehead, and his jaw tightens every time he moves. I wish he'd take something for the pain.

Everyone stares at Angus like he holds all the answers. He purses his lips and shakes his head. "What the doc was sayin' 'bout Wyoming sounds good. Be good game there, too. We'd be able to grow food in the summer. Down south, the soil's all clay and sand. Hot as balls in the summer. Make it tough for people who ain't used to it."

"What about the winter?" For some reason, I trust Angus's take on this. He knows about this kind of thing. Hunting and fishing. This is his element.

"Seems like places that secluded might have generators and wood-burnin' fireplaces."

Winston blinks and looks at Angus like he just sprouted a second head. "That's probably true."

"And we can load up on supplies before we go. We'll kill us some animals and use the fur." He scratches his head. "Indians did it. I think we could probably figure it out."

Axl nods once. His face scrunches up, and he inhales sharply. "Yeah," he manages to get out, but it's strained.

Joshua gets to his feet. "So we head north."

His shoulders slump. He doesn't look thrilled. No one does. Why would we? We're headed north with no idea of what to expect or where we're really going. We could run out of gas and get stranded, or we could get up there to find it just as overrun as Vegas.

"Gonna have to get some clothes before we get too far," Angus says. "We got us a map?"

"We have one in the front." Winston turns and hops out of the truck without another word.

Angus and Jon follow, and the little group around us slowly breaks up. Joshua walks away, mumbling something about checking on Al. Moira drags Nathan toward the back with the women and children. They're probably going to huddle together back there so they can all keep warm. It's getting colder by the minute.

Axl's in pain. It's written all over his face. In every move he makes. "What can I get you?" I ask, running my hand across his chest, stopping just an inch shy of the gauze.

"You're all I need."

I laugh. I can't help it. "That's good, because it looks like we don't have anything else."

"We're gonna be okay," he says fiercely.

"Are we?"

Axl moves closer to me, straining from the movement. "We gotta be. After all this shit we been through, we gotta catch a break. Right?"

"I never knew you were such an optimist."

"Never was. Not 'til I met you." He kisses my neck, and I shiver. "Never had nothin' good in my life 'til you."

"You had Angus." Axl raises an eyebrow, but I shake my head. "He's an ass, I'll be the first one to admit it, but he loves you, Axl. You're probably the only thing he's ever really cared about."

"I never really thought Angus gave a shit 'bout me except when he needed something. But after the last couple of days, I'm startin' to think you're right." He frowns. "You think he can change? That he can find a way to fit into this group?"

"I think he'll try. For you."

Angus and Winston appear outside the truck. Angus tosses an atlas inside, then hoists himself up. Winston follows. When they're both in, they spread the atlas out on the floor in front of us.

"We're going to head up this way." Winston trails his finger along the map. "We got over five hundred miles to cover."

"Then what?" I ask, staring at the atlas. The distance seems impossible. With no gas stations and no clothes, traveling into the unknown. It seems like the perfect way to get ourselves killed.

"Gotta hope we find a good place," Angus says.

My eyes sting, and I turn away from the map. I press my face against Axl's neck. "I guess that's all we have anymore, isn't it? Hope."

"We got each other," Axl says. "That's something."

Winston nods, and when Angus purses his lips, even he looks like he agrees.

I sniff and wipe away a tear that somehow managed to escape. "Then let's do it. Let's not hang around waiting for the dead to find us."

Angus nods, and Winston gets to his feet as he folds up the map. They both start shouting off orders. Axl wraps his arm around me tighter, and my heart pounds. People work together, gathering things so we're ready to go. This group we have here, it's like a family. Axl is right. That *is* something. It's so much more than we could ever hope for in times like this.

CHAPTER TWENTY-SIX

AXL

Being shot sucks. Not that I thought it'd be fun, but it ain't just the pain. It's seein' the worry on Vivian's face. It's realizin' Angus really does care and I'm puttin' him through hell. It's addin' to an already stressful night.

I lean against the wall while Joshua tightens the strap on my sling. Every time he adjusts it, a bolt of pain shoots across my back. I wince and he apologizes, but he don't stop what he's doin'. I gotta clench my fist to keep from hittin' him.

When he's done, I relax. Havin' the sling does help with the pain. But I hate sittin' here. Watchin' everybody get packed up. I use my free hand and try to hoist myself off the ground, but it don't work. More pain shoots through me. Vivian is at my side before I'm done cussin', holdin' my hand.

"Let me help," she says, and I can't argue. I'd be dumb as shit to pretend I didn't need it.

"What about Vegas?" Hadley blurts out.

Vivian is helpin' me to my feet and I turn too fast. The throbbin' in my shoulder turns into a pain that feels like a bolt of lightnin'. Shootin' down my arm and across my chest at the same time. I suck in a deep breath, and Vivian's arm tightens 'round me.

"You okay?" she whispers.

I press my lips together and nod. "Yup." It don't sound convincin'. Even to me.

"Vegas," Hadley says again. "All those women at the Monte Carlo. What about them? We're just going to leave them there? Run off and forget about them?"

"What you want us to do?" Angus asks. "We can't take 'em all in, and we're pretty outnumbered."

Hadley frowns and shakes her head.

Jon's standin' next to her, and he nods. "She's right. We can't walk away."

The pain in my shoulder is still there. A constant burnin' that throbs, almost takin' my breath away when I move too fast. I ease back and lean against the wall of the truck. Then I hold my breath until it eases a little.

"We killed a bunch of 'em," I manage to get out. "Might not be so outnumbered now."

Winston is starin' at me, then he looks over toward Vivian. Then Jessica. His daughter. I can read him like a book. "We have to do something."

Angus shakes his head and swears under his breath. He spits. "What you wanna do? Just go there and throw the doors open?"

Vivian's body is tense, and she's starin' at the floor. She nods slowly, and her blonde hair falls over her face. "Exactly. Do to them what they did to us. Open the doors and let the bastards in."

"No guarantee it will work," Nathan says. "The zombies aren't going to use the elevator to go upstairs. What if the men are all in their rooms? It's the middle of the night." That wife of his is clingin' to him like crazy, and her eyes are wild-lookin'. Like they're gonna pop outta her head any second.

I pucker my lips, and this time I don't give a shit that I probably look just like Angus. They're right. Much as I hate to admit it. We can't leave them women alone, and we did kill of a lot of their men. I got that bastard boss before somebody put a bullet in me. We could do it. Probably wouldn't even be that tough.

"We can start a fire," I mutter. "Make the fire alarm go off. It'd draw them downstairs." I move an inch, and flames of pain lick their way across my insides. All the breath leaves my lungs and

Vivian grabs my arm, but I shake my head and close my eyes. It takes a few seconds for the fire to die down.

"You aren't going anywhere," she whispers.

Wish I could argue, but she's right. I'd be useless. Not a feelin' I enjoy.

"So you want us to go to the Monte Carlo, start a fire, then throw the doors open and let the zombie bastards in?" Angus asks. His voice is tight, the way it gets when he's callin' you out on your bullshit. I open my eyes and meet his gaze.

He shakes his head and spits on the floor.

"We have to live in this truck, Angus," Vivian snaps.

Her body is gettin' more tense by the second. She's starin' at Hadley, who's twistin' a strand of hair between her fingers. Pullin' on it so hard I wouldn't be surprised if it fell out.

"We can't leave them," Vivian whispers.

Hadley nods, but she don't look up.

"What 'bout all them women?" I ask. "You gonna just leave them to fend for themselves, or you gonna bring 'em back with you?"

"We got 'nough baggage as it is," Angus mutters.

He acts like he's gonna spit on the floor again, then he looks at Vivian and heads to the back of the truck. The bastard actually spits out into the desert. Never thought he'd be considerate. Ain't really his style.

Hadley drops the hair she's been twistin', and her head snaps up. Her green eyes narrow on Angus, and she takes a step forward. "You bastard—"

"He's right," Winston says.

Everyone—Angus included—turns to face Winston.

Winston don't blink, and he don't look sorry. "We can't take them on. How many women were there?"

Vivian shakes her head. "Thirty, maybe."

Nathan's wife whimpers like a sick dog, and the doc swears. He's covered in Al's blood. And mine. We gotta get us some clothes.

"We can't take that many more people," Nathan says, ignorin' his wife.

"And it isn't just that it's thirty more people. It's thirty damaged women. They'd be exactly what Angus said, baggage." Winston rubs the back of his neck and looks at the ground like he's

225

ashamed to admit it.

But he's right.

"Shit," I mutter. "It's no good."

"So we leave them?" Hadley's voice is high, like a kid going through puberty. "We walk away and forget they're being used—" Her voice breaks, and she shakes her head. She goes back to twistin' that hair.

"No," Winston says. He looks up and his eyes meet mine like he's askin' permission.

"We ain't gonna leave 'em, but we can't take 'em," I say.

Winston nods.

Vivian stands up straighter, and her hand falls away from my arm. "So we get a small group together and head out in the Nissan. We start a fire, draw the men out, then let the zombies do their worst. But we leave the women? Do we even go up to that floor? Tell them the coast is clear?"

Hadley nods, but she don't look up. "Yes. We have to."

Angus is standin' at the back of the truck, and he spits again. "Shit."

"So who's going?" Vivian asks, ignorin' Angus.

My shoulders tense, and pain shoots down my arm. It's like a blade is bein' dug into my skin, and it brings tears to my eyes. I exhale, and Vivian's right there, askin' me if I'm alright. But there's no pain intense enough to distract me from what's 'bout to happen.

I grab her, workin' through the pain, and pull her against me. "No," I murmur, pressin' my lips against her head. Her hair tickles my nose, and I squeeze my eyes shut. "I ain't gonna let you."

"I have to," she whispers.

"I'll go," Jon says.

Vivian pries herself out of my arms and takes a step away. "Me too."

The pain in my shoulder has moved down to my heart. And that damn animal is back, clawing at me from the inside out.

I lean against the wall while I try to catch my breath. Winston volunteers. And Hadley. Even Nathan, which makes his wife start cryin' like a banshee. Then Angus says he'll go. He's lookin' at me when he says it, and his lips are all puckered up. There's something hard in his face, and I can't help rememberin' our conversation 'bout the Monte Carlo. Maybe he wouldn't be there if things were different. Maybe this is his way of showin' me.

Then his eyes go to Vivian, who is already gettin' ready to leave. No, he's doin' this for me. To keep an eye on her, 'cause he knows I can't.

Does he know I'd die without her? He must.

Still can't believe he cares.

I slump to the floor while everybody 'round me starts movin'. Makin' plans. My shoulder throbs and my legs are shakin'. I'm sweatin' even though everybody else seems to be covered in goose bumps.

Maybe I should let the doc give me something for the pain.

"You look like shit," Angus says, sittin' down next to me.

"Can't lie," I say in a voice that don't sound nothin' like me. "Feel like shit."

Angus clears his throat and puckers his lips. For once I don't think he looks like a monkey. Maybe I'm delirious.

"I wouldn't have you know." He ain't lookin' at me. He's starin' out the back of the truck like he's focusin' on something else, but I know my brother better than that. He don't like makin' himself vulnerable.

"I know," I mutter, mostly 'cause I don't wanna send him off to Vegas while things are still tense between us.

He puckers his lips even more. "I ain't like them sick bastards. I know I can be a hard-ass, but that's just for survival. Always had to be that way. I wouldn't take advantage of somebody weaker. That ain't right." He takes a deep breath and narrows his eyes on the horizon. "That'd be too much like *her*."

I shift uncomfortably, and even the pain shootin' through my body can't distract me from what just happened. Angus never talks about our mom. Never.

Just like it always does when I think 'bout her, my throat tightens. "She was a bitch," I manage to get out.

Angus nods, then spits on the floor. "But she was our mama. Only one we ever got." He clears his throat and gets to his feet, lookin' down at me. "I'll keep an eye on Blondie, don't you worry 'bout that."

"Keep an eye on yourself, too. Don't go doin' something stupid."

Angus grins. "Now, when have I ever done something stupid?"

When I laugh, the pain is so intense it leaves the edges of my vision black.

MY EYES ARE CLOSED AND I'M SWEATIN' FROM THE DRIVE. Every bump is agony, and by the time we pull to a stop, I'm havin' a tough time stoppin' myself from cussin'. My lips are raw from bitin' into them. The throbbin' in my shoulder is gettin' to be too much, but I don't want nobody to know.

Somebody kneels next to me, and I know it's Vivian before I even open my eyes. When I do, just seein' her face helps distract me from the pain.

"Let Joshua give you something," she whispers, brushin' the sweaty hair off my forehead.

I shake my head and try my best not to wince from the pain. It don't work, and the expression on her face is almost enough to make me give in.

"I'm okay," I whisper instead.

She runs her hand down the side of my face, stoppin' on my chest. "We're getting ready to head out."

I put my hand over hers. "Don't."

"I have to. You have to know that."

I squeeze my eyes shut when pain slices through me. It's got nothin' to do with the gunshot wound.

"I'll come back," she whispers.

I nod, but I can't make my eyes open. Then she presses her lips against mine and I pull her closer with my good hand. I grab a handful of her dress and wrap it around my fist. No. I can't let her go.

"I'll never make it if you don't come back," I say against her lips.

"I would never leave you. It would take more than a few zombies to keep me away."

My shoulder throbs, but I ignore it. I part her lips with my tongue and kiss her like I can change her mind. She runs her hands over my chest, and her lips are right behind. When they stop over my wound I inhale sharply, but it's got nothin' to do with pain.

"I love you," she says.

My throat's too tight to get anythin' out.

CHAPTER TWENTY-SEVEN

VIVIAN

Being back in Vegas has my stomach in knots, and being here without Axl just feels wrong. Like I left a part of myself behind.

Getting to the back of the casino was easier than it should have been. Winston knew what streets to avoid, and the back was practically deserted. We haven't seen a single live person since we pulled into Vegas, and the Monte Carlo is eerily quiet when we pull to a stop about ten feet from the back entrance.

"What you think they're doin' in there?" Angus says, peering out the front window.

Winston shakes his head. "Sleeping. Waiting for the other men to come back."

Angus spits into a can and shakes his head. "They're gonna be waitin' a long time for that."

I nod along with the others, but I can't talk. I'm too tense.

Before we left the mountains, we drove back past the shelter and managed to reclaim a lot of the supplies the men had stolen from us. There were no survivors that we could see. It's possible they'd retreated into the shelter since their vehicles were useless. Thanks to Angus's bomb and Jon slitting the tires of the other cars. But we didn't risk going inside. The air was too toxic, and we didn't know if anyone would survive long enough to salvage anything. Unfortunately. We could have used the clothes.

I tug at the short skirt I'm wearing and press my lips together. Pants would have been nice. At least I was able to get a pair of shoes from Anne, who had the foresight to put some on before she fled her condo. They're tight, but they're better than nothing.

Maybe we can stop at the gift shop before we head back. Right.

"Let's just do this," Nathan snaps.

He's sitting next to me in the second row, sweating like we're on the way to his funeral or something. I'm a little shocked he came. No way did I think Moira would let him out of her sight.

"Alright, then," Angus says.

He jerks the key out of the ignition and puts it under the visor, giving Winston a pointed look. He's thinking ahead. This way the rest of us will still be able to get out if something happens to him. Leave it to Angus. Damn.

I take a deep breath and grab the handle. God, please don't let anything happen to Angus. For Axl's sake.

Or to any of us, for that matter.

"Me, Winston, and Nathan'll get a fire started downstairs," Angus says. "Get that fire alarm goin' off. You girls and preppy back there can head on up to the suite. Let them girls out."

"Sounds like a plan," Winston says, grabbing his gun as he pushes the passenger door open. "Let's get moving."

I expected Hadley to crumble once we got back to the Monte Carlo. She's barely been hanging on since we left. But when she climbs out of the Nissan, the knife in her right hand is steady. Maybe this will be good therapy. Like closure or something.

I hope so.

Winston and Angus clear the way, and the rest of us follow behind. My heart's pounding so hard I can barely hear the zombies moaning over it. Too bad it doesn't do anything to cover up the smell. The air is ripe. Even worse than it was the last time we were here.

When we get inside, Hadley, Jon, and I break off from the others, then head to the back. Away from the casino to the staff elevators. Jon being with us is helpful. He lived in this casino for over a week before they managed to break us out.

"This way," Jon says, darting down a dark hall and motioning for us to follow.

Hadley is right on his heels, and I'm not too far behind. I can't stop looking over my shoulder. My jaw aches from grinding my teeth. Every sound makes me jump, and my heart pounds so hard it feels like a little jackhammer going off in my chest. This was a bad idea. We may have killed off a good number of them back at the shelter, but there's no way the six of us can do this without some casualties.

My heart pounds harder.

I don't want to say goodbye to anyone else.

Something clatters somewhere in the distance, and we all freeze. I press my back against the wall on instinct and a scream bubbles up inside me, but I manage to keep it down.

"What was that?" Hadley whispers. Her green eyes are huge, but she doesn't look scared. Just alert.

She puckers her lips in a way that reminds me of Axl, and my heart constricts. No. I can't think about that. Now is the time to focus.

Jon shakes his head, and I stay with my back pressed against the wall. We don't move. I count to ten while I wait for something to happen. Laughter breaks the silence and floats down the hall. The jackhammer in my chest goes into overtime.

The sound slowly fades away, but I don't relax. And I don't move. Finally, after a minute or so, we can't hear them anymore. I exhale, and Jon's shoulders relax. Hadley looks exactly the same.

"Let's keep moving," she says.

Jon starts running and I push myself off the wall, skittering to keep up. Tremors have started in my legs. No, this was NOT a good idea.

We're at the elevators when the fire alarm goes off. It's a loud shriek that makes me jump and squeal like a little girl. Red lights on the ceiling flash, making the hall look like disco. Only the light is red. A bloody disco.

"The elevator is on the seventh floor!" Jon yells over the alarm.

He presses the button and steps back, and my heart pounds when the number above the elevator changes to six. Then five. I hold my breath, but it stops on three and I know we're screwed.

"Someone else is getting on!" I shout.

Jon nods, and Hadley's fingers flex around her knife. I tap my toe on the floor and wait.

The number changes to two and we all take a step back. It changes to one and the elevator dings. It's barely audible over the shrieking of the alarm.

My stomach tightens as much as my grip on my knife. I bounce on my toes as the door slides open. Four men. They blink and scramble for weapons, but they are clearly unprepared. It gives us the time we need.

Hadley moves first. She lets out a cry and thrusts her knife forward while she runs. The man closest to her is caught completely off guard. She manages to sink her blade into his stomach before he has a chance to take a step back. Jon and I are right behind her. Jon goes for the biggest one, but the guy meets him halfway. He blocks the attack and sends Jon flying out of the elevator. He grunts, but I don't have a chance to see how he is.

The man in front of me is only a little taller than I am, but he has to outweigh me by at least fifty pounds. I don't bother with my knife, I go right for his crotch. The heel of my shoe slams into his balls, and he doubles over in pain. As soon as he's down, I bring my knife up. Right into his neck. Blood pours from the wound and drips onto the carpet. He straightens up and grabs at his throat, but I turn away.

Hadley's guy is on the floor, and Jon is struggling with his. The fourth guy is crouched in the corner with Hadley standing over him. For some reason though, she hasn't moved. I step closer and have the urge to spit when I see him.

"Brad."

His head jerks up, and he frowns. "Didn't think I'd see you folks again."

Hadley kicks him right in the nose. He groans and tries to scoot away, but there's nowhere to go.

"You prick!" Hadley shouts.

She's back. The Hadley who screamed at Mitchell when we first made it into the shelter. The one who kicked zombie asses on-screen for a living. I don't know why this trip helped her recover, but it has. If we get out of here alive, she just might be able to come out of this.

The alarm is still wailing and Hadley is still standing over Brad when Jon comes over to join us. My fingers wrap so tightly around my knife that they ache.

"We need to go," I say.

Hadley's looking at Brad like she's going to slit his throat. I'm not going to stop her, but if she's going to do it, she needs to get a move on.

Hadley nods and doesn't take her eyes off Brad. "Press the button. We'll take him with us."

Brad's eyes get huge. "What're you gonna do?"

Hadley puckers her lips while the elevator jerks up.

"Just kill him," Jon says.

"No. Let's see how things are upstairs before we get rid of our only leverage."

"He's not much leverage," I say.

Brad is still cowering in the corner like a little baby. I'm pretty sure he'd be willing to slit his own wrists to get out of this about now. Too bad he doesn't seem to be armed.

"Yeah," Jon says. "I doubt anyone will care what we do with this guy."

Hadley smiles and it lights up her face. "Zombie chow, then."

Brad's eyes get huge just as the elevator lurches to a stop.

The doors slide open, and the scent of death hits me, making my stomach lurch. It isn't just from the smell, but from the memories, too. Thinking about being here, about being dragged from the room. Not knowing what was going to happen. Remembering how defeated Hadley looked when she came back.

Thinking about Lexi and Megan...

The zombies are still chained up at the end of the hall when I step out. Jon is right behind me, dragging Brad. Hadley comes last. There are no men guarding the door.

"Everyone must have gone down when the alarm started going off," Jon says.

It doesn't occur to me that the alarm has stopped until he says it. "Yeah," I mutter.

Hadley passes me up, motioning for Jon to follow. My stomach is in knots and my legs are like limp spaghetti. The zombies at the end of the hall scream and pull at their chains.

"See." Hadley jerks her head toward the zombies. She holds Brad's gaze. "Zombie chow."

Brad starts to fight Jon, who tightens his grip. Jon's bigger than him. Stronger.

My stomach rolls, and I shake my head. Is this what we've come to? "Hadley—"

"Don't tell me you want him to get away with this," Hadley says, screeching to a halt. "Remember what happened? Think of how different things would be if we had listened to Angus. We should have thrown Mitchell to the zombies. The time for playing nice is over!" The final sentence hisses out of her like it's full of venom.

"No." I shake my head while I try to think of something to say. "But this isn't you. This is Angus. You're the person who fought for James when he was bit. Who stopped Angus from beating the shit out of Mitchell. You have compassion and a heart."

Hadley shakes her head, and her face scrunches up like she has a difficult time remembering who that person was. "I did, but I was wrong. I was wrong with both of those things, and as a result, James almost took a bite out of me and Mitchell destroyed our home. And this bastard helped." She jerks her head toward Brad, and for a second, I think she's going to punch him in the nose.

"So zombies it is," Jon says, stepping forward. Dragging Brad with him.

Brad screams, and I move after them. My heart pounds and I reach out, but it's too late. Jon shoves Brad toward the chained zombies. He falls to his knees, then scrambles back, trying to get away. He isn't fast enough. A zombie gets ahold of his arm and digs its nails in.

The scream Brad lets out sends a shudder down my spine, and I have to turn away. Hadley hasn't moved an inch, and she doesn't take her eyes off Brad. Her expression is hard and cold, and her body is rigid.

Brad was a selfish bastard, but the torture he's going through makes my stomach turn inside out. The moans of the zombies mix with his wails of pain. They get louder at first, then turn to whimpers. Like a little dog. The longer I listen, the more I think. Of what we've lost. Of what he did to us. How we could have all died this exact same way and it would have been his fault. How he knew there were innocent children in the shelter, yet it didn't stop him.

Seeing Jhett's body on the floor. Watching Arthur run to his death.

Brad wouldn't have lost any sleep over it.

My throat tightens. Maybe this is what he deserves. We live in a kill-or-be-killed kind of world now, and maybe men like Brad deserve to be ripped apart by zombies.

I turn around and face the mangled mess that was once Brad the truck driver. He makes a few gurgling noises, then he's silent. Gone forever.

The world is a better place now that he isn't in our lives.

Hadley nods like justice has been served and she'll be able to sleep easier now. Maybe I will, too. Maybe we all will.

"Let's finish this," I say, turning away from the zombies ripping apart the asshole who left us all to die.

Even though his death brings a small amount of satisfaction, the feeling doesn't sit well with me. None of this does. I want to hurry. To get away from the Monte Carlo. There are too many ghosts and memories here, and I need to be back with Axl. Where I understand who I am and who he is, and how we relate to this world of madness.

Every woman in the room jumps when I shove the door open. They could probably hear Brad's screams through the door. Even if they couldn't, I can't really blame them for being a little on edge.

"What's going on?" a redhead in her thirties asks. I don't recognize her. Is she new, or did I just not see her with all these other terrified faces staring back at me?

"This is your chance," I say. "Arm yourselves with whatever you can find and work together, but now is your opportunity to get out of here."

No one moves for a few seconds, then all at once women start getting to their feet. A few jump up like they'e ready to make an actual, physical run for it, and the tension in me lessens a little. I wish we could do more. Take them in or arm them. Do something to help. I don't know how many will make it, but seeing that there's still some energy in the group makes me feel a little better.

"Good luck," I mutter, turning to leave.

Hadley stands in the hall next to Jon. They both stare past me at the room full of women like we're sending them off to an execution by not saving them. I hate the look in their eyes, because that's exactly how I feel.

"Where do we go?" someone calls after me.

I don't stop. I pass Hadley and Jon and head to the elevator. My thumb slams against the button like if I press it hard enough I can transport myself back to Axl. I wish it were that easy.

When I look back, Jon is heading my way, but Hadley has gone into the suite.

"I want to get out of here," I say. "We did what we could."

Jon leans against the wall like he can't stand up anymore. "Just give her a minute."

"Is screwing her your way of getting over your sister?" I blurt out. I can't keep it in. It's been weighing on my mind. Jon's jaw tightens, but I put my hand up before he can say anything. "She's been through a lot."

"This was her doing. She started it."

Typical. Men always have to blame the woman. You're just too sexy to resist. I can't think with no blood flowing to my brain, so I can't be held responsible for my stupid-ass choices.

I roll my eyes, and Hadley comes out of the condo behind Jon. "Be careful," I hiss, slamming my thumb back into the button. "Keep in mind that the last man who pissed her off got thrown to the zombies."

Jon actually laughs, and even though the hall smells like death and there's a hotel room full of abused women, I can't stop from smiling. It is kind of funny, in a really dark and messed-up way.

But hey, isn't everything dark and messed-up now?

THE HOTEL LOBBY REEKS WHEN WE REACH THE BOTTOM floor. "Guess they threw the doors open," I mutter.

Hadley and Jon nod in unison. They both look about as terrified and ready to get the hell out of here as I feel. My palm sweats from gripping my knife so hard. I follow them out of the elevator, and the hair on the back of my neck stands up. There's screaming in the distance. A gunshot rings out, and I jump about three feet off the ground. But we don't stop moving.

"Stay alert," Jon yells back.

I nod even though his back is to me. My eyes don't stop scanning the area for a second. The scent of death gets stronger the further into the casino we go. Then we can hear the moans, and I'm really on edge.

We're on the tail end of all this. We just need to get to the Nissan.

And pray the others make it out too.

When we get to the main part of the hotel, we freeze. There are three zombies less than five feet from us. They're heading the other way until they catch wind of us, then it only takes them two seconds to decide we are a lot more promising than the screams coming from the other side of the casino.

Jon whips out a gun I didn't even know he had and fires off two quick shots while Hadley takes the third zombie out with her knife. It happens so fast I barely have time to react. When did I become the least effective member of this group?

Maybe not being with Axl has me off my game.

"Let's get outside!" Jon yells, taking off.

Hadley and I jog after him, but we've only gone a few steps when there's more gunfire. I don't slow down, but I do look over my shoulder. Angus and Nathan and Winston head our way, taking zombies out as they go. So far, I haven't seen any other men. Maybe we got them all. Maybe they suffered and got just a small taste of what they've put these women through.

I can only hope.

"You three do what you came for?" Angus yells.

"Yeah."

I slow down just a little. Not sure why. I've never really been a fan of Angus, and usually being near him just means I'm going to be pissed off. Maybe it's because he's Axl's brother or because we've been together from the beginning. Ass or not, he's like a twisted sibling that I have to put up with. And I don't always hate it, either.

"You guys have any trouble?" I ask when he catches up.

His face is red, and he's panting. There's sweat on his forehead, and the pits of his shirt are wet. He keeps pace with me, even though it doesn't look like he finds it all that easy.

"Nope. Now all I wanna do is get the hell outta Vegas."

"Can't argue with that," I say.

Jon and Hadley make it out the door first, but we're right on their heels. The area was relatively clear when we got here, but now it's crawling with the dead. At least fifteen of them are heading toward the open door. It's like someone's ringing a dinner bell only they can hear.

Jon starts firing while herding Hadley to the car. She's got her knife out, and she hacks away at any zombies that get near her, but Jon won't let her get far. He has a good grip on her shirt.

Angus starts cussing and firing away at the zombies too. Just like always. I'm starting to wonder if he really is enjoying himself. He sure looks like it as he pulls the trigger, practically cheering when the zombie's head explodes.

Nathan and Winston are behind me. Winston rushes forward, pushing me toward the car in a way that's similar to how Jon is moving Hadley forward. Axl must have asked him to look out for me. He's got such a good grip on my dress that there's no way it isn't hiked up enough to show off my thong and bare ass. Angus even pauses between shots to check it out. Figures.

"Quit firing and get to the car!" Winston yells.

For once, Angus doesn't argue. He nods and grabs my arm, then pulls me forward. Winston lets go of my dress and jogs next to us with Nathan at my back. Jon and Hadley are in, and Jon is already starting the car. We're going to make it. All of us.

Winston rips the door open, and Angus shoves me toward the car so hard I almost fall. I grab the door to keep myself upright, then haul my ass inside. I throw myself into the third row while Winston jogs to the other side of the car. Angus scrambles in behind me and starts to scoot over, but Winston is in his way. Nathan stands outside waiting for us to make room when a zombie comes out of nowhere. The thing's rotten teeth sink into Nathan's neck, and blood sprays everywhere. My stomach jumps to my throat.

He yells, and I scream. Hadley starts crying. Angus cusses, then he and Winston both fire out the open door. The zombie falls, and Angus pulls Nathan in, yelling for Jon to drive. It all happens so fast. Like someone hit a fast forward button. When Jon slams on the gas, I'm thrown back against the seat. Angus slams the door, and no one says a word.

The car is silent except for the occasional sniffle from Hadley. Nathan's neck and shirt are coated in blood, but he doesn't even bother trying to cover the injury. The teeth marks are like a death warrant, and we all know it.

We make it away from the Strip and to a more residential area before Nathan says, "Stop the car."

Jon jumps like he forgot anyone else was with him, then turns to look at Nathan but he doesn't stop driving. "What?"

"I said stop."

Jon presses his lips together and turns to the front, but he slows the car and pulls over. We all know what's coming.

Nathan opens the door and climbs out. When he turns to face

don't want to tell anyone before Moira hears it.

Joshua nods slowly, and his eyes cloud over. He glances toward the back, then lets out a big sigh. He already knows, though. He has to.

Moira starts wailing a split second later, my already cracked heart shatters a little more. Moira is annoying and a pain in the ass, but I know how she feels. I can't fault her for mourning.

I lay down on Axl's good side and rest my head on his chest. He doesn't move. I close my eyes. The air is chilly, but his body is warm. I move myself closer, trying to block out Moira's cries. Nothing can comfort me after all we've been through except Axl. If he dies, I'm pretty sure my heart will stop beating on its own.

Acknowledgements

Thanks to my amazing first readers: Tammy Moore-Brewer and Sarah McVay. I love how much you adore these books even though zombies are not your thing, and I'm excited for you to get to read the next installment. To Erin Rose who is not only my first ever reader, but also my personal consultant whenever it comes to anything medical. Thanks for believing in me before anyone else even knew I had written something. Jen Naumann, thank you for offering to beta read and for gushing about the story and tweeting about how much you love it. I'm so glad I was able to write your favorite zombie series!

Thanks again to my editor, Emily Teng, for continuing to work with me and doing such a great job. I know you have your work cut out for you on commas alone. I look forward to handing you many more projects down the line. And thanks again to Jimmy Gibbs for the cover art. I love my five dollar covers and you wouldn't believe all the compliments I get on them!

Again, thank you Daryl Dixon and Robert Kirkman, and the whole cast of *The Walking Dead* for making zombies so popular at just the right time. You guys all rock!

About the Author

Kate L. Mary is an award-winning author of New Adult and Young Adult fiction, ranging from Post-apocalyptic tales of the undead, to Speculative Fiction and Contemporary Romance. Her Young Adult book, *When We Were Human*, was a 2015 Children's Moonbeam Book Awards Silver Medal winner for Young Adult Fantasy/Sci-Fi Fiction, and a 2016 Readers' Favorite Gold Medal winner for Young Adult Science Fiction. Don't miss out on the *Broken World* series, an Amazon bestseller and fan favorite.

For more information about Kate, check out her website: www.KateLMary.com